By Dean Murray

Torn

Dean Murray

Copyright © 2011 by Dean Murray

Published by Fir'shan Publishing

ISBN 978-1-9393630-5-3

www.FirshanPublishing.com

Second Edition

For all of the fans of the series

None of this would be possible without all of you

Chapter 1

The silvery light of a nearly-full moon should have been comforting. For most people it would've been peaceful even, but it pulled at my anger with surprising strength as I bounded across the arid Southern Utah terrain.

Darkly furred, four-legged shapes ghosted through the darkness on either side of me as we slid between the softly glowing pillars of trees. Jasmin, arguably the closest thing I had to a best friend, dove through a latticework of light and then it was my turn to feel the undergrowth grasping at my fur in an effort to slow my progress.

The warm evening breeze carried a host of aromas too subtle for mere human noses to identify. In our four-footed forms each molecule was unconsciously sorted and cataloged, leaving us free to concentrate on the elusive scent of our prey.

The other pack, a portion at least, was less than a mile away, far enough into our territory for it to be a killable offense if they were caught. They'd become increasingly arrogant over the last few months, but coming in close enough to threaten our families was a whole new level of provocation. Even their leader, Brandon, wasn't usually so bold.

A stray eddy of wind played across my muzzle, and I knew they'd made their first mistake. I pressed into my second in command for a moment, conveying an order through posture and motion, and then nipped at Jasmin's heels, the two of us stretching out in a full sprint.

Free from the others, Jasmin and I streaked through the night with a speed the rest of our pack couldn't have matched. Jasmin pressed at my flank, curious at my decision until she caught the scent, and then an answering growl made its way past her fangs.

The trap was clever, but the other wolves didn't know the terrain well enough. I let my beast bubble up from the corner of my being where I usually kept it chained. Between one moment and the next, I went from running on four legs to two. As my transformation ended, a six-foot tower of muscle and claws sprang from the shadows. I ducked Vincent's first blow and retaliated with a gash that opened one side of his chest nearly down to the bone.

A dark-furred form leaped at Jasmin, but the other wolf mistimed the spring. Most of the other pack didn't appreciate just how nimble she was.

Jasmin dodged to one side and then the two of them were circling, looking for an opening.

Vincent, the other hybrid, attacked with the strength and fury that'd earned him the position of second in his pack, but he hadn't been expecting to face me in this form. As a wolf I weighed in at a solid two hundred pounds, but would've still given up more than a hundred pounds to him.

Now I had at least six inches and seventy-five pounds on my side of the equation, and he was the one pressed onto the defensive as the fight progressed.

I caught flashes of action from the other fight as we circled each other. Jasmin sprang at her opponent, catching her behind the shoulders as Vincent reeled away from me in a shower of blood. I'd finally managed a deeper strike on his arm.

The high-pitched scream of pain as Jasmin began trying to crush her opponent's spine was answered by rapidly-approaching howls. Vincent attacked with renewed strength at the promise of reinforcements.

I was bleeding in a dozen places now, but the rage insulated me from pain and weakness. Both sides of my nature were united in hating Vincent. If I ever did manage to kill him, my questionable humanity wouldn't grieve. The world would be better for his absence.

I could hear the other pack now, panting with exertion, our friends hot on their heels. Vincent overreached in his effort to claim the kill, and I sank my teeth into the muscled flesh of his shoulder as I finally made it around behind him.

My claws sank into his arms and legs as I repositioned to snap his neck, and then a hammer blow of weight struck me across the shoulders. Knocked loose from Vincent, I spun around in time to tear Simon from the air as he leaped at me again. It was the perfect opportunity to end a life nearly as evil as Vincent's, but one of the recent arrivals had bowled Jasmin over.

Leveraging a frame that was more than capable of picking up a small car, I threw Simon into the whirling ball of flesh and fangs. He didn't hit hard enough to snap his neck, but he knocked the other wolf off of Jasmin, and then Vincent was back on his feet.

The rest of the rival pack, save for Brandon their leader, came streaming past, but they didn't help their fellows swarm Jasmin and me over. None of them even slowed. Vincent took an angry swipe at the last, a small female, and then our pack burst from the trees. A second later, our enemies were in full rout.

I let my bulk melt down back into my sleeker wolf shape as I joined Jasmin and the rest. We quickly chased the other pack out of our territory and halfway through the neutral buffer, but failed to catch even the wounded wolves. Jasmin normally could've run any of Brandon's pack down, but she was limping.

TORN

Isaac, my ever-sensible second in command, brushed up against me, putting slight pressure on my right side even as he dropped his nose in submission. It was a small thing, but it pulled me out of the blood lust, and I turned our course back towards home.

I should have seen the problem developing. James never has been very level-headed. That's a bad thing considering that, as the third hybrid in the pack, he's dominant to all of the other wolves with the possible exception of Jasmin. As the rest of the pack altered course to follow me James failed to change direction. He knocked one of the others over when she wasn't quick enough getting out of his way, and in the next instant nipped at Isaac. Less than a second later both James and Isaac's wolf forms exploded into hulking hybrids.

Isaac has always been the most even-keeled of us. His ability to carefully pick his battles is what's always allowed him to edge James out when it comes to ranking inside the pack. Even so, he couldn't allow James to attack his girlfriend, Jessica, without responding. When it comes to no-holds-barred fighting, Isaac's margin of superiority is much slimmer.

The two males clinched and went at each other with claw and fang while I was still spinning around. My own hybrid form tore itself free, and I crossed the intervening twenty feet in two long bounds as both James' and Isaac's girlfriends circled each other warily.

James was on top, tearing at Isaac's writhing form with all of his considerable strength. My backfist knocked James into a tree. He rolled to his feet like he was ready to take both Isaac and me on at the same time.

Dominic, James' girlfriend, abandoned her posturing and wrapped her long feline body around James, calming him with a speed nothing else seemed able to accomplish. Even so, it was still more than a minute before Isaac and James had cooled enough to get them both moving again.

The girls ran in the middle of the pack, keeping the boys separated from each other as much as possible. I probably should have chosen that moment to reestablish dominance over both James and Isaac, but my shoulders itched the entire time we were motionless.

The sensation of imminent danger didn't lessen until we were back into our own territory. Even then it didn't disappear; it just faded back to its normal level, back to something I could mostly ignore.

Everyone but Mother was waiting for us as we limped across the vast expanse of ankle-deep grass that led up to the house. The parents, those present at least, breathed sighs of relief as soon as we were close enough for them to count noses. Jessica's father, Andrew, took in the bloody gashes along Isaac's chest, and her scratch-free figure with the same worried eyes. He tiredly pushed his wheelchair forward as soon as we stepped into the light.

Addison, James' mother, looked agitated. She took in her son's condition and then favored me with the kind of look some dominants kill over. She hadn't liked me for as long as I could remember. It had bothered me more when I was younger, before I realized she doesn't live in the same world as the rest of us. She actually still had friends in Brandon's pack.

She didn't really believe the other pack meant us harm. It was only one of the many reasons why she'd been given the guest residence several hundred yards away from the main house. Nobody really thought she'd go so far as to spy for her old friends, but it made us all sleep a little better to know she wasn't lurking in the next room. James was already conflicted enough. There wasn't any reason to court disaster by giving her an opportunity to make him choose once and for all between us and her.

Shifting more smoothly than most of us were able, Isaac melted back into his human form. Jess was next; she took Isaac's hand, leading him to her father, who clasped them both in a frail hug before breaking out into a series of racking coughs. The cold night air always aggravated the old shape shifter's wounds. Isaac picked Andrew up out of his chair and after looking to me for a nod of permission, carried him inside.

I followed the other three wolves, or rather the two wolves and Dominic, the rest of the way to the house. I wasn't looking forward to speaking to Addison, but squelched the urge to transform back to my hybrid form to hold the discussion. I'd already worn too many shapes tonight. The cramps were likely going to be bad as it was. Adding yet another change to the abuse I'd put my body through would be a very bad idea.

"You split the pack up and let James get hurt, didn't you?"

Donovan, the family retainer, made as if to hush James' mom, but I stopped him with a glance. The last thing we needed was to give her venom additional targets, especially targets who couldn't defend themselves against James.

"I split the pack up, but that isn't how James got hurt. His injuries came when he jumped Isaac while we were still only a mile or so outside of the other pack's territory."

Addison's eyes practically glowed at the thought of her son attacking the wolf just higher than him in the pack hierarchy. She was convinced I was holding him back, that he wasn't being given his due. She was going to get him killed at some point, but there was no way for me to convince her of that.

James looked like he was going to interject something indignant, but I cut him off before he could say anything.

"I was within my rights to break the two of you up, James. The other pack had plenty of time to regroup and return. The last thing you should have been doing was spilling our blood when we were so close to their home."

I could see comprehension begin to dawn. He'd never thought it through, never realized just how much danger we were in, just how easily the other pack could have appeared out of the darkness and torn into us. He'd assumed I was just too injured to press our advantage, and had resented Isaac stealing his opportunity for glorious, bloody battle.

Addison hadn't managed to follow the logic, but it wasn't a lack of ability, it was willful refusal. She envisioned a higher place for her son, a place beyond our small pack, wrongly assuming his obtaining it would result in true safety for the first time in her entire life.

She'd never understood that his achieving her impossible dreams would just set both of them in even more precarious circumstances.

"You know what my rights are, James."

Now I saw actual fear streak through his eyes. Fear and resentment. Dominic crowded closer to his side, concern written large on her expression, but obviously making an effort to calm both James and his mother.

I held James' gaze for several seconds and then waved him away.

Jasmin met my eyes and then limped into the house, leaving me alone with my sister Rachel and Donovan. I tiredly moved the rest of the way into the artificial lights and Rachel gasped as her human eyes were finally able to make out what Donovan had been able to see since I'd stepped out of the trees.

"Alec, you're hurt."

I smiled at my little sister and then looked down to take inventory of my battered body. My ha'bit was shredded, the important parts were still covered, but the garment showed the wear and tear from our high-speed chase through some of the thickest underbrush in the area. My skin had almost as many holes in it as the tattered fabric. Vincent hadn't managed anything crippling, but he'd been well on his way to bleeding me out.

Rachel slipped under my arm, trying to support me as Donovan led the way into the house. The gesture wasn't needed. Rachel was a small fifteen, nearly as slender as Jasmin and lacking the unnatural strength common to the shape shifters, but I appreciated her desire to help.

Jasmin's wounds had looked like the kind you could tend with your own set of hands. Even if they weren't, she wasn't the type to seek help. I'd have to remember to check on her later, but for now I was the only patient in the examination room.

Donovan reappeared with his graceful lurch, carrying a fresh set of towels and some water and then set about cleaning out the worst of the wounds. It'd become a longstanding ritual. I bled from one confrontation or another, and then while he patched me up, he updated me on the state of the family holdings.

Rachel handed Donovan tools with the expertise of an experienced nurse as he began his ministrations.

"The Montana situation seems to be resolving itself nicely, sir. Our factor there has managed to secure ninety percent of the water rights we're expecting to need for the first phase of the project, and there isn't any uptick in prices yet. He hopes to be able to come in under budget for the first two phases. With your approval, I'll tell him to put together a proposal for beginning construction?"

I grunted my assent, and then flinched slightly as his probing fingers found a particularly deep wound. I could see the gash in the overhead mirror, and it was all the way to the bone at one point. In a human it would be cause for concern, possibly hospitalization. For me, the worst would be healed within forty-eight hours. Impervious to all known diseases, and we healed back to one hundred percent from anything that didn't kill us. Almost anything. The thought made me glance at Donovan's leg. His immaculately-pressed pants hid a disturbing array of scars.

Donovan worked through the list of open business items, ticking off of a mental list as he applied butterfly bandages and gauze to hold the deeper wounds closed. I listened, approving his decisions or occasionally confirming previous discussion, until he wound down to the last item.

"Sir, I assume you remain resolved on the Paige matter? It does bring an element of risk with it. Each additional human in the town represents another set of eyes to be avoided by the moonborn."

"Yes, Donovan, I'm resolved. This town is already starting to implode. It's too stagnant. You saw how everyone responded to the new doctor and his family. If we don't get new blood into Sanctuary we're going to have people eating each other at some point. Unless you've found something worrisome in the preliminary background check, we go forward with making it possible for them to move in."

"Very good, sir. The background check, rudimentary though it's been, hasn't turned up anything concerning. I expect we'll have to make some payments. Brandon's bribed some of the local officials, but we should be able to get the Paiges safely into their new home for less than fifty thousand."

Donovan taped up the last gash deep enough to need attention, and then cleaned up. As he turned to leave I reached out and stopped him.

"The infighting's getting worse, isn't it, Donovan?"

The older shape shifter, the man who'd been my surrogate father for nearly as long as I could remember, looked up to meet my eyes with concern on his features.

"I wasn't present for the latest outburst, sir. That being said, it does seem as though they are increasing in intensity."

The weight of the night suddenly seemed to settle fully on me and I wanted nothing more than to go straight to my bed.

"What would my father have done?"

"That isn't a fair question. Your father never faced this. At that time the closest rival pack was more than a hundred miles away. Not only that, there were enough of us that exile or execution would have been feasible alternatives for anyone causing excessive trouble. Unfortunately in the current situation you need every wolf you can nominally count on, and James represents too great an asset to push away."

Donovan bowed gracefully and then limped out of the room leaving me alone with Rachel, who hadn't stirred since she'd helped put away the last of the medical implements.

"Alec, you wouldn't really kill James, would you?"

She deserved an answer, she'd suffered and bled almost as much as the rest of us, but I knew she wouldn't push, so I chose the coward's route and didn't answer. I didn't want to kill part of our extended family, but the pack wasn't healthy, wasn't balanced. We had too many dominants with too few submissives to serve as a buffer between the more forceful personalities.

"You should have been in bed hours ago, Rach."

"I tried but I couldn't sleep."

For the first time I noticed how red her eyes were, and cursed the preoccupation that stopped me from noticing it earlier.

"What's wrong? Did Mother say something?"

A brave smile met my words, but she couldn't hide the hurt. "No worse than usual. I just didn't react very well to it tonight."

"She doesn't mean to hurt you, Rach. She's sick."

"I know. Sometimes I think it would be better if I just stopped visiting her, but she really does seem to do better when we don't leave her in as much isolation."

It was a silent recrimination. I hadn't visited Mother frequently enough lately.

"I'm sorry I've left that for you to take care of. I haven't spent much time with either of you lately."

"It's okay, Alec. I understand. Brandon's been pushing and he's got more bodies to push with. The pack's being run ragged, you more than anyone. It's just lonely around here when you're all gone."

I pulled myself off of the examination table and hugged her. It only took a few minutes to walk her to her room and tuck her in, but even once I reached my bed I was unable to fall asleep. I needed to find a solution for Rachel's isolation, needed to chart a course through the coming war with Brandon, and solve a half-dozen other problems. My mind continued to grind away at the worries long after the rest of the house went quiet.

Chapter 2

The weekend hadn't brought any more excursions by Brandon's pack. The best-case scenario would be that the wounds Vincent and Cassie had suffered had caused some of Brandon's wolves to refuse to come up against us again. It wasn't very likely, but I'd been grasping at straws for months now. It was unlikely Brandon's pack was going to just self-destruct, but more and more that was looking like the only hope we had of avoiding everything he had planned for us.

Donovan's nightly updates had revealed that Brandon had somehow found out about the family's investment in our Colorado mining startup. We'd gone from having all of the necessary approvals and permits on Friday afternoon to having a whole slew of complications and roadblocks waiting for me when I got up Monday morning.

Someone needed to fly down and smooth things over. My best guess was that Brandon had bribed a certain highly-placed male we'd been working with. It was a rare male of any species who could resist Jasmin, so she was the obvious choice to fix the situation. Even so, I wasn't looking forward to telling her she had to go.

We'd just finished up with History when I got the text from Donovan. I pulled her aside as we exited the room, and flipped out my phone as a distraction. Shape shifter hearing was acute enough to catch subvocalized speech. As long as we were careful to make sure none of the other pack's wolves were nearby we could carry on an entire conversation with nobody else the wiser.

"We're having problems in Colorado. I need you to go down there and straighten things out."

Normally Jasmin enjoyed a chance to get out of town and use a combination of charm and money to undo whatever mischief Brandon's minions had caused. Everyone in school thought we were dating. It was a useful fiction when it came to keeping the humans at arm's length, but Jasmin seemed to miss the opportunity to flirt more than I did. Once she got out of Sanctuary, there was never any shortage of males wanting to lavish attention on her.

Even if she hadn't had the advantages common to our kind, that still would've been the case. Nature had gifted her with incredible looks and the thin, runway model build most girls had to starve themselves to achieve. Lately though she'd been fighting any assignment that took her out of town.

"I don't want to leave. Send Donovan."

"That won't work. Brandon's bribed the police commissioner, and he's launched criminal investigations on our principals down there. Unless we want to get into a bidding war for his questionable loyalty we need someone who can do more than just wave money under his nose."

"Fine, send Dom. She's plenty pretty enough to flirt her way into his office and bluff him into backing off."

"It has to be you, Jas. Dominic's too much of a submissive to carry something like that off. You can take one of the jets and be back within a day, thirty-six hours at the outside."

My logic was solid, but she was far too stubborn to back down without a battle of wills. I could feel the energy bubble off of her as she geared up for a full-blown argument, but I didn't need any extra hints. There were plenty of visual clues that she was mad. Her blue eyes, incontestable proof of her royal ancestry, had gone unnaturally pale. They were already nearly the ice blue of her wolf form, and she was bleeding light so badly it was visible even in this form.

Visible for shape shifters at least. Humans would see nothing out of the ordinary, but the moonborn lived in a world where every living organism gave off a soft glow. In human form the light was dimmer than when I was in my hybrid or wolf body. Normally with these eyes I'd have to work to pick out glow from anyone but Isaac, James or another hybrid.

She'd made her point that she was pissed, but this close to the full moon I was less willing to deal with her theatrics. I let my beast rise up until I was just a hairsbreadth from transforming. Power rushed out and beat against Jasmin with an almost physical force. It washed over her with a fury that left no question who had the power to enforce their will. It still took several seconds of futile defiance before she bowed her head in submission.

"Go this afternoon, go tonight. It makes no difference to me, but you will be on that plane, and you will do your best to bring things to a successful conclusion. Brandon already overmatches us in a straight-up fight. We can't afford to let him surpass us economically too."

Jasmin gave me a choppy nod and then turned and stomped off towards our lockers. To be fair she was far too graceful for it to really be a stomp, but the intangible plane gave the impression of unhappy obedience. Jasmin's power still whipped around her, opening a thin corridor of bodies through the crowded hall as I followed along in her wake.

The humans didn't realize they were moving out of her way, didn't understand why they felt inclined to move, but the vestigial instincts that'd once kept them alive in a world when far more threatening things had roamed moved them now.

Just before we reached our lockers I picked up a new scent. It didn't belong in the school, didn't belong to any of the students I knew. Worse though, it didn't taste right. For the briefest moment I smelled sickness, and then it faded back into a normal, if novel, smell.

The Paiges had a girl our age and Donovan had indicated they'd moved into the old Anderson home during the weekend. I scanned the familiar faces looking for the new arrival, and then my muscles tensed up as I saw Adriana Paige for the first time.

She was slightly taller than most seventeen-year-olds, with straight blond hair and a body that was only slightly curvier than Jasmin's. Her jeans marked her as different from the rest of the student body, nearly all of whom wore shorts all year, but that wasn't what raised every aggressive instinct I possessed to high alert.

She glowed. Not just the faint glow of a normal person or the slightly stronger glow of a wolf. She shone with the light of a powerful moonborn hybrid, and she didn't belong to my pack, so she was an intruder.

She met my eyes and then flinched slightly as if she'd been struck. It was the action of a human girl, not that of a rival shape shifter. The gesture was just intriguing enough to check the urge to attack, to rip out her throat before she could try and do the same to me.

I pushed my power out, thrusting it at her with more force even than I'd used on Jasmin just seconds before. It was the gravest of insults, not as severe as showing up on another pack's doorstep unannounced, but still the kind of thing that led to fights. Only she failed completely to react to the provocation. As my rage started to cool I realized that she didn't feel like another shape shifter. There wasn't any answering rush of power, no reflexive effort to establish dominance.

Jasmin had already left for her Literature class, too angry with me to notice the new arrival, but I waited, eavesdropping on her conversation with Britney Samuels as I dropped my History book into my locker.

"We *so* have to go down there soon. It's the only place within an hour and a half where you can do any decent shopping."

Britney's familiar voice was full of eagerness. She finally had a new set of ears to listen to her gossip, a new sidekick to help her flirt, sleep or otherwise scale her way closer to the top of the social food chain. I already thought less of the new girl for letting Britney latch onto her.

As I closed my locker, Adri's response came floating over.

"That sounds great; I can't wait to get out of this stupid town."

My locker door hit with more force than I'd intended. The closest kids edged away from me, but I was too mad to care whether or not they thought I was going to suddenly lose control.

I'd spent tens of thousands of dollars and called in three separate favors with local officials to get her and her mom past all of Brandon's efforts to block them, and this was what I got? Another self-absorbed Britney-clone who was too stupid to realize insulting Sanctuary wouldn't impress the people who'd spent their entire lives here?

I stalked off towards my art class, and this time it was *my* power that crackled through the hall clearing a way between the other students.

Art should have been a refuge. It generally was a place where I could forget about dominance posturing and pack business. It helped that it was one of two classes I didn't share with Jasmin. Donovan had implied that my father had likewise escaped the burdens of his life by fleeing to the act of creating. Of course his passion hadn't been anything as perishable as painting. Still, painting at least had the simplicity of being something I loved just in and of itself. For all that Dad had liked metalwork, he'd still mostly been driven by the hope of discovering one of our people's lost arts.

Sanctuary wasn't large enough for the high school to have a class dedicated strictly to painting. I'd had Donovan make some discreet inquiries to the school board, but no amount of implied donations had swayed them, so I was currently stuck sitting through a section on sketching.

Try as I might, I couldn't lose myself in my current piece. The indignity of having helped someone who wouldn't have appreciated the effort even had they known about it continued to worry at the back of my mind.

When the bell finally rang, I was out the door before most of the other kids finished putting up their supplies. I hurried down the stairs only to pull up short as Brandon turned into the hall six feet ahead of me.

We'd once been nearly the same size, but he'd put an extra two inches and fifty pounds on over the last year, and now he loomed over my six-one frame.

"And here I'd been hoping you'd still be limping."

Even subvocalized, Brandon's words carried his usual streak of disdain. My reply was equally inaudible to everyone else around us.

"No limp here. It's too bad your pack wasn't two seconds slower though. You'd be down Vincent and Cassie in addition to needing to explain to the Coun'hij why it is your pack is violating our territory."

I'd expected his pulse to jump at least a little at the prospect of facing the one group that held the power of life and death over every wolf in North America. It didn't vary in the slightest. There was no scent of nervous perspiration, nothing. He was either a dramatically improved liar, or he no longer feared the Coun'hij.

His silent, mocking laughter implied the latter.

"I wouldn't be running off to bear tales right now. You'll find that where you're concerned a slightly different set of rules is currently in effect. No aid is going to be provided to a pack that isn't strong enough even to police its own borders. Especially one so busy fighting among itself."

"I don't know what you're talking about."

It was a stupid lie, the kind of mistake I hadn't made in all too long, but his revelation had shaken me. If things had changed that much, then our pack was operating under even more of a disadvantage than I'd realized.

"Don't insult my intelligence, Alec. If all of the blood we stumbled across in the buffer had belonged to you and Jasmin you'd both be dead. Somebody, possibly more than one somebodies stepped out of line and you had to make them bleed to bring the situation back under control."

He was wrong, not by much but he was still wrong. Donovan said it was his biggest weakness. Brandon tended to assume that everyone thought like he thought, wanted what he wanted, and would act like he would act in any given situation. It was starting to seem like his only weakness.

"When I inform certain contacts that you've even started sponsoring additional human traffic into the town, over my direct objections and despite the fact that it increases our risk of being exposed to the humans, I think you'll find a blind eye will be turned to almost any activity I choose to undertake."

"You're wrong. There are limits to what the moonborn at large will accept. If pack leaders are no longer sacrosanct they'll have an uprising on their hands."

"Oh dear, stupid Alec. Always so secure in the nobility of your bloodline. Of course I can't do anything too overt, but that's the very reason why I've been given carte blanche where you're concerned. It was your father's undoing and it'll be yours as well. The Coun'hij can't afford to have a possible focal point for rebellion running around."

He was right. If I'd chosen to remain safely anonymous rather than rising to rule my pack, they'd possibly have forgiven my lineage, but now that they couldn't just execute me at will I'd become too much of a threat.

"I do hope you've found the Paiges to be all you'd hoped and dreamed."

His departing barb was too close to on target. I'd been practicing for years to control the myriad signs that stopped the moonborn from lying to each other, but the rage from earlier reawakened and provided Brandon with a stronger response than he'd expected.

He turned back to look at me, flashing a satisfied smile before disappearing towards the cafeteria.

The fact that I'd just accidentally painted a big target on the new girl's chest continued to bother me throughout lunch and into Chemistry. Considering just how much I currently despised her, it shouldn't have been a cause for worry, but I'd seen Brandon in action before. Adriana Paige was going to be used and discarded before she even knew what hit her.

TORN

Physics was my second favorite class, more because Mrs. Alexander was so absentminded than for any other reason. I slipped into class a couple seconds before the bell rang, only to pull up short when I saw the new arrival sitting in the back of the room.

Adriana Paige didn't exactly look excited to be in Honors physics, but the mere fact she'd signed up for the class was enough to raise her stock with me. It was the smallest class in the entire school and I had a sneaking suspicion at least a third of the students were going to drop out at the end of the semester.

I took my usual seat in the back of the room as Mrs. Alexander used the blackboard to diagram the different parts of an electromagnetic wave. Nothing earth-shattering there. My attention turned back to Adriana as the explanation wound down.

She was prettier than I'd realized. A lot prettier. It explained quite a bit actually. Girls that pretty almost never had a difficult go of it in life so they tended towards self-absorbed and lazy.

Jasmin was an exception to that rule, but she'd paid for her maturity. You couldn't go through the kinds of horrors she'd experienced without figuring out several times over that the world didn't revolve around you.

Adriana on the other hand probably resented the move to Sanctuary because it took her away from all of the malls and hordes of cute, admiring boys.

Mrs. Alexander finished her lecture and told everyone to start forming into our usual groups. I should have seen it coming. I'd managed to convince her I worked best alone. The fact that there'd been an odd number of students for the first month of school had helped, but with the addition of Adriana that was no longer the case.

"Miss Paige, you'll have the good luck of working with Mr. Graves."

Despite my best efforts, I allowed some of my distaste to show. It was only for a split second, but it was sloppy. Joni Winters and Susan Bower giggled nastily when they saw it, and for the first time I realized just how hard the move was for Adriana.

The emotionless mask that she'd been wearing slipped slightly and for a brief moment she was just a lonely girl who'd been torn away from everything she knew.

Mrs. Alexander turned back to me with a frown, as if I were the one causing all of the problems.

"I'm sure you'll enjoy working with Miss Paige, Alec. After all, you can't really expect to do everything by yourself. Occasionally a helping hand is exactly what's called for."

The elevated pulse that had been teasing my ears suddenly shot up to panic levels as Adriana went completely white. I was the closest to her, but she was still pretty far away and there were desks in the way.

By the time I realized she was really collapsing, it was almost too late to catch her. Without thinking, I sprang to my feet, knocking desks out of the way. It wasn't until I held her limp body in my arms that I realized what I'd done.

Full moonborn speed wasn't used where the humans could see. It was an imperative that'd been drilled into me since before my first transformation. I always moved with human slowness at school, only I'd just surged forward with nearly all of my unnatural speed to stop Adriana from hitting her head.

Mrs. Alexander was the first to my side. She reached up to check Adriana's pulse as the rest of the class started gathering around us.

"That was well done, Alec. I saw her start to fall, but was too far away to have done anything about it. I don't know how you got there before she fell, but you probably saved her from a nasty concussion."

Hopefully the rest of the class had either been focused on Adri or looking elsewhere as well.

"Alec, her pulse seems okay, but you should get her to the school nurse."

I gave Mrs. Alexander a nod of assent, and then started pushing my way through the crowd of other students. I was nearly to the door before I realized that Adriana had returned to consciousness.

"Put me down, I mean please put me down."

Her voice was a little breathy, and her heart rate was back up again. I looked down at her, trying to ascertain if she was about to go into convulsions or not, and felt myself pulled into a pair of the bluest eyes I'd ever seen outside of Jasmin or myself.

I nearly stopped walking, had to shake my head slightly to clear it.

"You need to see the nurse."

"I'm fine. That wasn't anything; it didn't mean anything. Please put me down."

The tone had changed. Even more amazing, her smell had changed. She'd tasted sick just a second before, and now seemed fine. I looked down to confirm what my other senses were telling me and found an emotionless mask looking up at me. It was as if there was an entirely different person behind those glowing features now, and all of her vitals were still too erratic for me to garner anything from them.

"What do you mean you're fine? People don't just collapse with no warning. You seemed fine and then you were falling. You s...you seemed hurt."

I almost bit my tongue. I'd nearly slipped up again, nearly told her she smelled hurt. I'd all but come to a complete stop now, completely outside of my realm of experience.

"It was just the heat here. I'm not used to it. Now *please* put me down."

She was actually fussing with her hair now, obviously afraid that it had been messed up. Suddenly I realized what had happened. People didn't just bounce back from the level of trauma I'd just witnessed. Not unless they'd somehow tricked their system into stuttering in the first place.

I wanted to scream at her for having tricked me into nearly outing myself, but I took a deep breath and just barely managed to contain my growing rage.

"It was all just a game for you, wasn't it?"

Her response was the perfect study of the spoiled, self-centered child I'd initially thought her.

"You bet. Think they bought it?"

Unsure whether or not I'd manage to get away from her before I finally lost control, I loosened my grip and set her down. I was out of sight while she was still trying to decide which feminine wile to use on me.

Chapter 3

We'd had another night of peace, but nobody thought it was anything other than a temporary reprieve. Brandon was probably just worried tempers would run too high among his pack this close to the full moon. The last thing he could afford would be for one of his wolves to make a mistake and do something that couldn't be ignored, either by the rest of the moonborn at large, or by the Coun'hij itself.

I should have awoken refreshed after just a couple of hours' sleep. None of the shape shifters required much in the way of rest, but I overslept by more than an hour and still felt exhausted when I finally arose.

There was too much to be done for me to allow several hours of nightmares to slow me down. Donovan and I went through our once-monthly extended business meeting. He brought me up to speed on all of the things that hadn't been pressing enough to bring up in our nightly discussions, and then we identified additional ways the family capital could be put to work.

Whoever Brandon had managing the tithe he was receiving from the pack was good. He hadn't managed to hit the kind of self-sustaining levels Donovan had achieved, but they were generating a hefty return. In fact, if Brandon hadn't been siphoning so much money off for bribes they'd probably have almost doubled their assets over the last two years.

Once I finished up with Donovan, I ran Rachel into school, and then there was a full day's worth of homework to work my way through. Just because I was skipping school didn't mean that I could forgo the homework.

I'd actually contemplated going to school, but my control had been so spotty the day before I just couldn't justify the risk. I didn't like the thought of Rachel being alone at school, but she was adamant about going, and not even Brandon would be stupid enough to attack her. The end result of that scenario wasn't pretty, but he'd lose most of his wolves before the dust settled.

Rachel was as defenseless as any other human, but Jasmin, Dom, Isaac and I all loved her dearly. Besides, even if the others hadn't, I was dominant to everyone else in the pack. It wasn't the kind of thing I liked to use, but they knew what would happen to them if they let Rachel get hurt.

Even with such an impressive amount on my to-do list, I managed to finish up my classwork and sneak in some painting time before Jasmin returned from Colorado. Predictably she wasn't happy. She stormed into my studio and almost knocked over my latest, still-drying piece.

"I understand that you're not happy, Jas, but if you ruin one of my paintings you're going to be sorry."

It wasn't often that I saw a repentant expression grace Jasmin's face. I didn't get very long to enjoy it.

"I got the permits and property rights issues all straightened out. It was the secretary."

Now that *was* a surprise. Brandon had certainly economized on his bribes there.

"I burst into offices of half the city council and no less than three regulatory bureaucrats, but just wasn't getting anywhere with threats or bribes. They were all claiming innocence and didn't seem to be lying. It wasn't until I'd made my second round that I realized he was way more nervous than the situation called for."

I nodded my thanks as I tried to figure out what the canvas wanted to become. I'd created a border, but was uncharacteristically stuck on where to go with it from there.

"You did excellent work as always. I appreciate your going out there and handling things."

Jasmin's anger was back, closer to the surface than before. Damn full moon. It was going to turn this into a much bigger deal than it had to be.

"You didn't have to send me out there, Alec. Donovan could have handled things. Even Isaac could have handled this one."

I shook my head as I finally gave up and started cleaning my brushes. "You're missing the point, Jas. There was no way to know at the outset just how sticky things were going to be, and aside from Donovan you're my best troubleshooter. Donovan has a number of other duties. I can't tear him away from those lightly, and if things had gotten dicey with Brandon's pack last night you would be missed less than Isaac."

And there was the rub. Jasmin was as stubborn as any hybrid ever born, but when push came to shove she was still just a wolf. Granted her bloodline, the one we shared, gave her certain advantages, advantages which weren't discussed with those not of the same descent. Even so, she wasn't my second, and never would be.

Jasmin looked for a moment as though she'd argue with me. "Okay, I get it. I'm not as valued as either of your muscle-bound hybrids. I'll try to keep that in mind. Do you want me to go get Rachel?"

"No, you just got back. I'll go get her so you can get caught up."

I was surprised when Jasmin indicated she wanted to go with me, but welcomed the company. A short time later we pulled up to the school.

Rachel was waiting for us. Or rather she was outside where she usually waited for us. The two

Sorensen boys were out with her. It took me several seconds to realize the dark item they were tossing back and forth was her math book.

The rage that had been lapping at the borders of my control all day came within a sliver of breaking loose. I slammed the car into the closest parking spot and was out striding towards them before Jasmin even had a chance to get her seatbelt off.

With my beast so close to the surface, my power flared up without any conscious effort, lashing out at the pair with enough force that they spun around. The math book fell forgotten to the ground as they turned and ran.

Rachel retrieved her book and went to the car without speaking. I stood on the sidewalk for several seconds, fighting the urge to run the boys down and tear them in half.

Nobody spoke until we were back home, and then Rachel turned towards me with tear-filled eyes. "Alec, you have to stop doing that. I'm never going to have a normal life if you keep interfering every time someone teases me."

"Rachel, they aren't your friends. People don't treat their friends like that."

"You're missing the point. Right now I don't have a chance of even developing a friendship because everyone is so worried about how you'll react."

"That's ridiculous. Nobody who really wants to be your friend would give me any reason to harm them."

"Please. No guy in the entire town would even dream of asking me out. You'd totally freak."

I wanted to deny her accusation, but I'd spent plenty of time around the boys her age. You didn't need especially acute senses to realize that they weren't worth the effort it would take to push them out of a speeding car.

"See, you can't even argue with me."

"They aren't worthy of you, Rach."

"I don't want someone worthy of me. I'm not looking to get married right now, I just want to be able to spend some time with people who are normal, who are human."

That was truly the underlying problem. It hadn't been as bad before everyone had made their first transformations, but since then Rachel had been on the outside looking into a life she couldn't have.

"I'm sorry. I know this all hasn't been easy for you. I'll try not to be so menacing."

"That's not good enough, Alec. I want your word as the leader of our pack that you won't take any action to interfere with all of the stuff that normally happens to someone my age."

Jasmin stirred for the first time as I met Rachel's gaze and finally nodded.

"I won't promise to forgo any action, but I won't interfere short of anything that will cause you lasting harm."

I let my beast rise back up to the forefront of my being as Rachel invoked the ritual words.

"This ye so swear, unto this you bind yourselves?"

A wash of power surged through me as I opened my mouth. "This we so swear. That we won't interfere with your fellows unless lasting harm is offered, that we will use all resources at our command to avoid becoming forsworn. Unto this we bind ourselves."

Jasmin completed the ritual in her own flare of power. "An oath sworn, a promise witnessed. We will stand in testimony."

Rachel hugged me and then bolted from the car, smiling at Donovan as she disappeared inside the house.

Donovan greeted me at the door, smiling until he felt the lingering traces of power. "You swore an oath. To Rachel, or Jasmin wouldn't have been able to witness it."

I nodded and Donovan's mouth thinned to a disapproving line. "That was rash at the very least, Alec. What did you promise her?"

My beast rose to the surface again, and I fought to keep from lashing out. Donovan had the best interest of the pack at heart. Not only that, he was right. I wasn't unusually anywhere near this impulsive.

"She's lonely, Donovan. Right or wrong, she's convinced she'll never have a chance at real friends until people can rely on the fact that the entire pack isn't going to jump all over them for looking sideways at her. I promised to stay out of all of the teasing, to avoid interfering unless it is something that will bring her lasting harm."

"And you, Jasmin? I'd have thought you'd talk him out of such an ill-advised promise."

Jasmin's chuckle was a dry, humorless thing. "Unless you've got superpowers hiding up your sleeve, Alec is still the boss. I've tried to talk him out of one stupid action after the other for the last two months and he's pretty much established that the only time he'll listen to me is if I'm supporting what he already wanted to do."

Her parting comment was tossed over one shoulder as she disappeared around the corner. "If he'd asked me, I'd have said it was foolish to promise the entire might of the pack to ensure that any dweeb in the town can hassle Rachel. I wasn't asked though, so I'll leave you to clean up the mess, Mr. Wizard."

Donovan sighed disapprovingly at Jasmin and then turned back to me. "I must discuss this with Rachel. Once she understands the gravity of what you've promised I'm sure she can be convinced to release you from the promise."

My beast rose to the surface in a hissing display of power. The promise hadn't been binding on just me. The 'we' in the ritual had included my beast, and it had a very black and white view of a promise. The beast would casually kill for food or to eliminate a rival, but once it had committed to something all other options ceased to exist. The gray areas where humans went when they needed to justify something were anathema to it.

My beast wouldn't allow me to bring pressure to bear against Rachel to get her to release us from the promise. Since Donovan was one of my submissives, letting him do the talking wasn't any different than me doing it myself.

"You get three minutes, Donovan, and there won't be any blackmail or emotional overtones. You can make your case this one time, and that's it. If she says no and I later find out that you've been trying to bully her into recanting, I won't be able to help myself."

Donovan looked as though he'd have liked to take offense at my calling his normal, well-reasoned arguments bullying, but this close to the full moon he knew better than to push any of us very far.

"I'm very aware of the effects of the binding ritual, Aléc. I'll be ready at your convenience."

Feeling more exhausted by the minute, I followed Donovan to Rachel's room, where his efforts were exactly as effective as we'd both known they would be. Rachel wasn't swayed in the slightest.

Donovan reached the end of his three minutes, bowed ever so correctly, and departed. I had one more duty before I could finally surrender to my bed.

The alpha of the Chicago pack hasn't ever believed in cell phones. It made contacting him somewhat tricky, but the antiquated landline he'd finally had installed a few years before usually worked sooner or later.

This time the phone cut off on the second ring. "Yes?"

"Is Ulrich available?"

Calling another pack leader was always risky business. There were dozens of different ways to offend someone, and the situation with the Chicago pack was even more touchy than most. "No. This is Shawn, though. Is that you, Alec?"

I felt a brief surge of relief. Shawn was Ulrich's son. We were approximately the same age, and he was decidedly modern American as opposed to his father's Old World upbringing. The odds of me putting my foot wrong with Shawn were much less than with his father.

"Yeah, it's me. I've got a situation developing over here. Brandon's insinuating the Coun'hij's decided to take a blind eye where he's concerned. It seems pretty far-fetched, but I thought maybe I'd better check and see if anyone else had any clues how the wind was blowing."

Shawn was quiet for several seconds, digesting my revelation and fitting it with everything else he knew before responding. "That's bad news. Agony made a surprise visit yesterday morning. Dad figured it for just another expedition to dish out some hurt for him having been friends with your dad. I'm betting it was at least partially designed as a message."

"And a nasty one at that. I'm sorry that you guys are bleeding again because of what happened with our pack."

"Nothing to be done about it now. History isn't going to remake itself. Just be careful, none of us are looking to have it repeat."

The conversation stayed with me even after I'd retired to bed. Shawn had touched, however obliquely, on the events that had destroyed my father's pack, and resulted in the murder of more than a dozen innocents.

My father's legacy should have been the dawn of a new age among the moonborn. Instead he'd left a pair of shattered, unhealthy packs and nothing else.

Contemplating the past didn't solve anything. There weren't any new insights to be offered after so many years of analysis, but it at least distracted me from the more pressing concerns of what to do about Brandon when the Coun'hij had all but signed my death sentence. He was little more than a jumped-up thug, but I couldn't avoid the feeling I was being carefully outmaneuvered on nearly every front.

When sleep finally found me, it was only a brief respite. Dreams hadn't been a place of innocence for nearly as long as I could remember. It was one more thing they'd taken away from us.

This dream seemed innocuous. I found myself in the grotto, the heart of the garden that Donovan and Andrew spent so much time maintaining.

It was evening, the time when the garden was the most peaceful. Night-blooming flowers and the tranquility pool mixed their scents with the myriad aromas that rose from the desert just to the edge of the family holdings.

As enchanting as the unseen choir was, the visual experience was even better. Tendrils of ivy, glowing with life, partially concealed the rock walls from which the grotto had been cut. An errant breeze carried with it another host of scents, and I turned and found my latest creation.

The potted rose still didn't have a name. I'd held off selecting one first because I'd wanted to see how hardy the cross was, and then because nothing had seemed quite appropriate. It was a different kind of art, a different manner of creation, but this was something I shared with Father.

It had been Donovan's gentle hands that had guided me, had taught me the breeder's art, but it was on Dad's foundation that we built. The most promising fruit was a white rose, edged in purple. It was thornless, with full, velvety petals, and a scent that seemed to magnify and enrich everything around it.

The parent plant had been gorgeous but almost completely scentless. The cross we'd brought in six years ago had changed all that. Humans would have found the aroma attractive, without realizing just how unique it was. Now, after decades of work across two generations, we had something that was beautiful and disease-resistant without destroying the characteristic scent.

I hadn't been giving the roses the attention they deserved lately. Donovan would wordlessly ensure that they were still cared for, but it was one more sign of failure, one more way in which I wasn't measuring up.

I sighed and stood back up, only to find Adriana Paige watching me. It wasn't fair, but she'd appeared at the same time as my latest round of bad news. She wasn't the cause of Brandon's machinations, but to some extent she'd become associated with them.

It seemed that my dreams were even less of a refuge than I'd hoped.

"Of all the places for you to intrude, why did it have to be here?"

The mask that she wore almost constantly seemed to slip slightly and I was struck again by just how attractive she was. The hint of light playing beneath her skin was incredibly alluring. In another shape shifter it would have marked her as powerful, desirable because it meant she'd be able to protect herself and future children.

In her it was merely an odd genetic quirk, and instead of dwelling on it I found my gaze drifting to an exceptionally symmetrical face, to beautiful blond hair, and a trim body that was perfectly framed by faded shorts and a thin tank top. The perfection ended as soon as she opened her mouth.

"Only you could see such beauty and think only of keeping it to yourself. Trust me, even with surroundings like this I'd much rather be elsewhere if you're part of the bargain."

The rebuke caught me completely by surprise. It'd been a long time since anyone outside the pack had spoken their mind so freely to me, and even the pack tended to be circumspect in their criticisms. Unlike Brandon, I wasn't the type to punish people for speaking their mind. Unfortunately, from the outside, the humans often weren't able to determine which power bloc was committing which atrocity.

Before I could fully process her statement, Adriana shot me another venomous look.

"At least you won't have to suffer my presence for much longer; we'll be gone all too quickly."

It was too reminiscent of something I'd heard time and time again. My dream mind was once again reminding me of why it was so dangerous to get involved with humans. Barring death in some kind of challenge or war, I could look forward to nearly three hundred years of young, vibrant life. She, just like Rachel, would be lucky to experience fifty or sixty years of existence before age and illness tainted the remaining decade or two of life.

"No, you're right, all too soon you'll go the way of so many others. If I can depend on nothing else, I can rely on that."

Another finger of wind darted down into the grotto and Adriana reflexively closed her eyes, almost like one of the moonborn tasting the air. The mask slipped a little and the simple joy that replaced it made me mourn for my own loss of innocence. Most days I'd trade everything I had to be able to go back to the time when I'd enjoyed the simple things of life, when I'd still had dreams.

I had one last glimpse of beautiful blue eyes and then I was ripped screaming from the dream.

Mother's sobs pulled me out of bed and into a full sprint towards her room before I was even fully awake.

Chapter 4

"He's gone. Oh, Alec. What are we going to do without him?"

The words pulled at my mind, burrowing their way deeper and deeper into my being. Mother had sunk into a full-blown attack. I should have seen it coming. 'Welcoming' was the last piece she'd ever played before the cycle ended and she started over again. Apparently I was too distracted to properly attend to my own mother either.

My earliest memories had been of the attacks. Even back then my presence had been the only thing capable of calming her. Of course calm was a relative term. For a child barely old enough to speak, even the minor attacks had been terrifying. The nightmares had lost most of their power over me since then, but still occasionally made an appearance.

Rachel continued to hold out hope that the shrinks were right, that the repeated cycles might eventually lead to her coming to terms with the loss.

I'd given up on that idea a while ago. How could she possibly come to deal with what she'd lost? Dad had been her entire world. She'd cut herself off from everything else with the abrupt completeness of the Ja'tell bond, and his death had simultaneously been the loss of her husband and her pusher.

She'd spent the night reliving the experience of being informed of his death. Rachel had tried to go to her before I arrived, but she'd turned away from her daughter with the unseeing eyes of someone who, however briefly, believed she only had one child.

On good days Mom acknowledged Rachel's existence, but the attacks were never good days. Even once I'd arrived she'd sobbed for hours, gripping me with a frail strength that couldn't possibly hurt a grown shape shifter, but which had been almost painful to a child still unable to understand what was happening.

By the time she'd finally lapsed into unconsciousness, it was too late to return to sleep. It was fortunate that the night of the full moon was now behind us. Still, I was so exhausted that the lesser pull of the moon was very distracting.

Shape shifters required less sleep than humans, but our sleep was consequently more important. My beast was prowling at the edge of my self-control, almost as though sensing my weakness. I shouldn't be going to school, but we couldn't afford to show weakness, and Brandon's pack already viewed our staying home from class the day of the full moon as a lack of strength.

Rachel and I rode into school with Jasmin in her Mercedes, and even before we made it inside the teasing started. One of the senior jocks on the football team dumped her books without looking up from his phone.

He'd done it without realizing who he was tormenting, or he wouldn't have dared. When he looked up to see the results of his handiwork he'd gone instantly white, but constrained by my oath I'd simply helped Rachel pick up her scattered books instead of throwing him against the wall and ordering him to pick them up for her.

Jasmin didn't look any happier about it than me, but Rachel almost glowed as the ox-brained jock turned and fled down the hall with his skin fully intact.

The morning went pretty much as normal except for the almost constant flow of incidents. Apparently word spread faster even than I'd expected. There was still enough fear of the pack for the teasing not to progress to the truly terrible things that teenagers could work themselves up to, but the sheer volume bothered more than just Jasmin and me.

By third period a click of girls had formed around Rachel, and they served as a kind of buffer between her and the rest of the world.

I was frankly amazed when I arrived at the cafeteria and saw the group with Rachel. I wouldn't have expected her idea to work at all, but it hadn't been quite the disaster I'd expected. The girls who'd surrounded her weren't the ones I'd have picked as friends. They tended towards the social climbers and gossips, but it was more acceptance than Rachel usually got from the school at large.

Jasmin and I loaded up with two slices of pizza and an extra-large serving of fries each and headed towards Isaac and the others. One of the benefits of being moonborn was the kind of metabolism that would let even the girls stoke up on thousands of 'extra' calories per day and still not build up any appreciable body fat.

We were nearly to our usual table when I heard it happen. Having extra acute hearing doesn't necessarily mean you can understand everything you hear. In especially noise-rich environments it can sometimes be hard to simultaneously follow so many different conversations. I usually coped by listening for specific voices. Like Rachel's.

I caught the tail end of one of the girls next to her.

"...Cassie wouldn't like that."

"Please. She doesn't own him. If you like him you should go for it. It's not like she'll provide any competition. I've never seen her keep a normal boy interested for more than a few days. Once they realize what she's really like they never hang around."

The giggling that followed was cut short as Rachel's 'friends' looked up to find Cassie standing at their table.

"Are you really that stupid? Did you really just make this about you and me?"

Cassie overturned the table and then shoved Rachel just hard enough to knock her chair over. As everyone else backed away to give the two girls plenty of room, I realized Cassie's anger was purely a show. She was creating an incident, but I had no way of knowing why.

The pack moved in to defend Rachel, to shield her from someone who could easily snap her back, and I nearly lost control of my beast.

My subvocalized growl was enough to pull everyone up short as Cassie resumed hurling insults.

"You're going to get what's coming to you, you little slut."

Rachel was bewildered. She looked calm, but I could smell the fear begin to roll off of her. She'd gone too long without adequate sleep. Or maybe she was just too enamored of the illusion of popularity to even contemplate releasing me from the bond.

Whatever the reason, her response came out calm and even.

"I haven't done anything to you, Cassie, and you know it. This is all just an excuse."

The crowd was pressing in closer now, filling in behind the two packs but leaving the usual no-man's-land between as they chose sides.

"Shut your lying mouth. I'm really going to enjoy this."

Cassie sent a challenging wave of power out and Jasmin started shaking slightly as she nearly lost control of her beast. I grabbed her arm before she could hurl herself forward. Stopping her sufficed, but my beast all but demanded I attack her from having come close to violating my bond.

Brandon shot me a satisfied smirk as Isaac moved up closer to my back. I knew the latter wanted to spare Rachel from what was coming, but I shook my head. Until and unless Rachel said the binding words I couldn't let him help any more than I could help myself.

I'd spent my entire life trying to amass the power needed to protect my family and my pack, and I was just as powerless as ever. Cassie spat something else venomous and pointless at Rachel, but it was evident Rachel was starting to realize just how bad things could get. She was shaking now, and almost tripped and fell when Cassie shoved her into me hard enough to leave bruises.

The situation was rapidly escalating out of control when someone stepped into the buffer zone between the two packs.

Adriana stepped into the circle, catching Cassie's attention and causing her to spin around and confront the recent arrival.

"Take off."

Adriana shook her head, clenching her fists a little tighter as she began trembling ever so slightly.

Isaac let out the briefest growl and I suddenly realized that the racing heart and trembling could be interpreted as something other than fear.

As she began to glow even more brightly than she had a moment before I realized there was a chance she was gearing up for a confrontation, and there was no way for Cassie to be sure that she wasn't facing a hybrid.

Adriana leaned ever so slightly into Cassie and uttered her first words.

"Leave her alone."

It should have caused Cassie to attack. She wasn't used to backing down inside her own pack, and she'd shown a willingness to fight Jasmin despite being woefully outclassed. For a second I thought she was indeed going to knock Adriana to the ground, but then Brandon reached forward and restrained her.

As quickly as that, the fight was averted. The spectators broke up as the two packs left the cafeteria through separate doors. Rachel started into shock before we'd even made it to the thicket of trees we routinely used when we needed to discuss pack business while still at school.

Jasmin slipped an arm around Rachel's waist and then all but carried her the last fifteen yards. Isaac and Dominic crowded around her to make sure she was ok. I wanted to join them, but my mind was spinning so quickly that I was frozen in place.

Donovan had gone to great lengths to try and train me to think beyond the immediate obstacles, and I was creating contingency plans, picking and choosing among ideas with a speed that sometimes didn't even allow me to fully contemplate an idea before my subconscious had judged and discarded it.

"They'll attack her. Maybe not now, but Brandon can't allow anyone to stand up to him and not punish them. Maybe not directly, but she's going to suffer for having stood up to Cassie."

Jasmin and Isaac looked up at me, obviously seeing where I was headed. They hadn't thought things through to that point by themselves, but now they could see the inevitable conclusion.

"I'm going to offer her our protection. Brandon won't attack her as casually if I bind her to us."

Jessica and James went from disinterested to enraged in the briefest of moments.

James crossed the distance between us and was in my face quicker than most humans were able to blink.

"You'll get us killed! She's not worth us bleeding over."

Isaac appeared behind James and threw him back into the closest tree.

"You don't have the right to challenge Alec until you've defeated me."

James' eyes were nearly the yellow of his beast; Isaac had already crouched down into a combat stance.

"Enough. As pack leader I invoke my right to stand in Isaac's place."

It was an old rule, one rarely invoked, but I was tired of Isaac bleeding to keep James in line.

As soon as the words were out of my mouth James sprang at me, but I rocked him backwards with a punch to the stomach and then stepped back and let my beast roar up to the surface in an explosion of power.

James rode his transformation to his hulking hybrid form at the same time that mine completed, and then we went at each other with claw and fang as the rest of the pack fell back to serve as lookouts.

James was big, and fast, but I was bigger, faster, and gifted with the blessings of the royal line. He rushed me and I sidestepped him, slashing up his arm with the semi-retractable claws on the end of each finger.

He spun around, sinking his left hand into my side, but I was already moving forward. I bowled him over, sinking my foot talons into his chest and right arm at the same time that I immobilized him with one hand and wrapped the other around his throat.

It was a killing position. We both knew it, and my beast thrummed through me demanding I close my right hand and rip his throat out.

He struggled, trying to buck me off, and I lost a sliver of control. The claws pierced his throat enough to increase the flow of blood, and he froze as even his beast couldn't deny the imminence of death.

"Yield."

My voice was harsh and distorted, coming as it did from a throat that hadn't really been designed with language in mind, but the demand was unmistakable.

The fury in James' eyes hadn't lessened, but he finally relaxed, raising his head to fully bare his throat in an unmistakable gesture of submission. I released him and turned to take in the rest of the pack.

"Does anyone else wish to dispute my decision to offer our protection to Adriana?"

One by one they all dropped to their knees and raised their chins, exposing throats. Jasmin was the last, unnecessarily courting punishment once again.

I felt a stab of pain as I let my shape shrink back down to the one I'd been born with. The wound in my chest wasn't immediately life threatening, but it was bleeding fairly profusely. I looked around, found the wreckage of my clothes and used what was left of my shirt to apply direct pressure.

James and I were both clad in only ha'bits, our clothes shredded from the transformation to hybrid.

"Jess, go get your Escalade. We need a change of clothes."

When we arrived at the estate, Donovan took in the gash in my side and shook his head. He waited until Jess left to drop James off at his mother's cottage before speaking.

"I trust it was worth it, and that you came out the victor?"

"You were right. I should never have made that promise to Rachel. Cassie used it to set Rachel up for the beating of her life. If the new girl hadn't bluffed Cassie into backing down, things would have gotten ugly."

Donovan steered me to the examination table and started taping up James' handiwork.

"Rachel released me from the promise as soon as James and I got done fighting, but I'm worried about what Cassie and the others will do to Adriana if we just leave her out on her own."

I got a nod as Donovan taped a large patch of gauze to my side. "Hence the challenge from James. You do realize his worries are not entirely without merit. Unaided, the Paige girl is doubtless going to regret her involvement in facing Cassie down, but offering her your protection brings its own set of risks."

My beast didn't like Donovan's words but I forced it down. He was just offering advice, not challenging our dominance.

"I know. If she becomes aware of what we are, Brandon won't have to play games with the Coun'hij anymore, they'll have the exact excuse they need to come in and wipe us out. Still, she stepped in and protected one of our own when we couldn't do it. That obligates us to assume some risk to protect her as well."

Donovan nodded wordlessly and then left me to make my way back to my room.

I tiredly pulled out another set of clothes, something similar to what I'd worn before the fight, and then retrieved the excuse slip that Donovan had just written out in my 'mother's' handwriting, and rejoined the others.

Jess looked just as pissed as always. James was more subdued than normal—presumably he'd just had his own 'debriefing' with his mother.

We made it back just in time for me to slip by the office, hand over my excuse slip and then rush off to Pre-calculus. Mrs. Campbell gave me an odd look when she saw me, but I couldn't think of any reason for her to think anything was out of the ordinary.

Once the last bell rang, Jasmin intercepted me before I'd even made it back to my locker.

"Alec, I know you're the boss, but I'm worried about this Adri girl. She doesn't feel like a wolf, but she glows like a Fir'shan and she faced down Cassie. I think you should consider the possibility she's not what she appears."

I needed to get back home and rest before I lost control. It was getting harder and harder to override the most basic instincts of my kind. Dominance, submission, fight, flight—it was all slowly slipping through my grasp.

"I understand your concern, Jas, but she risked more even than she knew standing up to Cassie. I'm offering her some kind of limited protection at least."

As soon as Jasmin nodded in acceptance I set off looking for Adriana. It wasn't difficult. I knew where her locker was; from there I just followed the freshest scent trail.

I actually almost collided with her as I came around the last corner before the tutor lab. The abrupt motion as I stopped pulled at my side, tearing the wound back open with a lance of pain.

She momentarily looked shocked to see me, and then her usual mask slipped back into place.

"Adri, I wanted to talk to you about what happened today."

There was the slightest blip in her pulse and respiration as I used the shortened form of her name. Interesting, it was the kind of response you expected when you caused someone pain.

Exhaustion momentarily sent me down a blind alley as I wondered why she'd reacted so oddly. Her words struck me with the suddenness of a crowbar.

"You mean when your sister nearly got beaten by that whore, and you not only didn't do anything, you stopped your friends from doing anything either."

I almost ripped her head off. Not figuratively either. Shape shifters weren't always completely safe to be around and apparently my control was even more frayed than I'd realized. She continued before I'd even managed to get myself fully back under control.

"The fact that I, a little waif from out of town, could defuse the situation and save Rachel no doubt sticks in your craw, which explains why you're lurking around out here waiting to talk to me. Because only then can you fabricate some reason for why everything had to go down the way it did, and thereby save face!"

It was unimaginable that this mere human had the guts to stand before me and verbally whip me while my power arced back and forth between us. I had to shut her up before she said something that pushed me over the edge.

"You don't understand."

"Of course. That's an easy comeback. I don't understand. You're right, I don't. I would've done almost anything to protect my sister, but you didn't even care that Rachel was going to get hurt."

I was trembling, which was a bad sign. Even worse, my voice had changed subtly as my throat lengthened and shifted inside of me. I acted without even thinking, lunging forward and grabbing her by the shoulders with more strength than was safe.

"I was going to offer you my protection against Cassie and Brandon, and you throw your supposed superiority in my face. Fine, but don't come crying back to me when the mask comes off."

I'd torn my side completely open now, I could feel a trickle of liquid making its way past the gauze. I spun around and left, only just able to rein myself in enough to avoid moving at unnatural speeds.

TORN

I pulled my phone out of my pocket and
dialed Rachel as I headed towards my Porsche.
"We're leaving now. I'll pick you up outside the
lab in thirty seconds."

Chapter 5

I made it home in record time, only to be 'sent' to my bed as soon as we arrived. Donovan was right about how badly I needed sleep, but it was all I could do to put a leash on my anger and retire to my room.

Just seconds after I collapsed into bed I was asleep and dreaming.

I found myself at the top of the mountain which marked one edge of the estate. My vision was keen enough to make out a multitude of tiny details on the valley floor. I was looking out over the far side, so I couldn't see the estate, but there was no shortage of local wildlife to watch. I already knew I could spend hours doing just that. Equally enjoyable, the cool, crisp air held a hundred thousand scents to savor. Even the air tasted different than the stuff further down the mountain. I'd idly wondered a hundred different times what the air would taste like at the top of the world's truly tall peaks.

The mountaintop had been one of my favorite places to go when I was younger, after my first transformation, but before the duties of the pack became too oppressive. I hadn't been up to the top for months.

Visiting it, even in a dream, felt like coming home. It was perfect in every detail except for Adri's presence no more than a foot in front of me. Her being here after my recent verbal humiliation at her hands was almost more than I could stomach.

Things weren't made any easier when she finally noticed me and responded with typical harshness.

"Why did you follow me here?"

It was just a dream. I found myself suddenly relaxing.

"Actually, I can't think of any place *I'd* rather not be. You seem to have a gift for making my sanctuaries inhospitable, and rendering my rest uneasy."

Even as my mouth warned her away, the rest of me was drinking her in. She hadn't become any less desirable. If anything the knowledge that she was willing to stand up for Rachel, even against me, put her in a class all by herself. I almost missed her next words.

"That should be remedied quite shortly. I rather expect that even *my* mother can't go on thinking she'll make a living for us down here after we've been evicted. I'm sure you'll be relieved to be able to go back to your stupid petty dominance games."

I was shocked awake as suddenly as I'd fallen asleep. It made no sense, but it matched completely with the feeling Brandon had been outmaneuvering me somehow.

I flipped my phone open. "Donovan, I think Brandon's moved against the Paige family. What other information have we turned up about them? Specifically about their home and the mortgage they took out to buy it."

"Actually, that's one of the items I'd planned on mentioning to you tonight. I've turned up a surprising dearth of hard information about either of them. Under other circumstances I might have dismissed it, but for someone who's moved into Sanctuary, it represents a possible concern."

"Because the only way for them not to have left more tracks than that is if someone has been hiding it."

"Correct, sir. Unfortunately it's going to require additional time and resources to determine who it was that turned them into ghosts, as it were."

"Keep on it, please, Donovan. I'd bet it was Brandon, but I can't understand why he'd do that. We need more information if we're to have any hope of not getting buried when the tsunami he's crafting finally breaks over us."

I pulled my phone out and dialed the local bank president as I headed towards Jasmin's room. I might not have any hard information, but eviction could only mean one thing.

"This is William Kard."

"Mr. Kard, I've recently begun to entertain nagging suspicions that I'm not being kept fully in the loop."

"I don't know what you're talking about, Alec."

"What's the status of the mortgage on the old Anderson home?"

"You can't seriously believe that I'm familiar with the circumstances surrounding a relatively minor loan among the several hundred in our portfolio? Even if I did happen to know its current standing I can't discuss that type of confidential information with you."

His voice was the perfect combination of indignity and sincerity, and I didn't trust it for a heartbeat.

"You're prevaricating, which generally means you're lying. We've had a fairly amicable relationship up till now, Mr. Kard, so I'm not going to press you to divulge anything you feel improper. Instead I'll make you a promise. For as long as you continue to co-operate with me, to act in our mutual best interest, our family will continue to use you as our primary banking resource."

"That's a very generous promise, Alec..."

I cut him off before he could finish. "If, however, you ever act in a way I believe not to be in my family's interest I'll immediately withdraw everything currently sitting on deposit with you and leave you better than six million short of your statutory depository requirements."

"There's no call to threaten me, Alec. You'll find I don't respond well to that type of talk."

"It's not a threat, Mr. Kard, it's a simple statement of fact. I'm aware that such an action would roll your bank up overnight, but quite frankly at that point it wouldn't be my problem. Please consider this your official notice that I'm very interested in Mrs. Paige remaining in our lovely town, as a resident of her current house. In light of that, is there anything you'd like to tell me?"

"Brandon isn't going to like this, and I can't survive him taking all of his assets out any more than I could if you carry through with your threats."

"You'll be even worse off when I get done talking to the federal regulators."

"There may be a slight irregularity in the Paige mortgage, now that you remind me of just how important their interests are to you. Apparently she lied about her employment on the original loan application. Something about a contract with the Mayor to do a tourism brochure."

"I don't think you understand just how important this matter is, Mr. Kard. I want you to take it upon yourself to personally see to it the issue is resolved in their favor. This evening."

It almost sounded like he was having a stroke. It took him several tries to find his voice.

"That's absurd. I haven't done anything to merit this kind of treatment."

"Yes, you have. You're alleging loan fraud and I know very well nothing of the type has occurred. Your people would have confirmed all of those details before you ever wrote the original loan."

"I've got a signed confirmation stating that she was never promised the contract by the city. My people have seen it. If I fail to call the loan, I'll have some whistleblower calling the Feds."

"You'll have a confirmation from the Mayor's office first thing tomorrow morning. The next time I catch you purposefully losing the original paperwork on a loan, though, I will shut your bank down. Please fax over a copy of the confirmation your office received from the mayor."

I looked at my phone for several seconds before punching in Donovan's number.

"Yes, sir?"

"Who's the member of the mayor's staff most likely to have been working on the tourism brochure?"

"I believe Peters has been taking point on that particular project."

"Thanks, Donovan. Can you put me through to him?"

"Of course, sir."

Peters didn't sound particularly happy when he finally picked up on the sixth ring.

"Mr. Peters, this is Alec Graves. I have reason to believe that you've been pressured to lie about a contract you recently signed with Mrs. Paige."

"I need to talk to an attorney."

"No, you don't. I'm not interested in seeing you prosecuted. I do want to see the Paige family dealt with honestly though."

Peters didn't respond for several seconds. For a second I thought maybe his conscience was going to lose the battle.

"I'd like that too, but even if what you suspect were somehow true, there's nothing I can do about it. I need this job. If Wilkenson fires me, I'm done for."

"On the contrary. I'll hire you as a factor for some of my holdings in Nevada. You can spend three days down there and work from home the rest of the week. When the honorable mayor comes up for re-election next year, I'll back you with at least three hundred thousand dollars' worth of campaign backing. You'll win in an unprecedented landslide."

Peters' swallow was audible even over the phone. "Even with that, I'm not sure I can win. Wilkenson knows where all the bodies around here are buried. If I did win though, I'd be my own man, not some kind of puppet."

"You might be surprised at some of the bodies that come to light during the period leading up to the election. As long as there aren't any skeletons in your closet that I should know about, then all you have to do is fax over a copy of the Paige contract."

Ten minutes later Donovan sent me a text confirming that both faxes had arrived.

I dialed the mayor's number as I slowly paced back and forth across the room.

"Mayor, Wilkenson?"

"This is he. Who is this and how did you get this number?"

"It's Alec Graves, Mr. Mayor. I think we should talk about the tourism brochure you've been considering lately."

"I don't know what you're talking about."

"I'm talking about your office awarding a legally enforceable contract and then lying in order to help Kard kick the Paige family out of their home."

"You have no proof of that."

"Actually, I do. I have copies of both the original contract and your personally signed denial that the bank was sent just yesterday. It really was quite careless for you to get so involved. Brandon must have offered you quite the bribe."

He was silent for a second. "Peters. That weasel sold me out."

"No, Mr. Mayor, Peters just guaranteed himself a job. If you move against him then I'll see you thrown out of office and sent to jail."

"You don't have the power."

"Mr. Mayor, you have no idea what I'm capable of. Go to the Paige house tonight, apologize for the...oversight and congratulate Mrs. Paige on winning the contract. If you ever mention this conversation to anyone I'll make very sure your career comes to a very sudden, very bloody end."

I needed someone to make sure the Mayor followed orders. Jasmin's room was empty. I turned to go follow her scent trail and almost ran Rachel over.

"She went with James. They're taking a foot patrol around town to establish our continuing right to be out there. Jasmin said they'd be fine because Brandon's pack won't try anything with all those potential witnesses around."

I almost swore. "The two of them shouldn't be let out unsupervised."

The Porsche took corners well into triple digits, but I still felt like I wasn't going to get there quickly enough. There was no way I'd find them while still in my car, so as soon as I reached town I bailed out and started running in the direction of the strongest scent trail.

Less than a minute later I came around the corner of the school just in time to see Vincent shove James. Even well into twilight as we were, it was obvious who was doing the baiting.

Cassie was circling Jasmin and Nathanial was standing back with a smirk on his face. I was still more than sixty feet away when Vincent backhanded James and began shifting.

James' figure began blurring into his own hybrid form even before he'd finished recoiling from the blow. Jasmin knocked Cassie back into the flagpole and dropped down onto all fours before Nathanial could do more than blink.

It was insane for Vincent to have pushed us into a confrontation out in the open, but I let my own hybrid form explode outwards as I covered the last few feet.

James was still injured from our fight earlier, and he was rapidly losing ground to Vincent, who was fresh and unwounded. Jasmin and Nathanial had locked already. It looked like she might have the superior position, but they were whirling about too fast to be certain.

Cassie spun around as she realized they weren't alone, but I grabbed her with one hand and hurled her into the brick of the outer wall. It would have been simpler to kill her, but we couldn't afford a death out here. Unless there was no question that they'd breached our territory, there was too much chance we'd be the ones punished for the fight.

Vincent had clinched with James, each wolf trying to immobilize their opponent's arms and legs while savaging them with their mouths. It was obvious that James didn't have much longer. I hit the pair of them with enough force to warp the heavy metal doors, knocking Vincent loose.

Vincent tried to spin around and attack me, but I already had a firm grip on his arm, and spun him around and slammed him into the wall before he could regain his footing.

James was back on his feet and he sprang at the closest enemy he could find. Nathanial let out a yelp as wicked, eight-inch claws tore him away from Jasmin.

"This is over. Go back and tell Brandon to police his pack better or next time he'll find himself explaining to the Coun'hij why it was the three of you felt it wise to use your alternate forms so close to the middle of town."

My voice came out low and threatening, but that wasn't what caused Vincent and Cassie to back off. With my arrival the odds had just swung soundly in our favor. The fact that both James and I were still bleeding was nothing compared to what Vincent and Nathanial had just received.

For a moment it looked like James was going to refuse to put Nathanial down, but even overcome with blood lust, his beast knew better than to tangle with both Jasmin and me.

James dropped the smaller wolf into a bloody heap that Vincent had to pick up and carry away. He was going to miss a day or two of school, but he wouldn't die.

As soon as the other three were safely out of sight we transformed back to our human forms and gathered up the scattered pieces of clothing.

I ordered James and Jasmin back to the estate, and almost thought Jasmin was going to argue. I followed them back to Jasmin's black Mercedes, just to make sure she didn't disobey.

James was in my face as soon as I pulled into the garage.

"We had them. Dead to rights. They started a fight in a neutral spot, and we would've come out on top. Why did you blow yet another chance to kill Vincent?"

"First of all, I didn't blow the last chance. Second of all I'm the Kir'shan here. You do what I say when I say it. Tonight wasn't the time to fight to the death. Especially not in the middle of town. You were stupid to have let them goad you into a battle right there, and only the fact that they changed first is saving you from a beating."

It wasn't the most politic of ways to handle the situation, but I couldn't tell him the truth. The only thing keeping the pack together right now was the belief that inside the ridiculous set of rules the Coun'hij had established we had a chance at beating Brandon, or at least goading him into the kind of mistake that'd cause them to take care of him for us.

If James and Jess knew the rules were being rewritten to favor Brandon, there was a distinct possibility they'd disappear on me.

For a second I thought that James was going to attack me, but he'd picked up a whole new set of wounds. He was even less of a match for me than normal and he knew it. The energy level inside the garage ratcheted up nearly to the point of a transformation, and then he turned and stormed out.

Jasmin clapped sarcastically, reminding me that she'd just served as an audience.

"Okay, now that he's safely out of hearing range how about if you tell me what's really going on?"

"No, Jas. How about if *you* tell me what's going on? We both know it was the height of stupidity for the two of you to go into Sanctuary by yourselves. What's gotten into you lately?"

"I don't know what you're talking about."

"You're lying. Lying and hiding something."

She was mad, but unlike James, she was capable of controlling her anger. From time to time.

"They've decided to come down on Brandon's side, haven't they?"

The abrupt change took me by surprise. I couldn't respond without telling her exactly what she wanted to know. Sometimes I could bluff Jas, or even use some misdirection to convince her of something that wasn't exactly true, but I wouldn't be able to lie to her. She gave me a second to establish that I wasn't going to say anything and then shrugged.

"It was bound to happen, Alec. I won't tell any of the others, but Isaac at least will probably figure it out."

"You're right. I'm surprised you're not heading for the hills, but you're right."

"Please. Isaac and I have both known this would happen sooner or later. They wouldn't have done what they did to your father and the rest of the pack if they weren't completely terrified of what he represented. You're a focal point. Not now, not with such a small pack behind you, but every day you hold Brandon off is another mini victory. Eventually the other packs will start noticing, and they can't afford that."

"That doesn't mean you all have to go down in flames with me."

"Yes it does. Maybe we could have defected to Brandon early on, but that's not an option now. We've become part of the symbol. Any reign of terror only lasts as long as resistance is swiftly destroyed. If they let us go, they risk losing control."

Whatever else Jasmin might have said was interrupted by my cell phone. I recognized Rachel's voice as I answered.

"Alec, Mom needs you. Where are you?"

"I'm in the garage. I'll be there in a moment."

Jasmin turned to leave. I thought about stopping her. She was hiding something, and that didn't bode well for her continued cooperation, but there was a limit to just how far I could press her. Bleeding both of us, her especially, to get my answer would be poor repayment for someone who'd chosen to stick her hand into the meat grinder we were headed towards.

Rachel met me just inside the front door.

"I'm really sorry, Alec. I tried to calm her down but she won't listen to me."

"It's okay, Rach. I should have remembered this was coming. It always happens within a day or two of the big breakdown."

I went to step around her, but she reached a hand out to stop me.

"Alec, I was wrong to ask you to promise that. I can see that now. I shouldn't have traded on the guilt you feel to get something that could have put the whole pack at risk."

My sigh was more expressive than I meant to make it. Her resulting smile was the one she used when she was just moments from crying.

"Anyways, thanks for being willing to stand up for me. Oh, and for being willing to stand up for Adri. I think maybe she and I could be real friends someday. She seems different than all the other girls."

It seemed cruel to deprive her of her latest hope. I couldn't help but think maybe I should do it regardless, but I didn't.

"Well, if the two of you are going to be friends you should probably know she doesn't like to be called Adri. I'm not sure why but her heart races every time anyone says Adri instead of Adriana."

Her smile had transformed to a happy thing, and I took my leave. Once I arrived outside Mother's room, I steeled myself with a couple of quick breaths and then knocked on her door, letting myself in after several seconds.

Mom was curled up on the window seat sobbing. She was always frail-looking, but currently looked even more fragile than normal. I gathered her into my arms and began rocking her back and forth until she registered my presence.

"Oh, Alec. My poor, poor child. Whatever will we do without your father? You're so young. You won't even remember him."

TORN

She broke into wracking sobs again and I wished I could hand this duty off to someone else. She was still replaying the past, but the worst was still to come. The loss had been the worst part for her. For me it was when she told a toddler she'd take care of him. I wasn't a toddler anymore, but she didn't even realize it right now. Didn't realize it and didn't understand that I already knew she wouldn't fulfill her promise to take care of us.

Chapter 6

It would have been bad enough if last night had ended with my futile efforts to console my mother. Instead I'd had a full night's worth of homework which had been cut short to go out on patrol.

Apparently Brandon hadn't been pleased by just how badly Nathanial had been hurt. With the sole exception of Nathanial, every other wolf in his pack had conducted an extended patrol around the edges of our territory. I'd been pretty confident when his scent told me he was along for the ride, that there wouldn't be any actual violation of our territory, but it was the kind of threat we had to honor.

Neither James nor I had been at one hundred percent but we'd gamely kept up for hour after hour as Brandon's pack had dared us to step over the line into neutral territory. Predictably it hadn't been easy to keep certain members of our pack from taking the bait.

Conducting such an exercise with a freshly reopened wound had made it all the more frustrating. Despite my slight fear that I'd bleed out before the night ended, I'd awoken to find that my side was mostly healed.

Depressingly enough, the high point of the night was when I found the answer to our physics problem in one of the reference books I'd purchased upon enrolling in the class. Luckily it was a fairly straightforward explanation and I was able to just barely complete typing up my solution before it was time to go to school.

Once I'd arrived at school, I'd dealt with the normal round of trash talk and posturing from Brandon. Dream Adriana had pegged us correctly. Nearly everything we did in public came back to some kind of dominance game or another. Most of the kids who'd grown up in Sanctuary were so used to it all that they didn't even realize what was going on, but I hated it. If Brandon hadn't been so set on shredding our pack and soaking up the remnants, I would have been more than happy to leave him completely alone.

It was foolish to attribute the insights she'd displayed in my dreams to the flesh-and-blood person, but I found myself looking forward to seeing her again. She was extremely frustrating, but in less than a week she'd noticed things that people who'd been here their entire lives hadn't ever even given a second glance. She'd drawn the wrong conclusions with most of it, but the fact that she'd come even that close was intriguing.

I walked into Physics more than a minute earlier than usual and headed straight to my desk only to almost stumble when Adriana pulled her desk close to mine and hissed at me.

"So very nice of you to come to class on the day our stupid assignment is due."

It shouldn't have been so shocking, I had plenty of people who really didn't like me, but her words were so different from what I'd been expecting that I felt my face freeze into the expressionless mask I used when I couldn't afford to let those around me know what I was thinking. I pulled my typewritten sheaf of paper out and set it on her desk so she could review it.

Looking astonished, but still very sure of herself, Adriana pulled several handwritten sheets out and all but threw them at me. She was right. There was some background information that she could have covered in more detail, but it was a very concise answer to the problem we'd been presented.

I felt a momentary pang at not having coordinated with her to avoid duplication of effort. I'd had a rough couple of days, but she had no way of knowing that. The charitable feelings I'd been working up to suddenly evaporated as she opened her mouth again.

"You were right. You never even came to class, and you got the right answer. Did you cheat? Is the answer to this problem out there somewhere on the Internet?"

I felt my expression slip into true anger for just a second before I managed to bring it back under control.

"No, I didn't cheat. I did the research to find the answer, presumably just like you did. Next time you feel like insulting me, please suppress the urge."

She choked back whatever denigrating response she'd been contemplating, and then Mrs. Alexander arrived. I'd always enjoyed the study of mechanical advantage. Levers, pulleys, ramps. They were simple things, but they'd allowed humanity to begin its first steps towards mastering the environment around them.

Unfortunately I couldn't take any pleasure in the lecture with Adriana radiating dislike at me from just a few feet away. The only event that even came close to pulling me out of my funk was when Patty and Sammy exchanged whispered rumors about some celebrity being in a massive car wreck. Adriana's pulse momentarily shot up at exactly the same time. It was ludicrous. There was no way that she could have consciously heard their whispered conversation. Human ears weren't that acute, but there was no other explanation for why she'd chosen that moment to almost enter a panic.

There was nothing to be done. For everything I learned about her two new, unfathomable things floated to the surface. Once the bell rang I followed her up to the front of the classroom to hand in my answer.

Mrs. Alexander's eyebrows rose slightly at the sight of not just one, but two reports being turned in for our group.

"Oh, Adriana. It looks like you've been busy."

As I passed over my typewritten pages she grinned conspiratorially at Adriana. "Somehow I rather suspect you both have the same answer, Alec just used twice as many words to get there."

Adriana shot me yet another dirty look that I hadn't earned. How was it that after just a few days even the teachers felt obligated to defend her? I'd spent my entire life trying to prove I was making my way on my own talents rather than my family's money and she won their approval with a few sheets and a smile.

My mood wasn't improved any when Jasmin slid into her adjacent desk at the start of pre-calculus.

"Word on the street is that the new girl got a ride into school from Brandon."

My desk creaked in protest as I felt a momentary surge of rage.

"Apparently she didn't need our protection after all. Too bad you didn't know that earlier or you could have saved yourself some pain and blood."

"That doesn't make sense. Brandon never does anything without a reason. Why would he befriend someone who stopped Cassie from hurting Rachel?"

Jasmin shrugged and fished out her homework assignment. "Beats me, but if she's stupid enough to fall for his lines then she deserves whatever happens to her."

I couldn't agree. Especially not once I stumbled upon the likely answer.

"He's doing it to punish her. He'll addict her to his touch and then he'll cut her off."

Jasmin's eyes suddenly got a little wider. "How did I miss that? That explains a lot. I thought some of those girls were being a little aggressive, but if he's formed Ja'tell bond with them, then that would explain it all."

"Damn incubus. His own pack should tear him apart for that."

"You know that'll never happen. He's got everyone but Vincent terrified of him, and it was probably Vincent's idea."

Jasmin's tone was a darker thing than just her words would have implied. She didn't like what Brandon was going to do any more than I did.

The idea of Adriana being reduced to something worse than a meth addict touched on all kinds of things I didn't want to think about. Forming Ja'tell bond with a human was always looked down upon. It was somewhat acceptable when the shape shifter in question did as my father had and married the poor human they'd addicted, but even then it wasn't a topic for polite company.

I was still futilely looking for a solution that would stop even more girls from being sucked into Brandon's clutches long past when school had ended.

Now that Rachel had begun staying after school for math tutoring every night I'd begun sending the rest of the pack home and finding an empty classroom within earshot of the lab. Usually it was a chance to knock out a good chunk of my homework, but after my conversation with Jasmin I found myself unable to focus.

I finally packed all of my things up early and headed out to my motorcycle. The shiny, blue Yamaha R1 wasn't a very practical vehicle, but it was more fun to drive than even my Porsche. Rachel exited the lab and all but ran to me. It was nice to have one person at least who was glad to see me today. I pulled out my blue helmet and the black motorcycle jacket that should offer her a margin of protection if we happened to wreck. She grimaced at having to wear safety items when I was blessedly unencumbered, but she knew the drill. I'd walk away from just about any accident conceivable, but she wasn't nearly as durable.

I handed the gear over with only a portion of my attention. My focus was on the pair of girls who had walked out of the school shortly after Rachel; more specifically on one of the girls. Britney wasn't of interest. I'd long ago established just how shallow and self-serving she was, but Adriana was a different matter.

I'd contemplated a dozen different plans to keep her out of Brandon's clutches, but none of them were viable. Adriana seemed to be returning my stare despite the fact that at this distance, with my eyes covered by sun glasses, there was no way she could be certain I was looking at her.

She was such an enigma. She stood up to Brandon's pack and then accepted a ride into school with him. She defended my sister and then chose Britney Samuels as a best friend. Not to mention the persistent lack of additional information about her. It seemed impossible in this day and age of computers and universal Internet access for anyone to have left no trace after seventeen years of life.

Her expression was mostly made up of the emotionless mask that she normally wore, but there was the briefest trace of something else. Something I couldn't identify at this range, not without scent clues, but which made me want to protect her.

Rachel swung up behind me, and then waved as she saw Adri for the first time. Adri's return wave was a little hesitant, but it seemed to satisfy Rach.

"Time to go, big brother."

The bike dropped into first gear with a satisfying clunk, and then I spun it around with a hiss of heating rubber and shot out of the parking lot.

There wasn't anything more I could do for Adri. She'd made her choices and was going to have to deal with the fallout.

Chapter 7

I'd spent a restless night after getting Rach home. There'd been more patrols, followed by a debriefing with Donovan, and a full set of homework. I managed to get enough sleep to function, but not enough to really feel rested.

The first couple of classes didn't do anything to move the day along more quickly. Wuthering Heights was one of the most depressing studies of how badly people could mess their lives up if given even a slight chance, and History was a complete waste of time.

Jasmin blew out of History so fast that I didn't even get a chance to say goodbye. Even more surprising she wasn't at her locker when I went to deposit my books. I could have tracked her down by following her scent trail, but we were finally scheduled to start a unit on painting, and I didn't want to miss anything.

Art almost made up for the previous few hours. I couldn't actually work on the kinds of stuff I was truly passionate about, but it was still nice to sit down, mix paints and apply brush to canvas.

My good mood nearly evaporated away when I met up with Jasmin and felt the traces of power on her.

"You swore an oath." Rage nearly brought my voice up into the audible range for humans.

"Yes, I did, but I'm not under any obligation to tell you what it was about."

"I can find out. All I have to do is figure out who witnessed for you."

"There was no witness, Alec. You may as well give up because I'm not going to tell you anything else."

Her words hit me like a physical blow. She wasn't lying, which was possibly the craziest thing she'd done so far. Oaths were always witnessed to ensure that someone could explain the circumstances of the oath. Once your beast was bonded to a course of action, it would complete that action regardless of right, wrong, or even questions of legality.

The witness served to give mitigating evidence in the event that the oath resulted in an action that brought punishment down on you. There wasn't generally much mitigation that could be taken into account, but if you were forced into an oath that could potentially result in your being killed, the last thing you wanted to do was forgo any possible defense.

There was a chance I could beat it out of her, but whatever else I held common with Brandon, I didn't like being a monster.

"You shouldn't have done that without consulting me. If nothing else, recent events should have taught you that."

"I'm sorry. I really am, but it had to be done. I'll undergo whatever form of punishment you decree, but I'm not going to budge on this."

She was right. It wouldn't matter what I did to her. Short of death, nothing was going to impact her resolve. I left, too angry to eat.

Rachel found me in the art room five minutes before lunch ended.

"Alec, are you okay?"

"Oh, fine, just watching the pack splinter around me."

"It's Jasmin, isn't it? Dom told me she could smell the ritual on her."

I grunted in response, assuming the matter was closed until Rachel wrapped her hands around my arm. She wasn't strong enough to stop me from moving, but her touch stopped me regardless.

"Alec, I know it's hard to deal with her sometimes, but she's got a good reason for what she's doing this time."

I heard a snap as the brush in my hand splintered. Rachel knew what was going on, but I already knew she wasn't going to tell me. She wasn't as strong-willed as Jasmin, I could have tortured it out of her, but if there was anyone in the pack I couldn't bring myself to hurt it was Rach, and she knew it.

I threw the brush into the trash and went to leave but she hadn't relinquished her grip on my arm. "Alec, everyone's talking about Adri having collapsed. What else have you heard?"

My laugh wasn't very gentle. "You forget, sis. For all that you feel isolated you hear more about what's going on among the student body than I do. I haven't heard a peep about any of this."

Rach looked for a moment like I'd gone too far. I finally reached out and pulled her into a hug. "I don't know what everyone is talking about, but she did collapse in Physics her first day here. It seemed like it was a trick, so I suspect she's just trying to cash in on her newfound fame as Brandon's latest toy."

She wasn't happy with me now. "Alec, she's not like that. We've talked a little after school and I really don't think she's pretending."

There was no point continuing the conversation. I disengaged myself from Rachel and headed off to class.

Rachel had a point. While I didn't really converse with anyone outside the pack, I had the ability to be in the know if I wanted to be, I'd just been tuning out the background chatter lately.

I spent part of my time in Chemistry listening to whispers and came away astonished. The girls in the school were being even more brutal than normal and it looked like Britney, Adri's supposed best friend, was leading the push. If Adri had really been hoping to generate popularity out of her attacks, it had just backfired on her in a major way. Somehow I'd gone from being disgusted by her antics to feeling sorry for her.

I hurried straight to Physics, and was pleasantly surprised to find Adri had beaten me to the class. She registered my presence about the time I sat down, and momentarily seemed confused as she reached for her notebook.

She looked over questioningly at me, and the sight of her with her mask removed actually drew an honest smile out of me. It had been so long since someone had returned my smile it took me a second to realize she was smiling at me. She blushed and broke eye contact as the bell rang.

Mrs. Alexander finished up the roll and opened up the floor for any questions that the class might have regarding the light unit we'd just finished up. Predictably, the first hand up was Sammy's. I'd shared three classes with her over the last four years and she'd been the teacher's pet in each of them.

Sammy launched into a question regarding glowing blue light around reactor cores that I promptly tuned out. We weren't going to be tested on it and when I was really ready to learn about it I'd just jump online and do some research.

As Mrs. Alexander finished up her explanation the next hand up was Adri's. Judging by the sudden jump in Adri's pulse she was nearly as surprised as I was.

"Is the light always blue? Is it ever a whitish-gold color?"

There wasn't any reason for the question to set off internal alarms, but it did.

"Not that I'm aware of. The water will actually emit quite a bit of ultraviolet light, but for whatever reasons, the electrons don't ever seem to release any electromagnetic radiation down in the lower energy levels like infrared, or even the visible red. You'd need red and all of the other colors to generate a true white light."

The reason suddenly became evident as Adri opened her mouth again. "What about some other mechanism? One that wouldn't just make water glow with a dancing gold light, but plants too. Do you know of anything like that?"

The pencil I'd been twirling between my fingers snapped into two pieces as I realized just how badly I'd been played. I didn't hear a word of Mrs. Alexander's response.

She'd just coyly described exactly what we saw when we shifted forms. Suddenly everything made sense. She hadn't been scared about facing Cassie down because she could have easily torn Cassie in half. She wasn't just a wolf, not with a glow like that. She had to be a powerful Fir'shan, one who'd knowingly impinged on the territory of two separate packs.

That explained the lack of history. Her identity, her mom's identity, they'd both been manufactured just before they'd moved here. They'd been detailed enough to pass Donovan's initial background check, but there hadn't been anything else to them.

Only things were even worse than that. She wasn't just some random Fir'shan. She had allied herself with Brandon after turning down my offer of protection. Suddenly I was completely certain who Brandon's contact on the Coun'hij was. There was no way of knowing which one she was. There were plenty of them who hadn't been seen by anyone.

I looked up in time to catch Adri's smug grin and almost threw myself at her. Rage washed through me but I kept the barest edge of control. I couldn't afford to act right now or they'd destroy the entire pack as retribution.

The show of confusion that flashed across her face gave way to understanding as she realized I'd finally seen through her facade. It was all I could do to remain seated through the rest of the class.

I tracked down the rest of the pack between classes, told them to stay clear of the new girl, and then spent the last hour refusing to answer Jasmin's questions. Her mood deteriorated in pace with the minute hand on the clock and by the time the day ended I wasn't sure I was going to be able to stall her long enough to explain developments to everyone simultaneously. Luckily the rest of the pack was just as antsy as she was, and they all but ambushed me.

I followed everyone to the cafeteria.

"Okay, you kept me in suspense the entire time I was trying to grind through stupid math problems. What is going on?"

"Adriana Paige, the new girl, she's a Fir'shan."

"That's impossible. Sure, she glows, but I've never got any kind of shape shifter vibe off of her."

James' tone was insulting but I let it pass.

"She's got the glow of a Fir'shan, a powerful one at that. She faced down Cassie when any normal human would have been running away in terror. Donovan hasn't been able to track down any information about her or her family that wasn't in the initial, basic background check we ran, and finally she just described exactly what we see in wolf form to the entire class under the guise of asking about the light unit we just finished up."

The reactions varied from outright disbelief on Dom's face to cautious doubt from Isaac. I thought for a second I was going to lose them, but then Jasmin, who'd been pacing since she came into the room, almost fell down.

"He's right. I saw her do something else today that didn't gel with normal human actions. She's got to be one of us, and extremely powerful to be able to hide the fact she's moonborn." The pack instantly devolved into a whispered argument.

Again, there was a range of responses. It was obvious that whatever Jasmin had seen was linked somehow to the oath she'd taken earlier, which didn't exactly endear her to anyone. Isaac was cautiously in favor of waiting Adri out until her purposes became more obvious, while James wanted to ambush her before school and kill her.

I let them bicker for nearly an hour before I finally shut them up and told them that we were going to adopt a wait-and-see posture. There were several questions, and it wasn't until I told them that I didn't want anyone leaving Rachel alone with her that I realized Rachel had just spent the better part of two hours in the tutoring lab, the same one that Adri had started working at just a few days earlier.

Chapter 8

Rachel wasn't happy when I told her our suspicions about Adriana. Somewhere along the line she'd decided that the new girl was going to be her new best friend and she refused to believe that Adri could possibly be someone sent to help Brandon bring us down.

My normally composed little sister ran the whole gamut of teen angst over the next two hours. She cried, yelled, threw things at me, and generally did all of the things I'd never have let anyone else get away with.

I left partway through the tantrum when Isaac sounded the warning that we had Brandon's pack inbound. Brandon's people proceeded to all but run us into the ground over the remainder of the night. We saw each individual in the pack at some point, but never all at the same time. It was obvious they were rotating people out on a regular basis so they could wear us down. Unfortunately knowing that was what they were doing didn't help.

By the end of the night we were all tired and sloppy. Vincent chose that opportunity to set up a little ambush and only sheer dumb luck put Isaac close enough to Jasmin to drive him off. I finally stumbled back home just before seven and found Rachel awake and waiting for me.

"Okay, Alec. Here's the deal. I won't fight you on this Adri thing on two conditions."

She didn't even blink at my exhausted stare, so I finally nodded for her to continue.

"One, I still get to go to tutoring. You can assign whomever you want as bodyguards, but I need to be able to go there or I'll never pass Mrs. Campbell's class."

I slowly shook my head. "We can tutor you here."

"That will never work and you know it. Everyone's already spread too thin trying to keep up with Brandon's latest series of provocations. The last thing any of you can do is spend an hour or two holding my hand through basic algebra."

"Not that I'm agreeing, but what's the second condition?"

"I need your help starting a rumor. A counter-rumor, really."

I already knew where this was headed, but Rachel went ahead and said it outright.

"Adri needs someone sticking up for her. Whoever started the gossip about her collapsing is ruining her life and we need to help."

"It was Britney, and the last thing she needs is help from us. You realize if we're right that she's probably one of the Coun'hij. One of the really terrible ones that nobody can put a face to because they can't risk what would happen to them if we all knew who they were."

Rachel shrugged unconcernedly and the matter was settled. I assigned Isaac and James to take turns chaperoning her, and then the two of us pooled what we knew about her and Rachel came up with a counter-rumor that I thought was a little over the top, but which she was positive would do the trick.

I showered and then we all motorcaded into school. Rachel filled Dom in on the plan on the way, and then it was time to execute.

I was surprised at how much fun it was. Dom and Rachel got started right away, but I didn't get my first opening until English. When I heard Tina Jones and Nikki Thomas begin discussing Britney's rumor I leaned over and interrupted them.

"You guys should really get all your facts straight before you go off half-cocked like that."

I thought it was a little gruff, but Rachel and Dom had both suggested I play the role of high-and-mighty king of the social food chain to the hilt.

"What do you mean? I've talked to three different people who saw her collapse in physics her first day here, and everyone knows she's odd. The only reason Brandon ever even noticed her is because she pretends to be clumsy and throws herself at him every chance she gets."

I shrugged nonchalantly. "I'm not saying she hasn't collapsed, but hasn't it occurred to either of you to wonder why it is she's doing so?"

"Um, like because she's a freak? I'd think it would be pretty obvious that's she's faking it for attention."

"Try again. Nobody's that good of an actress. There's something in her past that's got her pretty messed up, everyone else is just too dense to see it."

My script had run out after my second comment. I'd never meant to give any kind of reason for Adri's behavior, it had just kind of popped out of me. The startling part was that I wanted to believe it was the truth. It would be so much better if this really were a series of freakish anomalies. If she wasn't faking, maybe she wasn't a rogue Fir'shan intent on taking our pack down.

The only question was, if she wasn't faking, then why hadn't *I* ever wondered what was causing her panic attacks?

The question was one that stuck with me through the rest of the day. Our whisper campaign was highly successful. It seemed hard to believe, but in the course of just an hour and a half almost the entire school was abuzz with a new set of carefully-crafted rumors.

Physics was even more of a trial than I'd expected it to be. Adriana was back to pretending nothing unusual had happened. Mrs. Alexander was keeping a close eye on us for whatever reason, so there was nothing to do but watch impassively as she angrily moved her desk next to mine. Being within arm's reach of her made my skin crawl, but I refused to let her understand just how much I'd figured out.

Isaac nodded at the end of the day when I reminded him he was on Rachel watch. Rather than complaining about the duty he just added a few extra books to his bag and started towards the lab. I hadn't managed to catch the titles of any of them, but it was a good bet they weren't in English. Isaac spoke more languages than anyone else I'd ever met, and unless he was deep in the midst of learning a new one, he generally could be found reading a novel or history book in Italian, Spanish, German or Arabic. There were a few more rattling around inside his head but it was nearly a full-time job to try and keep up with his scholastic endeavors.

Arriving home was a distinct relief. I wanted nothing quite as much as to head to my room and catch up on the hour and a half of sleep I'd missed the night before, but there were more important things to be done.

Donovan met me at the door with a thick letter. He always knew when I was going to go visit her. At first I'd assumed he was just tracking the food shipments, but over the years there had been a couple of times when there hadn't been a food shipment to give me away. I quickly checked that nobody was within hearing range and then took the letter.

"How do you do that, Donovan?"

"I've had much of the raising of you these many years, Master Alec, but I'm not so vain as to assume that I have answers to all of your questions. Occasionally something pressing comes up that is completely outside of my ken. It's only natural to assume that when those times arise you'll visit our mutual friend."

I would have expected a level of sorrow to go with such a confession but Donovan didn't seem melancholy, at least not more than the occasion called for. I grasped his arm in a most unprofessional display of appreciation and then tucked his letter away and left.

Even after all these decades of service and care, he still didn't feel it proper for Rachel and me to embrace him, but sometimes it wasn't about what he needed. Sometimes we had to do it simply because we needed reassurance from the man who'd replaced a murdered father and an absent mother.

The R1 was crouched in one corner of the garage, sleek and low like some kind of shiny predator. I slipped a pair of sunglasses on, walked the bike out to the driveway, and then streaked down our lane with the instant power that you couldn't find anywhere else outside of a four-hundred-thousand-dollar car.

Once I turned off of the main road I opened the throttle up and felt the thrill of my front tire coming off of the ground at sixty miles an hour before the first corner came up and I had to lean on the brakes.

I threw the bike over with a heavy dose of counter-steering and then used both lanes to streak around the corner at a significantly higher speed than I could have managed in my Porsche. All too soon the trip was over and it was time to start checking my back trail.

I pulled up to the dilapidated shed that would serve as a hiding spot for my bike and then spent a few minutes with a pair of binoculars looking for signs that anyone had followed me. This stretch of road began well inside the pack's territory and didn't connect to another road for nearly sixty miles, so the only way for any of Brandon's wolves to stumble on it would be for them to either penetrate very deep into our land, or detour out nearly one hundred and fifty miles and come in from the other side.

I ensured that the road was well-maintained on this side through a stream of anonymous bribes to a couple of DOT employees, but the other side devolved into a pot-hole filled mess. The payments were technically illegal, but I made sure that they included enough cash to pay for the actual cost of maintaining the road, and so far my pet bureaucrats had been passing along the state's cut as instructed.

A few minutes later I was traversing the little-used path down to the cabin, and then knocked on the door.

Mallory answered, moving slowly as always. She favored me with a smile at the unexpected visit, accepted Donovan's letter and then motioned me towards one of the empty chairs in her tiny living room.

"Much as I enjoy your visits, I know you don't stop by for an unscheduled trip unless something is bothering you. What's happened, Alec?"

"I think we've got one of the Coun'hij in town pretending to be a normal human while she aids Brandon in his effort to tear the pack apart."

Mallory's face was wonderfully expressive. It was one of the few parts of her battered body that didn't hurt and she used it in place of the body language more common to the moonborn.

"You're sure she's a shape shifter?"

"It's all circumstantial, but it's adding up. She's got no history, doesn't show up on any of the databases we've managed to get access to so far. Her glow is stronger than Brandon's, but she doesn't ever seem to raise any power, which would hint at a control so solid that it's almost unimaginable. She faced down Cassie in front of Brandon's entire pack and then turned around and seems to be dating Brandon. She knows things she shouldn't know."

For several seconds Mallory didn't respond. The room began to arc with power as she brought her beast back under control. Mallory's control was good. It hadn't always been, but the injuries she'd received the night my father had died made shifting form excruciating, and she'd had to master her beast to avoid unnecessary agony.

"I'm probably not the most objective individual when it comes to the murderers on the Coun'hij, Alec."

"You were there. You saw what happened; you are the only living person who fought them instead of just bowing down and waiting for the ax to fall."

Mallory looked up with fire in her eyes and for a moment I saw the powerful hybrid lurking inside the frail woman I'd known nearly my entire life. The hybrid who had been one of my father's most loyal supporters, the one who'd attacked Agony when he'd been bleeding my father to death.

"That's not fair to Donovan. He stood up to them."

"You're right, but Donovan didn't have the seniority to know what was going on in my father's council when Agony visited. I need to know what made him make the decisions he made."

Mallory exhaled slowly and it was like she shrank down inside herself. The powerful woman I'd seen just a second before disappeared and all that was left was the tired, crippled old woman who had met me at the door.

"Alec, it would be pointless for me to tell you everything we discussed leading up to Agony's visit. It all boils down to one thing. The Coun'hij has ruled our people with an iron fist for centuries now. They don't even really play by their own rules. If they want something, you'll have no choice but to give it to them and hope they're satisfied. If this girl is really one of the Hidden as you fear, then you should stay as far away from her as possible or eventually she'll swallow your entire pack."

It wasn't the kind of warning that you just idly shrugged off. Fact of the matter, it wasn't the kind of warning that you could even just process and move on. We sat in silence for a few moments before it became apparent that neither really had any more to say on the subject.

My chest tightened up in anticipation for what I knew was coming up. A regular wolf was nothing less than superhuman. A hybrid was physically the next best thing to invincible. Sure, there were things that could bring one of us down, but they were the kinds of things that had become so scarce that humans for the most part didn't even have myths about them anymore.

If my contest with Brandon had just been a purely physical match, my situation would still have been precarious, but nothing like it was now. Hybrids weren't in and of themselves the very top of the food chain. A very small percentage of hybrids manifested an ability to go along with their raw strength and speed.

My father had been one of them, Mallory had been another. The abilities weren't all created equal, and could take an almost infinite variety of forms. My father's ability had been that of regenerating from wounds even faster than normal for our kind. Mallory on the other hand was actually able to see the abilities of other hybrids.

Ultimately there was no guarantee that manifesting one would make you any more powerful than any other hybrid, but there was more than one account of someone's power making a decisive difference in some key battle or another.

Father and Mallory had made a good team. He'd been able to face challenger after challenger without ever getting worn down, and she'd been able to warn him when he faced someone with an ability that might change the course of a given fight.

Isaac, James, me, none of us had manifested any kind of ability yet, which wasn't necessarily surprising. The odds were honestly very much against us. Plenty of packs did just fine run by hybrids who'd never manifested any kind of unusual ability whatsoever. It wouldn't have necessarily bothered me that I was *just* a hybrid except for the fact that Brandon *had* manifested an ability and it was a heck of a power.

His power had somehow bonded to the strength and speed expected of a hybrid and supercharged them to the point where no normal shape shifter had a prayer of standing up to him unaided.

I always anticipated and dreaded the end of my visits with Mallory, and this time was no different. I took a deep breath, knelt in front of her chair, and waited as she placed her palms on either side of my face.

After several minutes she slumped back into her chair.

"I'm sorry, Alec. Nothing's changed. You've got the potential. More potential maybe than I've ever seen in anyone, but it's still just potential."

Chapter 9

I returned just in time to hand Donovan Mallory's letter and then join the others as Brandon once again attempted to use his superior numbers to wear us down. This time we were more prepared; I ordered Jasmin and Dom to lag back, pretending greater exhaustion than they actually felt.

The ruse paid off in that Nathanial and Simon had fallen from the rest of the pack in an effort to taunt us. Jasmin and Dom had put on a burst of speed that allowed them to run the two wolves down just short of Brandon's pack.

The rest of us had been only a couple of seconds behind and we'd arrived just ahead of Brandon's people. Dom wasn't one of our better fighters, but she'd done her job, delaying Simon just enough for James to get there and savage him. She limped away when we were forced to fall back, but we'd left a pair of motionless piles in our wake.

It was doubtful we'd managed to kill either Simon or Nathanial, but Brandon only had so many truly aggressive wolves. If the most aggressive kept taking beatings maybe his pack would start to show some of the cracks that were in danger of tearing *us* apart.

We'd been quite handily winning the skirmish until Brandon had doubled back and entered the fray. We all left bloodied, but feeling as though we'd come out on top. At the very least it cut the night's activities short and allowed us all to go home and get a full two hours of sleep.

The next day didn't start out any better. Our rumors seemed to have taken on a life of their own. Even the groups of kids that didn't normally get involved were discussing Adri and the manufactured "tragedy" that'd befallen her.

More surprising was just how quickly perception of her had changed. She'd gone from being perceived as a total freak to someone who, it was generally agreed, was polite to everyone. I waited, expecting it would only be a matter of time before she began capitalizing in some way on her recent fame, but I didn't overhear anything to indicate she even realized just how much she could have gotten away with.

Physics was even more nerve-wracking. I'd taken a fairly serious blow to my right shoulder and another to my left arm when Brandon had knocked me away from Vincent. The wounds would be healed in a day or so, but right now they made me even less happy to be within striking range of Adriana.

Once again I slid my body ever so slightly away from her and launched into a simulation of what we were likely to face for our project. She was still maintaining the charade that nothing had changed, but her mask was starting to slip more often. She sat down and double-checked my math, seemingly becoming more and more furious with my failure to react to whatever Machiavellian game she was playing.

I heaved a profound sigh of relief when I was finally able to leave the class and allow my abused nerves a chance to calm down slightly.

Later that evening Rachel bounced into my studio in high spirits.

"The rumors totally worked. Dom and Jasmin both said they heard people talking about them all day."

Rachel ducked backwards as I absently reached out and made as if to paint the end of her nose.

"Yes, you're a genius. Your plan worked as intended."

"You're waiting for the other shoe to drop aren't you?"

"I have to, Rach. I don't think I'm wrong, but even if I do, we're better off treating her like a threat and being wrong than letting her position herself to hurt us."

For a second it looked like she was going to argue with me, but instead she shrugged and turned to leave. Just before she disappeared she turned back.

"Alec, Les Misérables is coming to Vegas. Can I go?"

At my somewhat hesitant nod Rachel broke out in a big grin. "Aren't you at least impressed that Adri hasn't let all of this go to her head?"

I pushed the question out of my head once Rachel was gone and tried to concentrate on my painting. There was no telling how long our reprieve would last. Apparently Brandon's people had taken too severe of a beating last night to push us again tonight, but it was only a matter of time before he bullied them back into another series of provocations.

I fully intended on using the time to finish off as much of my current piece as possible, but I was already running into problems. I'd never had a hard time painting before. Normally I just let my hand begin a piece and it took shape almost of its own accord.

This time that worked only up to a point. The borders were all progressing nicely with a series of dark, almost black colors, but the center remained steadfastly blank. I'd heard about artists, painters and writers who lived in near-constant fear that they wouldn't be able to continue to create, but I'd never thought it would ever be an issue.

I wasn't there yet, but I was beginning to glimpse some of what they must experience. I wouldn't be able to move on until this piece was done and it was beginning to appear as though it would never fully take shape.

Chapter 10

I still hadn't made any progress on the mystery painting and the effort was starting to get in the way of other things. Even so, I spent nearly the whole day thinking about the project. Only physics, and the danger represented by Adri, if she was really what I was afraid of, sufficed to tear my mind away from the painting.

Adri smiled at me as I slipped into class and took my seat. It seemed impossible that she was happily plotting the destruction of everything I held dear.

Mrs. Alexander brought the lab equipment over and I began setting up for the lab. I tested the breaking point of our string and then began running through calculations on just how many pulleys we'd need to pull the weight up our ramp and over the other obstacles.

I made sure I was using the coefficient of starting friction and then acting more on a hunch than any solid calculations, I loaded the system with an extra sixteen grams and then caught Mrs. Alexander's eye and waited for her to come grade us.

Once she'd arrived I smoothly ran the weights through the obstacle course she'd stipulated.

"Sixteen grams. Most impressive, you two. An entire gram more than I would have ventured to risk myself, and done before anyone else. I thought the pair of you would make a great team."

I expected Adriana to keep her mouth shut. That's what people usually do when they are given credit for something they really had little if any part in, but amazingly enough she didn't remain quiet.

"Mrs. Alexander, I didn't actually do any of it. I kept making mistakes."

Mrs. Alexander laughed so hard that the pencil that was habitually behind her ear wobbled and nearly fell off.

"I rather suspect you're understating your accomplishments, my dear. Didn't contribute indeed. As if Nora's favorite student would just sit around while there were equations to solve."

I couldn't help but stare at Adri. She hadn't taken credit for my work, and then turned out to be Mrs. Campbell's favorite student. Nora Campbell wasn't anyone's dummy. There were a few teachers who hadn't clued into the tension between the two packs, but she wasn't one of them. In fact, she'd occasionally let information drop that hinted at a rather better grasp of the situation than I would have liked. Rachel was relatively easy to fool, but it seemed much less likely that Adri had managed to fool Mrs. Campbell as well.

I fielded the call from Mayor Wilkenson between Physics and Pre-cal.

"Graves, I've got a note for you."

"I don't think we've really got that kind of relationship, Mr. Mayor."

"It's from the girl. I went over and told her they had the job as you instructed and she started asking questions about why things turned around so quickly. She tried to blackmail me into telling her who her benefactor was but I set her straight. Only she wanted me to pass along a message."

A sudden chill ran through me. Somehow it hadn't ever crossed my mind she might have the resources to realize what was happening; that it was me who'd just helped her.

"I don't think it will be necessary for you to physically give me the note, Mr. Mayor. Please read it to me now."

"It says, 'Whoever you are, thank you so much for what you've done. Not just for the job, but for smoothing things over with the bank as well. I wish there was some way I could repay you for everything.' And then she signed it Adriana."

"Is there perhaps any type of symbol on the note? A picture, anything other than the words?"

"Looking for a secret message, Graves? Nope, that's all there is to it."

"Thank you, Mr. Mayor, you've been most helpful."

Rachel came to my room when she got back from tutoring.

"Alec, thank you so much for helping Adri. I know you're taking grief from Jasmin over it, but I really appreciate you doing what you could for my friend."

I leaned back in my chair to consider her for a moment and then turned on the white noise generator that would allow us actual privacy.

"Rachel, how can you be so sure Adri's a normal human being?"

"I just am. I can't really explain it, but she doesn't feel like a shape shifter. Why are you asking all of a sudden?"

"I got a note from her. She realized something had to be up with the sudden reversal of the city's decision to make the brochure. In hindsight I probably didn't help the situation by using the mayor as an errand boy, but it's too late to do anything about it now. She blackmailed him into passing along a message to her mysterious benefactor."

"What did it say?"

"That's not important, sis. What is important is that I'm finally fully realizing just how good of an individual she is if she isn't a shape shifter. I'm no longer content with just letting events play themselves out. If she's a human, then she deserves our help for everything she's done."

Rachel's eyes were bright with excitement. "That's great, Alec."

"No, I'm afraid it's not great, but it's the only path left open. Can you think of anything that she wouldn't miss for the world?"

Rachel's answer came immediately. "She'd never in the entire world miss a showing of Les Misérables."

Chapter 11

The arrangements were surprisingly easy to make. Each member of the pack had at least one fake ID, and a credit card to match. I pulled the black American Express out of my wallet and headed to Donovan's office and the computer he'd had set up to spoof a fake IP address. It probably wouldn't stand up to a full-blown federal investigation, but it would shelter the transaction from anything short of that.

I ordered five tickets on the third to last row of the main level, one on the very back row, just to the side of the first five, and then thirty in an uninterrupted block up on the mezzanine.

The date didn't look important at first glance, but I'd very carefully picked the night of the next full moon. If Adri really was one of us it wouldn't matter how strong her control was. If she came to the performance I'd know for sure what she was. Either she'd give off a noticeable tingle of shape shifter energy, or she'd remain the same, normal human that she generally appeared to be.

My mind shied away from what I'd do if she did turn out to be one of us. First things first.

I left for school before any of the others, arriving more than half an hour before classes were scheduled to start. Mrs. Pendely looked up in surprise as I walked into the office.

"Oh, hello, Alec. What brings you into school so early?"

"Hi, Mrs. Pendely. Could you please see if Principal Gossil has a few minutes available to speak with me?"

"Oh, dear. I'm afraid you'll need to come back a little later. Maybe around lunch?"

"It really is important. Maybe you could just ask him?"

I let a hint of steel touch my voice. Mrs. Pendely was a nice lady, but she was used to taking orders. After just the slightest bit of hesitation she nodded and walked over to knock on the Principal's door. I quietly followed her, thereby negating the first line of defense.

Principal Gossil was busy telling her why he couldn't meet with me when I slipped around her and stepped into the office.

"I'm really sorry, but this will only take a second."

I had him. He didn't want to talk to me, but he wouldn't appear the ogre to the people he worked with.

"Very well, Alec, what can I do for you?"

I waited until Mrs. Pendely had retreated back out into the main office area and then pulled out thirty-one of the tickets I'd printed off earlier that morning.

"I'd like to make a donation to the school's art program."

"Fine, leave a check with the secretaries and they'll see it gets to the right people at the district level."

"It's not that kind of donation, sir. I've come across a number of tickets to the Vegas showing of Les Misérables. I propose that you offer them to the student body at a discounted rate and then after you've deducted the transportation costs of getting everyone there the remaining funds can go to the art program."

It was a reasonable offer, but any hope of things going smoothly evaporated as he leaned back and shook his head.

"I know your type, Graves. You're just like the Worthingfields. What are the strings?"

"Nothing to worry about, sir. I would like to remain anonymous of course. Also, I think you should conduct a free drawing for the top five tickets."

"Let me guess, you already have the five individuals who'll be winning the tickets picked out don't you?"

"I would like you to make sure that Adriana Paige is one of the winners."

He leaned forward with a satisfied grin. "Absolutely not. You want to make a donation, make a donation. You want to play puppetmaster, go somewhere else. You don't own me, and I'm not going to let you start dictating how I'll run my school."

I'd been hoping it wouldn't come to this. I didn't really enjoy playing the heavy, but some things were more important than the hypocritical self-righteousness of one small-town principal.

"That's an interesting stand. I think it's especially enlightening when coming from someone who's recently racked up more than ninety thousand dollars in gambling debts. How do you think the school board would react to finding out you've been betting against our football team? I'll bet you've been giving the football coach all kinds of ulcers. Unless maybe he's in on it too?"

He was gasping like he'd just been punched in the stomach, but now wasn't the time to let him collect himself. I dropped the tickets on his desk and stood up.

"Make the trip happen, keep my name quiet and make sure the Paige girl is one of the winners when you do the drawing tomorrow during fifth hour."

I pulled his door shut again behind me and smiled at Mrs. Pendely as I left.

The next piece of unpleasant business was something I put off dealing with until lunch. I waited until the entire pack was assembled and then calmly began.

"At some point today the Principal is going to announce a school-sponsored trip to Vegas on the night of the next full moon. I'm going to be on it."

Instant, if quiet, chaos was the predictable result.

"Are you crazy? Brandon's pack always spends at least part of that night pushing us really hard. How do you expect us to stand them off without you?"

Jasmin was the one who voiced the question, but it was obviously heavy on everyone's minds. I verified that none of Brandon's pack were within hearing range before responding.

"Isaac will be in charge during my absence, so it will ultimately be his call, but I expect that he'll decide to run a patrol right up to the border of the other pack's territory. If we temporarily take a more aggressive stance it should push them off balance enough for my departure to go unnoticed."

James' fingers had gone white on the table as he tried to stop himself from ripping fist-sized chunks out of it. The disagreement had raised the discussion up into the audible ranges as everyone tried to shout each other down, but the crackle of the loud speaker interrupted the rapidly escalating fight.

"This is Principal Gossil and I've got an exciting announcement. The school is sponsoring a trip to Las Vegas to see the production of Les Misérables that just started. Tickets are available at a discounted rate in the office for the next two days."

The pack turned almost as one to shoot me a look of unhappiness, but I paid no attention, instead focusing on the rest of Mr. Gossil's speech.

"We'll be holding a drawing for five free tickets. All those wishing to be entered into the drawing should stop by the office between today and noon tomorrow."

The cafeteria at large seemed completely disinterested in the announcement, but there was a high-pitched sound of delight immediately heard from the direction of Brandon's accustomed table. I somehow knew it originated from Adriana Paige.

The pack as a whole still wasn't happy but I allowed my beast to bubble up to the surface, just a sliver away from transforming, silencing them all with a hurricane of power. My point made for now, I stood and left, my food uneaten on the table.

Since I shared most of my classes with Jasmin, the departure bought me only a temporary reprieve. All too soon I was sitting next to her in Chemistry and wishing there was a way to permanently shut her up.

Her subvocalized monologue wasn't entirely without merit. I *was* endangering the pack, and I hadn't really given them good reason. It was a good thing she didn't know the next step I was considering.

TORN

If Adri really was from the Coun'hij, then returning her note, especially with my sigil on it, would give her exactly the opportunity to execute me she'd been looking for. Considering the fact that she very much appeared to be dating Brandon these days, even if she wasn't moonborn, there was still an element of risk to it all.

I tuned Jasmin out for the rest of the hour and tried to decide whether or not to go through with it all. I'd essentially decided against it by the time the bell rang; but when I made it to Physics, Adri looked up at me with the barest trace of a smile and almost without conscious thought I turned around and left the building.

The fact that we had a sub was convenient, but it wasn't the full reason. It was as if something compelled me to act in opposition to my best judgment.

I left my car a quarter mile from her house and ran the rest of the way in just over a minute. There wasn't a vehicle out front, which was pretty good reason to believe the house was empty, but I still felt exposed as I walked up to the door and pulled out the heavy stock I'd brought just in case.

The pen felt good in my hand as I wrote. Not as good as a paintbrush, but still right and proper. A minute later I pulled back and looked at what I'd written.

Adriana,

Your words of thanks were altogether unexpected, but decidedly appreciated. You're most welcome for whatever small part I might have played in helping events to unfold as they would have in a perfect world.

My actions were not such as to merit any large boon from you, but still I must ask one. Please never show this note to anyone. I ask not for myself, but for the others such knowledge could affect.

I hope your circumstances continue on much as they are now, but on the chance they do not, I can be reached by leaving a note in the hollow of the lightning-struck tree half a mile to the east of your house.

—@

I signed it with my personal sigil, the symbol of my family altered ever so slightly to make it mine, and walked away without looking back.

Chapter 12

I hadn't intended on returning to school, but James called as he headed into his last class. Apparently Dom's drama teacher was being a jerk again and she needed help finishing up the props for the school's production of a Midsummer Night's Dream. I agreed to come relieve him from guard duty at the tutor lab, and then turned around and headed back into town.

Once I arrived, I sent James a text letting him know he could leave, and then waited outside the tutor lab and listened to everyone inside. Rachel was muttering to herself about whatever problem she was working on, and the sound brought a grin to my face.

A few minutes later I heard books rustling and then Rachel's cheery voice filtered through the window.

"Are you ready? James had to leave early, but don't worry, we've still got a ride home."

Adri responded after just a short pause.

"Great. Britney's been avoiding me like the plague. I didn't even see her leave today."

I didn't hear Rachel laugh very much anymore. It happened so infrequently I'd forgotten just how much I missed it. It was one more thing to put on the ledger. A plus if Adri was a human, a negative if she was about to disillusion my sister even more than life already had.

"She left about five minutes before James did."

"Was she still chatting up her prime candidate for the big dance?"

"Yep, she's definitely settled on Tim Parsons, who is perfect if you like your men fairly handsome, moderately popular, and built like an ox."

I wondered for just a moment if Rachel was quite that feisty with anyone else, and then the door was opening and both girls were blinking in the blinding Utah sun.

"Alec!"

Rachel ran over and gave me a hug. She knew better than to tie my arms up around a potential hostile shape shifter, I moved slightly to the side and wrapped one arm around her for a second.

"You didn't think I'd forget, did you?"

"Not forget, no, just maybe be a little late."

It was a slightly painful reminder of just how little I'd been around lately.

The three of us walked over to my Porsche and Rachel slipped into the back seat, leaving the passenger seat open for Adri. The last place I wanted a potentially hostile hybrid was behind me.

"Did you enter the drawing for Les Misérables tickets?"

There was a slightly knowing quality to Rachel's voice as she leaned up between our seats and looked at Adri. No telling whether the rest of the pack had filled her in on our argument, or if it was pure intuition.

"Yes, but so did everyone else. My chances are so dismal they're not even worth mentioning."

I heard a slight movement off to my right and Adri's voice came out pitched higher and more breathless than normal.

"Rachel, you should be wearing your seatbelt."

"Why? It isn't like anyone is going to pull us over and give us a ticket."

The sudden spike in Adri's pulse reminded me of the rumor we'd manufactured. The rumor which had been partially based on Adri's reaction to people talking about car wrecks. Without intending to, I found my mouth opening.

"She's right, Rachel. You should be buckled in."

A quiet click attested to the fact that Rachel was buckled in, but as soon as Adri's pulse had settled back down, she turned back to me.

"Isn't that a bit hypocritical? I mean you tell her to buckle up, but you're not buckled up yourself."

I wanted to laugh. It would take one heck of a car wreck to put me down. In fact, even without a seatbelt on my odds of walking away from an accident were better than Rachel's with one. I managed a shrug.

"Yes, I suppose it does look hypocritical at that. Let's just say that Rachel would be missed if we hit another car, but nobody would need to miss me."

I reached the lane back to her house and turned into it, filing away the fact that she'd reached for the door as if expecting to have to walk.

Rachel jumped out of the car as soon as it slowed down and opened Adri's door for her. "Enjoy the rest of your night, and don't lose hope on Les Misérables. You never know when you're going to beat the odds."

That was a bit too obvious. Rachel needed to learn to play things closer to her chest. Adri looked for a moment like she was going to say something else, but then just thanked me and exited the car.

I pulled out of the driveway before Rachel could see Adri find the note.

That night was another hellish experience. Brandon and his wolves pushed into our territory and then just waited for us to come to him. It was an out-and-out bid to destroy us, but we couldn't ignore him or we'd be admitting we couldn't control our own territory. It was only a short step from there until the carrion birds would be circling us.

We crept towards his pack, paying special effort to keeping downwind of them. He should have had scouts out, but was probably worried about having them cut off from the rest of the pack. That or maybe his wolves were more scared of what we'd do to them than his threats.

TORN

It's hard to truly get close enough to surprise another wolf. By the time you're into what humans would think of as unarmed combat range they can hear your heartbeat. We did the next best thing by approaching as close as we thought we could get away with and then springing towards them with all of the inhuman speed of our kind.

James, Isaac and I were in the van, and we rolled up the three closest wolves while everyone was still trying to figure out what was going on. I'd tangled with Nathanial of all people, and took great pleasure in sinking my claws deep into his guts.

Before I could go for the kill Brandon hit me with roughly the kinetic energy of an SUV. I was completely outmatched and only Isaac's abandoning the bloody mess that had been his opponent saved me from being maimed.

I dodged roughly half of Brandon's attacks but the ones that landed were deep. I caught glimpses of the rest of the fight in between blows. Jess and Dom seemed to have locked up with their opponents. It was hard to tell who was winning, but the sheer amount of motion indicated that neither fight was close to over yet.

Jasmin had clinched with her first opponent, torn their throat out and already moved on to another. Isaac and I launched a flurry of blows at Brandon but he dodged most of them and blocked the rest with enough force to knock us back a step. A flicker of motion brought me partway around and reflexes that I'd spent the last two years training whipped my left hand up just in time to rip Simon out of the air.

Brandon used the distraction to attack, raking long furrows down my back, and then I was back around and his blows were raining down on Simon. Seemingly overcome by blood lust, Brandon struck again and again until his claws finally caught on Simon's ribcage and ripped him from my grasp.

The sight of their leader shredding one of their own caused two of the remaining wolves to break, which further eroded the morale of both Dom and Jess' opponents.

We had the edge in numbers now, but James had definitely come out for the worse in his fight with Vincent, and none of the rest of us were much less marked. It was anyone's guess as to whether or not we could take them, but Cassie and Vincent seemed to have lost their stomach for the fight. They began backing away, and not even Brandon was capable of taking all five of us.

Brandon and Vincent each picked up two of their fallen comrades and then backed away from us. I expected an argument when I ordered everyone back to the house, but apparently we weren't any more desirous of continued bloodshed than they were.

I was feeling strangely weak by the time we made it back to the estate. The last thing I remember before collapsing was Donovan limping out from the house in an effort to catch me.

Chapter 13

It would have been nice for them to have picked a weekend for their attack so that everyone at least had a chance to heal up before having to go back to school. We'd all come through without any visible wounds, but underneath our clothes everyone was a mess of gauze and bruises, and I was still a little shaky on my feet from having lost so much blood.

All four of the wolves we'd hurt the worst were absent from school and I had a few moments to wonder whether or not we'd killed them. Vincent passed me in the hall, much of his normal arrogance restored, and informed me that all four would be back for another round within a couple of days.

The wounds across my back were especially tender. They combined with the healing itch across most of the rest of my body to make it extremely difficult to concentrate on anything. Still, the closer it got to fifth hour the more my mind kept returning to the drawing. I'd specifically told him to run it during Physics, but now I worried that the instruction hadn't been explicit enough.

The end result would be the same, but I wanted to see her expression when her name was read. I left Jasmin after fourth hour and went directly to Physics without even stopping at my locker. Once I found my seat I tried to distract myself, but anyone that knew me well would have seen just how anxious I was.

Adriana arrived a few seconds later and it was all I could do not to stare at her. Despite my best efforts my gaze wandered over to her several times and it wasn't until I saw her glaring at me that I finally got myself under control.

The loud speaker kicked on and Principal Gossil cleared his throat before proceeding. "It's my pleasure to read off the names of the five winners in our drawing for tickets to Les Misérables."

There was a pause, and I heard a rustle of paper as a name was drawn, unfolded, and smoothed out.

"The first winner is Pam White."

The resulting explosion of noise a few classes down was loud enough that I was pretty sure even the humans could hear it from here. Thankfully Mrs. Alexander pulled the door shut as Principal Gossil drew another slip out of the box.

"Also winning a ticket to Les Misérables next weekend, Mr. Andrew Webbs."

I was starting to get a headache as another round of screaming broke out. Thankfully the two from our class that cheered gave up quickly so as to better hear whether or not their names were next.

"And the third lucky person is Suzanne Bergerman."

Adri's pulse had skyrocketed over the last few names. I could hear her breathing pick up with each new name, it almost drowned out the sound of the next draw.

"Congratulations goes to Amy Birch."

This set of yells was thankfully on the other side of the school, and I wondered for the first time if Gossil was going to defy me and just not give the last ticket to Adri. It was too late to do anything about it, but I felt my grip on the desk tighten to the point where the wood let out a slight groan.

Principal Gossil finally cleared his throat and continued. "The fifth winner is Ms. Adriana Paige."

As the room broke out in half-hearted cheers I realized there hadn't been any rustle of papers before he'd read her name. Had all of the other drawings been loud enough for humans to notice them? Would anyone notice the lack if they had?

It was too late for worry to accomplish anything. I watched as Adri thanked everyone, and then turned towards me.

"Congratulations, Adriana. Les Misérables is one of the best. I hope you enjoy it."

The undertone of anger as she thanked me defied understanding.

Chapter 14

Lately Adri smelled like she'd rolled in Brandon. The rest of the pack liked it even less than I did. It was extremely unsettling to be sitting calmly in a class and then suddenly smell Brandon coming towards you. Jess was getting especially jumpy. We'd been fairly careful to set our schedules up so that we'd have as limited contact with Brandon as possible, and it suddenly felt like he was everywhere. Mentally knowing it wasn't him didn't help much when stacked against more than ten thousand years of instincts.

I was sitting in my art class, unsuccessfully trying to recapture the simple joy of painting when I once again had Brandon's stench assault my nose. The curious gait just outside the classroom wasn't heavy enough for him so I knew it was probably Adri running errands for Mrs. Campbell again.

The bell rang a few seconds later, but I wasn't in any hurry to put my supplies up. I kept hoping I'd be able to abandon the currently-stalled piece

I was working on, but every time I tried to start something else I ended up just futilely throwing colors on the canvas.

The rest of the class trickled out as I finally gave up and quickly began cleaning up. The normal din of several hundred students traveling towards the lunch room nearly caused me to miss the collective gasp on the stairs just outside the art room.

Even when I heard it I didn't necessarily think anything of it until I felt the conflicting surges of power that signaled a fight.

"What are you looking at, freak?"

Vincent's bellicose tone identified exactly who'd faced off against Isaac's cool pool of power. It was hard to believe anyone from Brandon's pack would risk an actual fight out in the open, but Vincent was becoming increasingly restive over their failure to absorb us. I didn't have any idea what Brandon was doing to keep him in line, but the leash was starting to wear thin.

I threw the rest of my supplies into my drawer and started out the door as Vincent whispered something only barely audible from my new position. "After we kill you and Alec I'm going to lay claim on Jess. She's scared enough to be all the sweeter when I break her."

He'd done his research well, there was really only one thing guaranteed to get through Isaac's control, and I felt Isaac's beast surge forward to within a whisper of breaking loose.

I was within sight of them now, surrounded by a cluster of nervous teenagers. They were carefully circling each other, hardly noticing the uneven terrain the steps provided.

"Vincent!"

My voice hit him at the same time I cut loose with my own power and sent it down the steps like a crackling wave. Vincent backpedaled from Isaac faster than anything human could have managed, and the people ahead of me pressed back unconsciously against the unseen pressure flowing from me.

Vincent was attempting to edge away from us now, but Isaac shifted just enough to cut off his egress. For the first time in ages I saw actual fear on Vincent's face. He'd assumed he'd be able to continue to provoke Isaac at will without paying any kind of price, but Isaac apparently wasn't willing to just ignore the latest threat.

We worked in tandem, closing in on Vincent with the inevitability of time. I didn't want a fight here in front of all these witnesses, but Isaac was within his rights to want satisfaction from Vincent, and I wasn't about to leave him alone with a killer like Vincent.

Vincent suddenly grabbed Blaine Casperson and shoved him towards Isaac with enough force that the kid nearly went over the railing. Isaac grabbed Blaine, but Vincent was already moving. He used the distraction to escape down the stairs and what seemed like half the student body surged around Isaac to congratulate him.

I wasn't interested in the kind of fawning that usually followed a fight, so I quietly slipped past everyone and down to the cafeteria. Rachel found me as I finished paying for my food. She stretched to get close to my ear and whispered.

"You need to find Jasmin right now. If you don't hurry she's going to do something stupid."

Most alphas wouldn't have even dreamed of taking orders from a human, sister or not, but Rachel had earned my trust a hundred times over. I left the food where it was and headed towards Jasmin's lit class. Her scent trail led me outside into the parking lot just in time to see her Mercedes go roaring out onto the main road.

I raced to my Porsche, turned it on and hit fifty before I had to break to get onto the road. She was headed towards Brandon's pack's territory and I knew I had to stop her before she gave him an excuse to bring the Coun'hij into the picture.

Jasmin had all of the enhanced reflexes of a moonborn, but she'd never spent enough time behind the wheel to acquire an intimate knowledge of what her vehicle was capable of, and I used that against her ruthlessly.

She blew through a four-way stop at fifty and I followed right on her heels. She slowed to thirty to take a ninety-degree turn and I slung the Porsche around at fifty with all four wheels squealing as the high-performance rubber fought a losing battle with inertia.

I had an edge in acceleration and I caught her about the time she hit eighty. The face that looked back at me in the rear-view mirror wasn't rational, so I took the only route remaining and put the front end of my car into the back corner of hers with enough force to push her off into a fallow field.

I hit my head hard enough to see stars, but still managed to pull myself out of the car before Jasmin. She wasn't much behind me though, and I had to muster every ounce of speed to tackle her before she broke away across the field. We hit hard enough that the energy converted into a roll and she came up spitting and hissing.

She lunged at me but I sidestepped her and used her momentum to bring her around and down onto her stomach. She tried to spin around, but I kept pressure up on the arm bar I'd put on her, and after four or five minutes she calmed down enough to talk.

"You can't stop me. You don't know what he did. I'll sneak away and kill their parents while you're not looking."

"You're right, I don't know what he did, and I probably won't unless you tell me; but I can and I will stop you."

The look in her fierce blue eyes seemed to promise terrible things, but I reached down and coaxed my beast close enough to the surface to raise power and then pushed it at her like a metaphysical slap.

"Jasmin, I don't want to have to repeat myself. If you bring their parents into this they'll attack Donovan and Andrew. They'll come after James' mother and mine. If that happens I'll disavow you so quick that you'll have the Dark Hunt on your tail before the day is out."

She stopped struggling and there was hurt in her manner for the first time since I'd pinned her. "I wouldn't want anything to happen to Donovan or the others. I just didn't think about their likely response."

"That's the problem, Jas. You don't think when you get really mad; you just react. Usually you keep it under better control than this. What's going on?"

She shook her head as tears started to gather at the corner of her eyes. I hadn't seen her cry for years. Even when she'd been young, with all of the terrible things her father had done, she'd rarely cried.

"I can't tell you. I won't."

I finally let go of her and stood up. "We both know I don't have the leverage to really force you to do anything, but you're on thin ice."

She rolled to her feet and stalked back to the Mercedes without saying anything. We pushed both vehicles back onto the road and then she headed back towards school. I examined the mostly cosmetic damage to the Porsche with a sigh, and then followed her.

We'd missed Chem. I was missing a lot of class lately. Donovan would cover for me, but there were limits even to what he could do. Eventually I'd bump up against the state's mandatory attendance policy. I supposed I could always get my GED, if I somehow lived long enough to make that a necessity.

I stopped at a bathroom and repaired the worst of the damage to my clothing. Luckily I was wearing dark colors, so the wear and tear from wrestling a crazed wolf didn't show all that badly.

We had a sub again in Physics. I almost turned and left, but I felt a hunger to be treated like a human being. Not the protective older brother, or the domineering alpha, just a regular person. I didn't truly know what Adri was, but either way I could count on her to treat me at least as poorly as she'd treat anyone else.

I probably would have left regardless if I'd realized what kind of reception I was going to get from the rest of the class. A number of female hearts sped up as I weaved through desks to get to my corner in the back. I assumed my seat with a silent prayer that the sub would keep everyone under control.

I couldn't have been further off base. As soon as he'd finished with the roll he released us all to work on our 'group projects'.

The girls were the first ones to head back to my corner. Apparently Vincent was even more disliked than I'd realized. I was almost immediately surrounded by normally sensible females who suddenly couldn't say enough about how brave Isaac and I were.

I politely answered their questions and tried to deflect their admiration, but they were like bloodhounds on a scent, and the boys from the class quickly joined to turn it into even more of a zoo.

I managed to sneak a couple glances at Adri, who seemed thoroughly disgusted. She'd given up on studying and was sketching something.

Surrounded as I was, there was no way to stop the girls from brushing up against me, and I was beginning to think rudeness was going to be required to break things up before they started addicting themselves to my touch.

Luckily the sub chose that moment to intervene. He slammed his hand down on the desk like a gunshot. "I told you all to keep it to a dull roar. I want everyone away from that back corner. Get back to your seats."

Adri was drawing again. I found myself overcome by curiosity. This wasn't something I'd known about her. Without thinking, I cleared my throat to get her attention and ventured a smile. She tilted her head to one side as if to tell me to hurry up and get to the point.

"Sorry, I can tell you're not really in the mood to work on our project, especially with all of the racket today, but I saw you limping down the stairs just before lunch. Are you okay?"

Impatience was replaced with disgust for no apparent reason, and she turned back to her drawing.

"I'll be okay. Just a little sprain."

I flipped open a book and pretended to read while watching Adri out of the corner of my eye. I was just able to make out the drawing as it took shape. She wasn't exceptional, but seemed completely immersed in the experience, and the picture actually wasn't all that bad.

An oblong pond surrounded a tiny, crescent island. A number of trees served as the only other detail, but my study of the piece was interrupted when I realized that Adri's heart was once again racing to dangerous speeds. I'd had enough experience with her attacks now to realize one was in the offing. I opened my mouth and said the first thing that came to mind in an attempt to distract her.

"Hey, that's really pretty good. Is that a real place?"

She nodded wordlessly, but the attack was even closer.

"What's it called?"

Her response was so quiet as to almost be inaudible. "Monster Lake."

I was losing the battle, but I wasn't sure what else to do. Another question popped out of my mouth without conscious effort on my part.

"Was that close to your house in Minnesota? I..."

She suddenly stopped breathing, and I lunged towards her just in time to stop her from hitting her head on the ground.

Her breathing resumed as I picked her up and started looking for a way out through the sudden thicket of bodies that was forming as everyone rushed to see another of the actual attacks that the rumors had made famous.

Her eyes flickered open and for a brief second her mask wasn't in place. She looked up at me with such complete trust it felt like something reached inside of me and rearranged pieces that hadn't moved in years.

"Stand back, everyone, and let me through!" The sub was yelling like an ox, but making little actual progress. I registered my surroundings, but my attention was focused on Adri. I saw the mask click back into place as she came fully back to consciousness.

The substitute had finally pushed his way through to us, and based upon his breathing and elevated pulse was only a few seconds from a panic attack of his own.

"What's going on? Is she okay?"

I stood, Adri still in my arms, and began pushing my way out through the path he'd just made. "I think she'll be fine, but maybe I should get her to the nurse. Just to be sure."

Adri started squirming in my grasp, trying to get free as she realized she'd made a spectacle of herself again.

"There's really no need. I'm fine. I don't need to see the nurse."

She tried to thrash around, but I carefully immobilized her and continued onwards. I paused at the door to get final permission to leave.

"You hit your head pretty hard; I really think we should get you to the office. Sir, with your permission?"

He nodded and I headed out into the hall, but I was busy making a note of the fact she'd calmed down instantly when I'd mentioned the possibility of a head injury.

"Let go of my hands."

Mindful of the fact that she'd been limping, I gently set her down, and then had to restrain a chuckle as she began probing the back of her head.

"What are you doing? You didn't actually hit your head. I caught you before you hit the ground."

"Please, every other time I've dropped that quickly I've totally banged myself up. You were on the other side of my desk, there's no way you got all the way around it and managed to catch me before I hit the ground."

I felt my expression freeze as I realized I'd once again risked exposure to save her. "Believe what you will. There's no reason to worry about a concussion."

"Then why did you tell the sub I'd hit my head?"

There was honest curiosity in her voice and I looked away, buying myself time to decide whether or not to tell her the truth.

"I presumed you wouldn't want to stay and be subject to everyone's questions. You seem not to like people prying about your attacks, and you were less happy than usual today. I thought you could use the break."

I hadn't expected gushing praise necessarily, but I didn't expect the amount of venom she rounded on me with.

"*I* looked unhappy today? You, who never crack a smile unless you're going to get something out of it, were concerned about the fact I wasn't all smiles and giggles? Maybe you should flunk a test or two. Only it doesn't really count unless your dad, you know, the one who used to make your birthdays really special, is gone."

I was too stunned to respond. I started to reach out to her, but she stepped away before I could touch her.

"Don't try and pretend you're sorry. You were just looking for an excuse to get out of class once all of the hero worship dried up. Well, I got you out and you helped me avoid all of the stupid questions everyone would've asked, so we're even."

I watched her stomp off, and then turned around and headed back to Physics. I reassured everyone that she'd be okay, and breathed a mental sigh of relief when nobody pushed for more information.

Everyone was still clustered around the front of the room talking. Nobody had gotten around to righting the fallen desks, so I picked them back up and then gathered her books. The Monster Lake picture had torn free of her binder, and I hesitated for just the briefest second before pocketing it. The bell rang as I pulled my things together.

Pre-cal passed by in a haze as I replayed Adri's attack and our resulting conversation again and again. It was remotely possible she really was that good of an actor, but more and more I didn't believe it. Only if she was a human, then I was starting to realize just how big of a mistake I'd made.

More subdued than I'd been in a very long time, I followed Jasmin home. Donovan came out to meet us, and frowned at the obvious damage to both vehicles.

"I took care of it, and it's not worth talking about, Donovan. Can you please have them both repaired?"

There were unanswered questions in his eyes still, but the code he lived by wouldn't allow him to push. He nodded and then retired back into the house. Jasmin followed him, but I was too unsettled to go inside myself.

I wandered out to the green house and began pruning some of the roses that I'd been neglecting lately. The cool, white petals seemed to reach inside me and pull at things that were fresh and wounded. I tried my best to put the thoughts, the lingering scent of Adri out of my mind, and started working my way down the aisle.

Rachel's arrival interrupted the first measure of peace I'd managed to find in what felt like weeks. "Alec, you have to help her."

I shook my head in confusion as I tried to transition back to reality. "What are you talking about?"

"It's Adri. Something is wrong again. It's her birthday, but it's more than that. She seems so sad. I'm worried about her."

Of course. How could I have not realized her earlier reference meant today was her birthday?

"She said something to that effect earlier, but I didn't put it all together. I think she's still mourning whatever happened to her father."

Rachel nodded in sudden understanding as her eyes started to brighten with unshed tears.

"Her mom isn't around very much. She's kind of like us, a bunch of near-orphans with too much baggage."

I pulled Rachel into a hug and then blotted her tears with the edge of my sleeve. "It's okay, Rach. I'll do what I can for her."

It wasn't the kind of promise I should be making. Even if she was just a normal human, there were so many other things that should be taking priority, but I wasn't talking as the pack leader anymore. It was just Alec who was making that promise, who wanted to help for more reasons than just making Rachel happy.

I sat motionless for several seconds after Rachel left, and then finally picked out the best specimen of all the roses and cut the cane down near the base of the plant. The petals were just starting to unfold enough for the scent to make its way out of the purple-edged prison.

I leaned forward to smell it, and the fragrance of the rose mixed with the remnants of Rachel's tears to make something that created an ache deep inside me. It wasn't Rachel's tears I was thinking about, it was Adri's. I suddenly had the answer to a question that had plagued me for months.

Lagrimas del Angel. It was a perfect name for the plant that none but another shape shifter would ever truly understand.

Pushed by a growing urgency to carry out my errand, I returned to the house, quietly raiding the drawer where Rachel kept all of her stationary and ribbons. A few minutes later the note was written, secured to the flower with a dark green ribbon, and traveling on the front seat of our Escalade.

I backed the vehicle in between a pair of trees that would partially shield it from prying eyes, and then started cross-country to get to the Paige house. I stopped at the tree I'd referenced in my last note, and found with mingled relief and disappointment that it was empty. It was good that things weren't bad enough for her to need the services of her mysterious protector, but I found myself hungering for more contact with her.

I crept up the steps, only to nearly stumble as I realized the cause of the erratic heartbeat just audible from inside the house. She was experiencing a series of attacks one right after the other.

I carefully set the rose down on the doorstep and then knocked firmly on the door. I'd covered the distance to the nearest set of trees and taken up position behind the dense underbrush by the time she made her halting way up to the door. It almost caused me physical pain to see how bad her limp had become, but I found a measure of relief as she read my note and then brought the rose up to her beautiful, tear-streaked face.

I watched until long after she'd retreated back into her home.

Chapter 15

It was amazing just how quickly you could get a Porsche fixed if you had money to burn. Donovan spent an alarming amount of money accomplishing his magic, but my car was ready when the time arrived to go to Vegas.

Unfortunately a new wrinkle had arisen. When I'd promised Rachel she could go to Les Misérables I hadn't known I was going to be using the production to test Adriana's humanity. I would have still been agreeable with the idea of her going if there'd been a way to ensure her safety. I'd always planned on clearing the seats to either side of Adri, I didn't want to put any more innocents in the line of fire than I had to, but when I offered to swap tickets with Suzanne, I'd been surprised to find out that she'd already traded spots with my little sister.

Rachel had tried every combination of guilt and tears known to man, but I'd remained unmoved. She could still go if we drove together and she was seated safely on the Mezzanine, but under no circumstances was I going to allow her to sit next to a possible hybrid when the full moon would be amplifying every homicidal urge native to our kind.

In the end she decided it would be more likely she'd be forgiven for just not going at all than for going and snubbing Adri.

I hadn't enjoyed the fight, but I wasn't going to run the kinds of risks with Rachel that I was willing to run with myself.

I made the trip from Sanctuary down to Vegas in near record time, and even managed to push concerns about what the rest of the pack was likely going through mostly out of my mind.

I pulled up to the opera house a few minutes before the production was to commence and handed my keys to the valet. Even when Rachel had finally acknowledged the fact that she wasn't going to sway me when it came to her sitting next to Adri, she'd still held out for one last victory.

As a result, I found myself going to Les Misérables wearing a full tux. I'd wanted to refuse, especially when she pulled out the blue tie and pocket square, but I hadn't had the heart to refuse her after I'd just finished denying her something she'd had her heart set on for weeks.

The moon was heavy in the sky as I took one last look upwards before entering the building. Even separated from its pull by marble, steel and wood, I could still feel my blood all but boil from the energy of the night.

I tried to leash my power, but it was crackling about me wildly, causing people to turn and look as I walked into the front entryway. I'd gotten glimpses of gargoyles as I'd driven up, but my attention had focused primarily on the large fountain that had dominated the front courtyard. The graceful curve of the horse's neck had been underlined by the mythical creatures gathered at its feet.

I ignored the stares and whispers long enough to take in my surroundings. The marble of the floor was polished to such a high sheen that I could see the painted murals on the vaulted ceilings. I followed the wall around at eye level, taking in the gilded molding and intricate detail that would have been instantly discarded as an unnecessary expense in almost any other building.

I was close enough to hear the whisper of velvet on clothing as people passed by the rich, burgundy drapes that framed the archways deeper into the house. I could have stayed there enjoying the visual and auditory buffet for quite some time, but I could hear the sound of the orchestra warming up, so I finally moved away from my wall and proceeded to my seat.

I slipped into the back row, and quickly found Adri sitting two rows ahead of me. She was stunning in a pale sun dress, not as formal as the full tux Rachel had forced upon me, but still a definite step up from what most of the patrons were wearing.

Now that the time was here, I almost couldn't bring myself to act. After several seconds I finally loosened the leash I'd been using to try and hold my power in check, and let it roll out and down towards Adri.

I heard her heartbeat, difficult though it was to pick out among so many, race slightly at the sensation, but that wasn't any different than dozens of others. She didn't turn and throw herself at me, there was no answering lash of power from her, nothing that would have indicated she was anything other than the lovely teenage girl she seemed to be.

I felt a black mood descend upon me as I realized just how badly I'd handled things. If I'd behaved differently, if I hadn't assumed she was a Fir'shan out to destroy my family, maybe I'd have had a chance at winning her interest, but the opportunity was long past now. She'd already accepted Brandon's invitation to the Ashure Day Dance, which he'd executed in his typically ostentatious style.

I almost left before the performance started, but superhuman reflexes or not it was a bad idea to be on the road in such a mood. A few seconds later the house lights came down, the orchestra finished warming up, and it was too late to leave.

Unfortunately, not everyone was as worried about courtesy. The two college kids immediately in front of me had been going on and on about their supposed escapades since before I'd walked in. I'd been ignoring them up until now, but their testosterone-poisoned brains were quickly using up my store of patience.

Almost against my will, another wave of power arced away from me with enough snap that even the humans shifted uncomfortably in their seats. Adriana looked back and caught me staring at her, but even worse, her action afforded the pair sitting in front of me their first view of her lovely face.

"Dog, get a load of the looker."

"Oh, baby, it almost hurts. I need to tap me some of that."

Their whispers carried back to me, but I could only hope they were too faint for Adri to hear. As the production started, the entire audience quieted down and I temporarily lost myself in the experience.

The lead actor had a force of personality that validated his selection for the part. He wasn't quite Broadway material, but it was quickly apparent that the cast was going to give us a quality performance.

The music helped lull my beast back into a state of near dormancy and even went a little ways towards improving my mood until it came time for Fantine's descent into prostitution.

The idiots sitting in front of me fixed not on the tragedy her life had become, but on the baser nature of the events, and quickly were whispering the kinds of things that weren't brought up in polite society.

The patrons in the immediate area were starting to evidence signs of discontent, but predictably that just egged them on to greater efforts and additional volume. Adri turned around and shot them both a dirty look, but that just served to give them a new target.

"Oh, sweetie, don't you worry, we've been aching to get our hands on you all night. We're saving plenty of loving for you later. Meet us out back after this crap is over and we'll give you a real show."

My control snapped as I saw her blush in embarrassment. The integral instincts, the ones that I'd fought to keep suppressed all night roared to the forefront and I reached down and placed a hand on each of their shoulders.

My grip wasn't as hard as I could have made it, but it was still forceful enough to cause them pain. They both tried to turn around to confront me, but I increased the pressure and yanked them back into their chairs as another snap of power filled the area around me.

The hiss of pain I drew out of the one on the right was fortunately drowned out by a sudden crescendo in the music, and then I was leaning forward and speaking deliberately into their ears.

"You're both not worth the effort it would take to kill you. You can either shut up and stay, or you can leave, but either way you will show respect to everyone here or I will hunt you down and rip your arms out of your shoulders."

As threats went it didn't feel especially impressive, but it was backed up by the steadily increasing pressure from my hands, and enough metaphysical juice to make them nearly wet themselves. I released them and then leaned back to see what they would do next.

I half expected them to turn and confront me, but they were so unnerved that they remained shaking in their seats for several seconds. The arrival of an usher shook them out of their shock and they turned back as though intending to demand my ejection from the theater.

I allowed the waves of power hammering at them to peak again. A few seconds later they got up and left, leaving behind a noticeably relieved audience.

The rest of the play was well performed. In another time and place I would have enjoyed it immensely, but my thoughts returned again and again to the simple fact that I'd misjudged Adri. Only now, when it was too late to do anything about it, did I realize just how badly I wanted her to think more of me than she did.

The sense of desolation quickly grew, and when the curtain finally closed on the performers for the last time I exited the theater with such speed that I got questioning looks from both of the ushers I slipped by.

TORN

It wasn't until I handed my token to the valet that I realized just how tired I was. It'd been so long since I'd spent time among humans on the night of a full moon that I'd forgotten how exhausting it was to try and keep up the facade of humanity.

I climbed into my car as soon as it was brought around and let my control slip somewhat as I dropped it into gear and pulled out in to traffic. It was an incredible relief to let the power run off me in sheets, but I had nearly two hours of driving still ahead of me, and as the night progressed I found that even the effort of just retaining my form was becoming increasingly draining.

When I finally pulled up to the estate I didn't even bother pulling my clothes off. I simply staggered out of my car and let the change rip through me. I drunkenly speared the scraps of clothing with my claws, and then stumbled back to the grotto and curled up on the hard rock surrounding the pool.

Mere seconds later I was asleep and dreaming. It'd been a very long time since I'd shared a dream with Adri but it no longer bothered me when I saw her running through the underbrush ahead of me. I wasn't positive it was the real Adri, but I knew she wasn't a shape shifter.

Lost in the perfect joy of running and being with someone I couldn't be with in real life, I bounded along behind her. I maintained enough distance that she wouldn't realize she was being followed, but stayed close enough to watch the lithe perfection of her form as she skipped from rock to rock across the stream or jumped a large ravine that would be impassable to any mere human.

I wanted to stay there, to follow her forever, but reality called me back all too soon, and I awoke to Rachel shaking me.

"Alec, you need to get up. Jasmin and the others are back and they're not very happy."

I thought about shrinking back down to my normal shape, but decided against it. If they were truly unhappy then I'd be better off remaining as a hybrid.

"How was the opera?"

"It was good. Exhausting, but good. She's not a moonborn."

Rachel's smile was sincere without being smug. "I knew that, Alec, but I'm glad you're convinced finally."

Jasmin and the others came around a corner as we finished speaking, and they were all in their human forms so I allowed mine to shrink down as well.

"So was your little field trip worth all of the bleeding we went through?"

I didn't like her tone, especially not on the night of a full moon when my beast was so close to the surface, but I forced the anger away.

"She's definitely not a shape shifter. What happened tonight?"

Isaac came to the fore and I realized that his arm was heavily bandaged. Jasmin didn't give me much of a chance to process the information. "Oh nothing much, we just ran your patrol and then got jumped by nearly the entire pack while still in neutral territory."

I rechecked to make sure everyone was standing there, and felt a wave of relief as I verified that nobody had been killed, or even wounded so badly as to be confined to bed.

"Not Brandon though?"

Now Isaac spoke up, as befitted his right as second of the pack. "No, but Vincent and the others pressed us pretty hard. This time they had the initiative and we were heavily outnumbered. Vincent used one of the submissives as a distraction and then nearly chewed my arm off before we managed to beat a fighting retreat."

If Vincent had managed to get fangs into Isaac's arm then the odds were very good that Isaac had some fairly deep gashes to his chest and back. I'd have to be mindful of that and ensure that James didn't challenge until Isaac was fully healed.

I bowed my head slightly in respect for what the pack had accomplished without me, and then clasp Isaac on the uninjured shoulder. "I appreciate what you all did, and I'm sorry for the injuries you sustained. Now that we know for sure Adriana isn't from the Coun'hij we can begin laying long-term plans again."

Jess crowded next to her boyfriend, shooting me a dark look as she led Isaac away, but she didn't voice whatever she was thinking, and they all split up to go to their rooms. A human would have assumed that was it, but I knew we'd just experienced a shifting point. I'd burned up some of the goodwill I'd garnered with them over the years, and there wasn't anything I could do in the short term to affect that.

Rachel hugged me again and headed into the house. I knew I had things inside that needed done, but my nap had refreshed me more than I would have expected and I found myself wanting to stretch out my legs and run.

I dropped down onto my hands and knees and shifted over to my wolf form, taking off through the darkness with all of the speed inherent to my kind. I thought I was running just to run, that there was no purpose to my direction, but all too soon I found myself close to the tree where I'd told Adri I would check for notes if her situation worsened again.

I approached it cautiously, but there were still no scent traces to indicate that Brandon's pack had come through the area. There wasn't anything to indicate Adri had been here either.

It was a foolish, pointless thing to do, but I found myself jumping up to the burnt-out crook of the tree to verify that there really wasn't a note from her. I'd spent most of the night with her and yet still more time while I'd been asleep, but I found myself wanting more, like an addict who'd just come down off of a high and needed another dose to avoid facing the world once more.

I loped slowly in the direction of her house, unsure what I'd do once I finally arrived. I slithered between trees as I got closer, careful to stay out of sight of the pool of light from the pole-mounted light off to the side of the house. The lights were all off inside, but I could smell the hot metal of their Jeep's engine even from here, so I knew that Adri had safely arrived.

It almost seemed like I could feel her presence calling out to me. I somehow knew exactly which window was hers and without really thinking about what I was doing I allowed my forms to shift once again and resumed my hybrid form. I crept close enough to the house to hear both heartbeats. The constant, slow beating of sleep assured me enough to climb the thirty-foot pole and carefully unscrew the large light bulb just enough for it to go dark. I looked down at the house and realized I could see into Adri's room less than ten feet away.

I meant to leave, I told my body to lower itself to the ground, but something about the view had sent my heart racing. The view was familiar somehow, but I needed to be closer.

It was a pretty good reach, even for a six-and-a-half-foot hybrid, but I sank the talons on my feet into the pole and carefully reached out with first one hand and then the other, fastening my claws into the wooden overhang of her roof.

I spread my weight as broadly as possible and then let go of the pole and swung across the empty space. I sank my newly-freed talons into another section of the roof and finally looked down through the window.

I almost lost my grip and plummeted to the ground as I realized what I was seeing. Adri was peacefully asleep on her bed, covered in a thin tank top and a well-worn pair of shorts. The full moon made it easy to make out the graceful curve of her arm and the slow rise of her chest.

She glowed with the light of life, the only living thing in the dark room, and I knew that somehow this was what I'd been trying to draw. The window frame, the vague details I'd filled into the corners of the room, they were all the same. The only thing lacking was the beautiful figure that, despite my best efforts, seemed to be more and more central to my life.

I stayed too long. I lost track of time as I watched her breathing and listened to the sweet gurgle of her heartbeat. By the time I came back to myself even my tremendous strength was starting to flag as my arms began to shake. Suddenly I wanted nothing so much as to be home, to be in my studio painting the unearthly beauty before me. I took one last long look at Adri and then quietly dropped the twenty feet to the ground and headed for home.

Chapter 16

I was a man possessed. My sense of duty and Donovan's respectful nagging served to tear me away from my painting long enough to accomplish most of the tasks waiting on me. We caught up on a number of different items pertaining to the family holdings, I spent some time with each member of the pack, ground through all the homework that had to be finished up, and then retreated back into my studio and locked the door.

I mixed paints until I had a range of silvers and whites that seemed like they might do Adri justice, and then became frustrated when I failed to get the curve of her side or the angle of her head right. Normally I had a visually photographic memory, but as my lack of success continued I began to wonder if it'd failed me or if my talent just wasn't equal to the task.

It was a quiet night with no sign of Brandon's pack. I released everyone to range about our territory as they willed, and then snuck off towards Adri's house. It was a stupid thing to do. She was an incredible distance outside of our territory, but it was almost like I wasn't in control of myself anymore.

The light hadn't been fixed, so I shifted to my hybrid form and quietly scaled the pole. A few seconds later I was once again able to see the source of my inspiration. I'd only had a few moments to drink in her beauty before a stray breeze brought me the smell of Vincent and Simon rapidly approaching from the direction of town.

The dreamy, unpractical side that'd led me out into the trap was instantly displaced as I realized there was a reasonable chance I was going to die out here. I dropped to the ground and shifted back to wolf form on the fly.

It didn't matter whether they'd come by last night and smelled me, or if they'd just chanced upon me tonight. My only concern now had to be getting back to our territory before they caught me.

I could hear them now, panting as they ran several hundred feet back. They weren't gaining, but there was still a lot of ground to cover before I was safe. The underbrush that normally slid by with only the merest whisper of contact now seemed to be pulling at me, trying to slow my progress.

I was less than a minute short of our land when they sprang the second prong of their trap. I smelled Nathanial a split second before he pounced, which was the only thing that allowed me to dodge his attack. He still got a piece of my shoulder, but he missed the neck hold he'd been going for, and even as we went rolling from the force of the impact I let my hybrid form explode out.

His fangs lost their hold on my shifting flesh, but not before they tore huge, bloody gashes in the muscles that shielded the joint. I chose flight rather than attempting to kill Nathanial, but still only made it fifteen or twenty seconds further before I heard the others closing in.

I spun around just in time to catch Simon as he lunged at me, but Vincent shifted forms and hit me like a wrecking ball. Simon let loose with a pained howl as I took him to the ground, but I was forced to let him go in order to roll back to my feet.

It was a hopeless fight. Nathanial was mobile again and circling to my right at the same time that Simon was moving around to the left. Vincent was dancing just out of striking range as he waited for his companions to get into position.

I attacked before they could get set, moving into Nathanial with every bit of speed I could muster. I caught him with the claws of my right hand and nearly managed to make it back around in time to catch Simon. The motion threw off Simon's aim. He wasn't used to lunging at targets so tall, and his fangs fastened on my arm with accompanying spikes of agony.

Vincent was only a half-step behind, but I brought Nathanial up and used him as a club. The attack nearly succeeded in knocking Vincent over, but he barreled on in and knocked me to the ground again.

I scrambled furiously, attempting to get out from under Vincent. My talons and claws were finding purchase on his body, but he'd fastened his fangs onto my arm, clamping down with enough force that I knew I only had a few seconds before he'd manage to rip it off.

I redoubled my efforts, raking him with such frenzy that hot blood washed over me, but he didn't even flinch. I felt his teeth meet inside my arm, and then suddenly a loud shriek caused both of us to start.

I lunged back to my feet as Vincent released me and spun around to meet Isaac's attack. On paper the others had the edge against us, but Isaac was fresh, and I was still more than capable of handling whichever of the wolves got too close.

I knocked Nathanial away again as he sprang at Isaac, and then Isaac and Vincent clinched in a whirlwind of claws and blood. I spun just in time to duck Simon's attack, and then Nathanial was back again. Somehow he'd locked on my leg without me seeing the attack coming, and Simon spun around and hit me in the chest hard enough to knock me over.

I caught a glimpse of Isaac's fight, just enough to see that he was winning, that he'd pinned

Vincent and was working his way into a lethal hold, but my situation was turning serious. Simon had a hold of my good arm and was stretching me out so that I couldn't get at him or Nathanial, either one.

It wasn't the kind of thing that would grant them a quick kill, but all they had to do was keep me stretched out between them and sooner or later I'd bleed to death even if they didn't manage to rip me in half before then.

They chose the second option, and dug their paws in as they whipped their heads back and forth. The agony as my joints were strained nearly to the point of breaking wrung a cry out of me and suddenly Isaac was there knocking them off of me.

Vincent was back on his feet, looking unsteady but more than ready for another round, but Jasmin's howl announced approaching reinforcements. Vincent and the others disappeared into the night as I limped home after Isaac.

Jasmin joined us and then raced off to find the others. Everyone was waiting for us back at the house. I made it almost to the lawn before accumulated blood loss and shock brought me to my knees. The last thing I remembered before the blackness overtook me was James approaching with his ears laid back and the blood thirst in his eyes.

Chapter 17

Rachel was waiting next to my bed when I finally came back to full consciousness. She'd been crying, and still looked worried, but she mustered a brave smile as soon as she realized I was awake.

"Alec, I was so worried. What happened?"

I shook my head, wincing at the way the motion made my stomach clench. I hadn't known it was possible for one of us to get a concussion.

"We can talk about that later. What's the status of the pack?"

Jasmin walked into the room before Rachel could answer.

"Pissed off and worried, or maybe worried and pissed off. It probably depends on who you ask. What in Adjam's name were you thinking running about into the neutral territory by yourself?"

"As I recall you didn't think it was so unreasonable when it was you and James that struck out on your own."

"That was different. There were two of us and Brandon's pack hadn't been acting quite so aggressive. By all rights you should be dead."

I nodded my head, more gingerly this time. "You're right, Vincent and the others would have killed me if Isaac hadn't happened to be so close."

Rachel shook her head at me. "That's not what she's talking about. James was mad, or scared. When you came back he almost challenged Isaac right then and there."

I felt a shiver work its way up my spine as I realized what Rachel was saying. James couldn't attack me until he'd beaten Isaac, but Isaac had been injured. If he'd beaten Isaac, or if Isaac had just declined to fight, there wouldn't have been anything to stop James from killing me. He'd have inherited a pack that was only days from destruction, but he'd have finally achieved his mother's ambitions for him. Rule in hell indeed.

"So why didn't he?"

Rachel answered again. "Isaac refused to stand aside for him, and Jasmin told him that she'd challenge him just as soon as he finished with Isaac, and that she'd kill him if Isaac proved unable to do it."

I looked up at Jasmin and nodded in thanks. Isaac and I enjoyed a better working relationship than most alphas and their seconds. He knew I was a slightly better fighter, but even more than that he didn't have any desire to lead the pack. In any other pack he'd have either been killed early on or forced to become something entirely different than he was now. I kept the dominance games between him and James to a minimum and in return he generally backed me far past the point where most hybrids would have been looking to increase their own status and power.

Despite the capital I'd burned up with him lately, he'd acted essentially as I'd have expected. Jasmin was a different matter altogether. Her personality was much more aggressive than Isaac's and she very much resented being fourth in the pack. With the erratic nature of her actions lately I was almost surprised she hadn't joined in with James' attempted coup.

Some of my thoughts must have been mirrored on my face, Jasmin looked away after only a second of meeting my eyes.

"Don't look at me like that. I wouldn't have let him kill you."

"I never said you would. I'm just realizing I can't predict your actions as well these days as I used to."

"I could say the same thing about you. Going out there by yourself was seriously stupid."

"I don't want to talk about it, Jasmin. I appreciate what you and Isaac both did for me, but the reason I was out there is off limits."

Jasmin flipped me off and stormed out of the room. Rachel tried to make small talk, but quickly realized I wasn't in the mood and followed after Jas.

Now that I was safely by myself I pulled the sheet back and took an inventory of my wounds.

There were more than I remembered. The massive ones on my leg and each arm were about like I expected, but there were a whole host of slashes across my chest that I didn't remember receiving. Apparently Vincent had gotten in more blows than I'd realized.

Jasmin was right; by all rights I *should* be dead. I'd be back up and fully mobile within another twenty-four hours at the outside, but it had been a close thing.

I was shaken by what'd happened, but I pushed those concerns out of my mind and stumbled over to my studio, running my finger over the biometric lock. I needed to make another attempt at the painting while Adri's face and form were still fresh in my mind. Given what'd just happened it was unlikely I was going to get another chance to see her asleep.

When I finally staggered back to my bed and collapsed into an exhausted sleep I was only slightly less frustrated than I'd been after the last attempt. It was better. I had more of her essence, most of the sweet innocence that made one think of the angelic, but it still wasn't perfect. It still lacked so many of the essentials that made her perfection.

The distress over the painting dissolved as I floated away into a calming dream. I was at the pond on the far end of the estate. It was possibly the only natural spring in sixty miles, and was deep and wide enough to support a type of long, slender fish.

It was another refuge I hadn't been to in more months than I cared to think about, but it was made all the more calming by the fact that Adri was there as well. She walked up the path from the hedge maze and then smiled in delight at the sight of the pond.

I was momentarily worried she'd smell me and bolt, but in this dream Adri didn't seem to have inherited our sense of smell. I crowded ever so slowly forward to find a better vantage point from which to watch her.

She carefully walked up to the bench, and then as she placed one toe in the water, she was suddenly clad in a swimsuit rather than the jeans and tank top she'd been in just a second before. I felt my pulse speed up as I took in the gorgeous expanse of pale skin that the blue two-piece revealed. Fortunately her hearing was likewise human-dull.

She suddenly dived into the pond with a bravery and zest I'd seen only hints of previously, coming up sputtering and then diving back under to pursue the darting slivers of light that were the freshwater fish.

She moved with the smooth, sure strokes of an Olympic swimmer as she chased and then finally settled back to just float in the center of the expanse of water. I remained motionless, silently watching until my healing body finally determined it'd rested sufficiently and sent me back into the real world.

The next couple of days were a frenzy of activity. I'd chosen not to go to school, partially because I had too much to do to spend my day sitting through pointless lectures, and partially because I was hoping that Brandon would assume I was even more injured than I actually was.

I'd just discovered that the old saw about necessity being the mother of invention had a very important corollary. While self-preservation was capable of focusing the mind to an incredible degree, sometimes inspiration required a higher cause than mere survival.

For years we'd been hoping that we could defer the coming confrontation until I'd had time to manifest my power. I'd been hesitant as a result, often choosing to bend rather than face Brandon down over things that didn't directly relate to our survival.

It would have been tempting to blame Donovan. Flexibility and misdirection were the usual tools of the submissives, but that wouldn't have been fair. It had been my decision, just like it was now my decision to alter our tactics.

Donovan and I sat down, pooled our knowledge of Brandon's fiscal operations and assets, and then came up with ways to begin causing him problems in each area. It wasn't anything overly aggressive, but he was about to find his net worth declining abruptly.

I slogged through hours and hours of homework, and then did something I hadn't tried in ages. The rest of the wolves were at school, so I couldn't spar with them, even supposing that was a good idea considering their recent frustration with me, so I went out back to my father's old workshop and strapped myself into the machine.

Weightlifting had long been viewed as worthless among shape shifters. When you're easily able to bench-press a small car, there doesn't usually seem to be much point in becoming two or three percent stronger.

My father hadn't shared that belief, and with the advent of science and weight machines he'd been vindicated. It'd taken several years to design and build a machine capable of stressing the strength of even a full-blown hybrid, but metal work had been one of his great loves, and he'd persevered.

The result wasn't pretty, but it allowed me to lift massive, almost inconceivable amounts of weight in either of my two-legged forms. When I'd first manifested my wolf form I'd spent hours in the machine attempting to compensate for Jasmin's increased strength and power. I hadn't been entirely positive that my royal traits would breed true with only one moonborn parent, and it'd seemed the only hope of retaining control of the pack when faced with Jasmin's royal heritage.

I'd even continued working out on the machine for a short time after I'd manifested my royal hybrid form. Strength led to speed, and the two were vitally important in any shape shifter fight, but all too soon Brandon had manifested his power, and it had seemed pointless to continue to train when no amount of muscle growth could hope to compete with his unnatural strength and speed.

That no longer mattered. Even if I never manifested a power, I faced more threats than Brandon. Assuming we somehow survived the coming storm I'd still be faced with other challengers, other hybrids, and it was vitally important I be able to face them down.

I pushed, pulled and twisted for almost two hours, long past the point where my limbs were weak and trembling, and then took a brief break to drive into town. The thought of leaving the pack's territory, especially by myself, brought a pang of fear arcing along my spine, but I pushed the feeling away.

This was during the middle of the day, surrounded by plenty of witnesses, and if I let fear rule me now, the end would be all that much quicker.

I called Jasmin as I crossed into town.

"How's everything going?"

"Just peachy. You were right, Brandon and company seem pretty positive you're completely out of commission. I expect they'll launch another major raid tonight."

"Okay, we'll be waiting for them and see if we can't roll them up and put some fear back into them. Anything else important happen?"

"Just a little intra-pack strife on the other side. Brandon nearly ripped Vincent's head off. Apparently he's not too happy with the fact that Vincent's the one turning in the wins lately. First Isaac and then you. He just stormed out of the cafeteria with your new girlfriend."

I spared a moment of thanks for being out of scent range from Jasmin. If she realized how close to on target her barb was things would get even worse than they already were.

"Right. I just wanted to check in and make sure that things were going okay. I'll see you guys after school."

I hadn't really planned on swinging past the school but Jasmin's words were too much of a lure. I slowly rounded the last corner, and then pulled off behind the shelter of one of native juniper trees. From my position I could just make out the school and identify Brandon and Adri as they walked a slow circuit around the school.

Seeing him with her roused protective instincts that usually only threats to Rachel or my mother brought out. I nearly lost control of my shape when he leaned in as if he were about to kiss her.

I kept myself together enough to see him pull back before actually making contact, but it was as if the sight had somehow closed a circuit inside me. There was no longer any denying what motivated me.

I wanted Adriana Paige, and I was going to do anything I could, short of a full-blown war between our packs, to protect her from Brandon. Even if she fought me the whole way.

Chapter 18

The ambush went down essentially as I'd hoped. Brandon and the others came barreling through our territory so secure in their belief we were down a hybrid that they were even running with the wind.

We plotted their course and then hunkered down in a shallow wash. I'd taken a nap earlier in the day and was fully recovered. We waited until the other pack was parallel with us and then came up over the top of the wash and tore into the wolves closest to us.

The strongest pack members were up at the front of the group and we did even more damage initially than on our last ambush. I didn't even slow down as I hit the first wolf. I felt my talons sink into flesh, and then felt a foreleg snap as my full weight came down on him.

Jasmin was just to my left, and she brought down another of the submissives, latching onto his neck and whipping him around in a failed effort to snap it before she threw him in to a tree with enough force to impale him on one of the lower branches.

Cassie apparently was counting on Vincent to distract me. She came arrowing through the darkness directly at my throat, but I dodged the attack and got a claw into her as she sailed overhead. Vincent was intercepted by Isaac before he could come to her aid, and Dom of all people pounced on Cassie before she managed to turn and spring at me again.

Dom was normally the most submissive of our entire pack, but she latched onto Cassie's shoulder and set about ripping into her with the claws that were a cat's biggest advantage over us wolves.

Brandon came barreling into me and I fell back on three years of aikido training, absorbing his momentum, converting it into a leg throw that sent him more than twenty feet behind me.

He completed less than half a rotation before righting himself and lunging back towards me. Trading blows with him was a losing proposition, but we'd taken enough of his wolves out in the first two seconds of the fight that I didn't need to beat him.

I dodged what I could and blocked most of the rest of the blows, the force of which nearly knocked me to the ground each time. The first exchange couldn't have lasted more than a second or two, but seemed like an eternity.

Just as I slipped on a pile of shale, and went down into a three-point stance, I saw Jasmin dart in and rip at the back of Brandon's leg. He spun around with inconceivable speed, but he wasn't used to fighting a royal wolf, probably didn't even know it was possible for anyone to be as fast as Jasmin. She took a nasty-looking group of slashes to her flank, but avoided the majority of the force.

The attack bought me enough time to right myself and charge in with both arms swinging. I scored several deep slashes into Brandon's back and arms before he turned, and then it was my turn to be beaten back while Jasmin circled and looked for another opportunity to attack.

Vincent, Simon, Nathanial and a few other injured and severely dazed wolves were being handled quite handily by Isaac, James and Jess, while Dom continued to angle for a killing grip on Cassie.

Isaac finally managed a favorable clinch with Vincent, and was rewarded with a scream of pain as his claws burrowed towards Vincent's heart. Moving almost quicker than I could follow, Brandon spun around and tore Isaac off of Vincent.

Nathanial darted past Jess, forcing Dom off of Cassie, and then the five of them fled the scene, leaving the rest of their pack to follow as they were able.

I called Jasmin and James back before they could outdistance the rest of us, and then turned back to Brandon's three wolves who hadn't been able to flee with the rest. Now that we were past the heat of the battle I was able to stop and see who'd been abandoned.

Jack Peterson was the undersized wolf whose foreleg I'd broken while Sam Giles had been impaled by the tree branch and Alison Whitaker had been hamstrung and savaged.

James' eyes lit up as he took in the wounded wolves, but I ordered him away before he could act on years of pent-up anger.

"We're not going to kill them. They're free to go, or to stay here with us if they so desire."

A chorus of growls sounded from the girls, and even Isaac didn't look overjoyed at the thought of letting roughly a third of Brandon's pack leave when we had the ability to kill them and equalize the odds.

I walked over to Sam and carefully pulled him off of the tree, wincing a little at his yelp of pain. He reverted back to his human form as soon as I set him down, partially to speed the healing process and partly because in wolf form his wounds would pull more than as a human.

"Why would you let us live? Brandon would never do that for one of you he caught wounded and isolated."

"You're right, but I'm not Brandon. I've never caught the three of you approaching the excesses of Nathanial or Simon. I'm going to let you live now so you can think about the choices you're making, about the fact that you've got other options."

"More like you are going to let us live and send us back there so that Brandon will kill us for you and you can keep your lily-white hands clean."

Jack had shifted back to his two-legged form, but in keeping with the defiant tone of his words he wasn't curled up on the ground like Sam, and I felt the first streak of discomfort. Brandon's pack didn't wear the ha'bit, instead like most other packs dealing with the casual nudity and increased fights that it could have prevented.

"I won't lie and say you're not going back to suspicion and distrust. Brandon won't really believe I let you go out of sheer decency. If you go back he'll suspect you've become double agents, or maybe were double agents all along, but I don't think he'll kill you."

Alison had shifted back now, curled up in a ball either out of shyness or due to the pain of her wounds.

"We have to go back. If we don't, our parents will suffer. You don't know what it's like there."

I managed a shrug with the massive shoulders of my hybrid form. "I can imagine, but that isn't the point. The point is I'm not going to compel you either way. You can stay or you can go, but remember that it doesn't have to be like this. The packs are evenly matched now, but if the balance were to change slightly we'd all be looking at a completely different world."

I watched while Sam pulled himself to his feet and picked Alison up. Their progress was slow and erratic, but they started back towards Brandon's territory followed by Jack.

As we returned to the estate, Jasmin ran at my side, and I was surprised to feel some of the anger dissipate from her over the course of the few minutes it took us to arrive. I wasn't so fortunate where James was concerned, and he was in my face as soon as we stopped running.

"Why would you let them go? We could have killed them and tilted the odds in our favor."

It was Jasmin who spoke up before I could respond. "The Coun'hij, James. Alec couldn't risk doing something that would cause them to come after us. They were in our territory, but given how aggressively Brandon's been operating lately I think it's a safe assumption he's confident they are going to support him over us unless he really screws up."

Her words gave James enough of a pause that I was able to insert my follow-up reason. "If we'd have caught Vincent, Brandon, Nathanial or Simon I would have killed them. Even if it had been Cassie that we caught I'd have probably executed her and dealt with the Coun'hij if they chose to become involved, but those three aren't the murderers that Nathanial and Simon are. If we can convince them to defect it will swing the balance of power even further in our favor than just killing them would have."

The argument finally subsided into surly unhappiness and I let Donovan bandage me up. A few seconds after he finished I collapsed into my bed again. Although the wounds would have been cause enough to get some additional rest, they weren't my real reason for retiring so early.

I was vindicated when shortly after dropping off to sleep I found Adri once again participating in my dream. It seemed silly now. I was about to talk to a figment of my subconscious mind, but I'd already promised myself I wouldn't let any possible avenue go unexplored.

She was sitting on the edge of a cliff on the extreme south edge of the pack's territory, gazing out over the arid landscape. I approached to within thirty feet of her and then called her name.

"Adri, would you mind some company?"

She turned around guiltily, and then shrugged. "I thought maybe I was finally done with you in this place. You haven't been here in a while."

I took that as a yes, walked over, and sat down with her.

"I'm not going to apologize to you. I'm grateful for what you did at the opera house, for shutting those guys up, but that doesn't change the fact that your sister totally stood me up."

My heart sped up as I realized this was the first actual conversation we'd ever had that didn't include hurled insults and instant anger.

"I don't know what to say other than that she's sorry."

She turned away from the view long enough to give me a questioning look. "I never would have expected that out of you, not even out of dream Alec."

"You're welcome. I hope those idiots didn't ruin your experience the other night."

"They didn't. They would have if you hadn't stopped them, but it was the most amazing night. The show was everything I'd hoped it would be."

I nodded in satisfaction, and joined her in watching the breeze cause the sparse vegetation to sway back and forth.

"This is usually the part where you tell me that it wasn't as good as the London version, or that the seats weren't as soft as the theater on Broadway. Surely even here and now you'll find a way to offend the rest of us mere mortals."

Asking forgiveness wasn't usually a key part of my nature. I wasn't so proud as to refuse to admit my shortcomings, but this was different. I didn't care about right and wrong with Adri as much as I wanted to ensure she was happy, that she didn't grow to hate me even more.

"I'm sorry if I've rubbed your face in my family's wealth. It wasn't intentional. If it were possible I'd go back and do things differently."

She'd turned her attention to an ant that was making its way manfully across a small stick in its path.

"I wish things could have been different. Especially at the start. I'm in completely uncharted waters these days. The geeks all hate me, the popular kids are convinced I'm sleeping with Brandon to climb the social food chain, and my boyfriend hangs out with some of the worst bottom-feeders in the school."

It was too good of an opening to pass up, even at the possible expense of the goodwill I'd just built up.

"In my experience we tend to congregate with those who are most like us, regardless of whatever shell we may present to the outside world."

She looked up at me with real curiosity in her eyes, and I felt something inside me wrung dry to provide the moisture needed for future tears.

"You aren't talking about me, you're talking about Brandon."

I nodded slowly, and she tilted her head to the side deliberately as a gust of wind whipped her beautiful blond hair around.

"What if that isn't the case? What if he's where he is because he's driven by duty to them? Duty to his family, duty to the town? *Your* friends aren't the best character references, buddy. Jasmin is a complete sociopath and Rachel is scared to death of losing your goodwill."

"Jasmin isn't petty. I don't always understand why she chooses the path she takes, but there is always a good reason behind it. One doesn't go through the things she's gone through without developing an incredible capacity for empathy. I'd back her morals over almost anyone else I know."

It wasn't what I'd planned on saying, but as I said it I realized it was true, and the knowledge freed me to go on.

"As for Rachel, I can only say she's better than me in almost every way. I continue to fail to live up to my heritage, but she's stood by me despite that. I believe that means she sees a seed of something good inside me. Someday I think I may manage to live up to that potential. For now, whatever good I do have inside me worries about what Brandon will eventually do to you."

Adri's pulse was smooth and unhurried as she reached out and placed one hand on the side of my face. The contact sent little thrills of rightness through my being, but even that wasn't a match for what I felt at her words.

"You really believe that. You may not be right, but you're not lying."

"No, I'm not lying. That is the truth as far as I know it."

"I can tell. Your heart remained steady through it all."

Chapter 19

Rachel found me covered in paint, slumped against the wall in the gallery that separated my studio from my bedroom. I'd finally given up ever finishing up Adri's sleeping portrait. My mind's eye had utterly failed me when it came to reproducing an actual likeness.

"I think maybe it's time to give this one up, big brother. I haven't ever seen you so frustrated and consumed by a project."

I reached out and brushed a stray hair back behind her ear and then shrugged. "I think you're right. It had the most potential of anything I've ever painted, but I just can't seem to get it right."

"So do I ever get to see this near-masterpiece?"

My mind instantly shied away from the idea. Apparently my unease was obvious; Rachel held her hands up in surrender. "It's okay, there's no need to feel guilty. If it never ends up in the gallery, it never ends up in the gallery."

TORN

The week had been incredibly busy. I'd eventually had to go back to school. The tactical purpose of my absence had been accomplished on Monday night, and after that I couldn't continue to justify remaining home. I'd used my time at home, however, to get far enough ahead in my studies that I could spend more time with the rest of the pack.

I'd sparred with James and Isaac, spent additional hours in the machine, and slept more than at any other time since I'd first manifested a second shape. Everyone assumed it was a result of the tremendous abuse I was putting my body through in my strength training regime, but while I was extra tired each night, the real reason had been the hope each night that I'd share my dreams with Adri.

Only there, safe from the dominance games and worries about how Brandon would use her against me, was I able to open up and talk to her.

In real life she'd remained just as cool and distant as always, and after one or two abortive attempts to talk to her I just hunkered down and did my best to ignore the yearning tearing at me.

Inside the dream world things were different. I quickly learned just how dry her sense of humor was, that she talked with her hands when she got really excited, and that I had to be very careful of mentioning her father, her sister, and car accidents in general.

It had been a wonderful, hellish existence, but I'd been neglecting Rachel. I looked back up at my younger sister and caught her eying my clothes.

"I think I'm going to have to start buying you stuff a half size up from what I normally get you. That weight-lifting program seems to be working."

My laugh was nothing more than a courtesy to show appreciation for her humoring my latest wild attempt to save us all from Brandon. It was impossible for me to have put on the kind of mass she was indicating in such a short time.

"Rach, did you and Adri have a fight on Monday?"

She hung her head like she expected to be kicked and I was momentarily reminded of dream Adri's assertion that I bullied Rachel.

"Yes. She wasn't happy about my not going to Les Mis. I can't really blame her, but I haven't managed to find a way to make it up to her."

"Why didn't you tell me?"

"You've been really busy this week. Besides, there wasn't anything you could have done about it and I didn't want you to feel guilty for it."

"Maybe I should feel guilty. She's just a normal human. You could have gone and been okay, but I was too busy jumping at shadows."

Rachel shook her head and hugged me. "No, you were being my protective big brother, the one who lives in a dangerous world so that he can keep me safe. I understood even before you told me I couldn't go that it was likely my friendship with Adri was going to be the price I had to pay to convince you she wasn't a threat."

Her tone had taken on textures I couldn't really place. I opened my mouth to tell her she wasn't making sense but she talked over the top of me.

"She's my friend, and when you are someone's friend you do what's best for them even if you have to make sacrifices to see that happen. Our friendship was a small thing to sacrifice in order to convince you she wasn't a shape shifter. She's going to need your protection very soon, and you'd never have given it if you still thought she was like you rather than like me."

It was the oddest thing I'd ever seen out of Rachel. She turned, looking a little lost, and left the gallery before I could ask her what she meant, and once she was gone I couldn't bring myself to chase her down.

Jasmin knocked on my door as I was stripping down to my ha'bit. "You're leaving then?"

I hadn't consciously made the decision, but as she asked the question I realized she was right.

"I have to, Jasmin. I'm sorry, I can't really explain it, but I need you to trust me. I've realized you must have a good reason for the crazy things you've been doing lately, and I need you to trust that I've got a good reason for this."

For a moment I thought she was going to argue with me, but then she sighed and nodded. "If you've got to do something stupid, I guess tonight's as good of a night to do it as any.

Brandon's people will all be at the kegger. Vincent's too much of a party animal to miss a bash as big as this one is supposed to be."

I nodded my thanks and hurried out to the garage. The Hummer didn't boast all of the comforts of its shinier sibling, but it was the same vehicle the military opted for when the mission called for the ability to go almost anywhere.

It was already dark, so I didn't need to worry about anyone seeing me running around in my wolf form, but something compelled me to take a vehicle at least part of the way. I visualized the rough map that had been passed around the school earlier in the day, and then checked it against the prevailing wind. I was going to have to detour quite a ways off of the shortest path, but I couldn't risk anyone catching my scent and deciding tonight would be a good opportunity to take down the rival alpha.

I pulled off of the road and dropped into a ravine that was sometimes used by jeepers when they were looking for a new challenge. My progress slowed as the terrain became increasingly rugged. I knew that I could make better time if I dismounted and took to four legs, but stubbornly kept to the Hummer. When I got to within three miles of the party site I finally parked the Hummer and slipped out into the night.

It had cooled down somewhat over the last few weeks. It wasn't what anyone from Idaho would call cold, but some of the oppressive heat had left, and I found myself invigorated by the clean, crisp smell of the breeze.

I bounded over fallen trees, splashed through the tiny trickles of water that passed for springs, and otherwise enjoyed the trip until I got close enough to hear the thrumming beat of the music and smell the crowded bodies and spilled alcohol of the truly drunk.

Brandon's pack was ever-present on the wind as I slowly advanced forward. Brandon's heavy musk especially burned my throat and made me want to be elsewhere, but I sought it out regardless because floating along like an aromatic accompaniment was Adri's enchanting scent.

I spent nearly an hour hunkered down in the middle of a group of night-blooming cacti that was especially pungent and which would go a long ways towards hiding my scent if someone did happen to circle around and get downwind of me.

I'd almost decided I was the worst kind of crazy. I couldn't hear any conversation over the music and there wasn't anything to be learned by scent. I stood to leave when the music suddenly skidded to a stop.

"You should forget your stupid lies. If you repeat them you'll be sorry. Every single person here will vouch for Brandon."

Cassie's shrill voice was impossible to miss in the sudden silence. It rang through me with the subtlety of an amputation and I somehow knew who she was talking to.

"Get out of here. Don't wait around, don't ask anyone for a ride. You had your chance with Brandon and you blew it. He's mine again, and if you're not out of sight in the next five minutes I'll kill you myself and end this stupid experiment once and for all."

The last was spoken more quietly. With the wind pulling it away from the rest of the party, it was possible nobody heard her death threat, but I felt a surge of anger crash through me as I realized I didn't believe that. The kids who hung out with Brandon were completely cowed by the dominants.

Adri was moving now, her steps clearly audible over the continuing lack of music. I heard her fall and nearly left my hiding spot. It was incredibly unfair for her to go through this at all, let alone by herself, but she wouldn't welcome my presence in my current form. It was safer for both of us if Brandon's people didn't scent me.

She was moving at right angles to the wind, so the possibility was slim, but it still existed. My resolve was tested as the music resumed, drowning out the sound of her flight, and then I got the first smell of blood on the air.

My beast roared to life as part of me classified her as prey and therefore good only for running down and consuming, but I'd had years of practice sublimating those urges. I shoved my baser instincts down and walled them away behind control very nearly the equal of Isaac's.

TORN

I was attempting to follow Adri's progress on the wind when a low howl most people would have mistaken for a wolf floated to me. I lurched to my feet and took off at a sprint before I'd fully even classified it as belonging to Nathanial.

They were hunting, either out of pure sadism or because they lacked the inclination to dominate the wolf's desire to capture fleeing prey. The second howl didn't really surprise me although it dramatically worsened my odds. Simon was Nathanial's usual partner in depravity.

A fight between a hybrid and a wolf was usually a foregone conclusion, but a fight between a hybrid and two wolves was more like a matchup between sledgehammer-equipped glass rods. They would both look for the golden window of opportunity in which they could obtain a killing grip and I'd attempt to kill one of them fast enough that there was no chance for his fellow to kill me in turn.

I should have been scared. I was scared for Adri, worried I wouldn't be in time, but not afraid for myself. Nathanial and Simon had helped Vincent kill two hikers earlier in the year. There were other incidents in St. George and Vegas that I suspected were related to Brandon's pack, but that one I'd been able to positively tie back to those three.

The trip to the coroner's office hadn't left me, even all these months later. It was finally time to rectify the wrong I'd let slide out of my fear of the Coun'hij.

I was close enough now to hear Adri running along ahead of me. She slipped again as the wolves closed to within a few dozen feet. I heard her crash down the slope and then her journey was arrested by a meaty thump as something semi-yielding connected with a rock.

A yelp of pain followed a second later as she tried to stand, and then I was shifting forms as Nathanial sprang towards her. He never even saw me coming, but Simon had already adjusted to my presence and darted in to try and hamstring me.

I threw Nathanial into the canyon wall and then swiped at Simon, just missing as he dodged behind a large rock that drew a shower of sparks off of my claws. A growl escaped me as I tried to spin back around and intercept Nathanial.

I was a fraction of a second too late. Powerful fangs latched onto my shoulder only just before a second impact nearly knocked me to the ground. Nathanial's refusal to release my shoulder and go for a new grip was his undoing. I reached up with my left hand and sank my claws into the softer flesh of his stomach at the same time that my own fangs latched onto his neck.

Simon's efforts to transform his attack into something lethal left me bleeding and savaged, but I largely ignored him as I pulled and ripped until an abrupt snap caused Nathanial's jaws to loosen.

Even through the pandemonium of the fight I still heard Adri's pulse peak and then abruptly stop.

Chapter 20

My sudden worries Adri had somehow died were unfounded. After a short pause her heart resumed a thready, irregular cadence.

As Nathanial had dropped to the ground I'd absently grabbed Simon and held him at arm's length as I surgically ended his life as well. Most of my attention was on Adri, and once I was sure both wolves were dead I hurried over just in time to catch her as she came out of the attack.

In my haste I'd forgotten to switch forms, and her eyes had no sooner fluttered open than plain, old-fashioned shock took her away again.

I knew the results of my actions would come crashing back down on me later, but all I could think of in that moment was getting Adri away to safety. Mindful of the slashing claws on the end of my fingers, I picked her up and began running back to the Hummer.

I wasn't nearly as fast carrying her in my hybrid form as I would have been on four legs, but I pushed myself nearly to the point of collapse. My wounds were opening back up and my lungs were burning, but I had to get her to the Hummer with enough of a lead for us to get out before Brandon's wolves found the bodies and pursued.

When I finally stumbled into the wash containing the Hummer I wanted to lie down and sleep but instead I shifted back to human form, buckled her into the passenger seat, flipped the vehicle around and started back out the way I'd come.

With each second that passed I expected Brandon to come bounding out of the darkness and tear the Hummer open like a coconut, but after what seemed like an eternity we finally reached the road and I was soon throwing the vehicle around curves at the top speed it could handle.

I breathed a sigh of relief as we finally pulled up to the estate. Adri was still breathing and her heartbeat had steadied slightly. I yelled for Donovan as I unbuckled her and hauled her into the house.

Donovan and Rachel both met me at the examination room, and Rachel's surprised gasp was mirrored in Donovan's wide eyes and suddenly graceless movements.

"It wasn't me. She was at the party with Brandon and the rest. They kicked her out and sent her off in the dark. This was all from falling down, except maybe the leg. Nathanial and Simon were after her. I killed them and ran."

His shock finally starting to give way, Donovan moved to check my wounds but I shrugged him off. "Make sure she's okay first."

Rachel calmed me down somewhat while Donovan cleaned and bandaged Adri's scrapes, and then disappeared to grab Adri some new clothes.

"They were going to be for Jasmin's birthday, but they should do for Adri until we can get her something better."

Donovan helped Rachel dress Adri and then came back around and started on my wounds. They'd already started healing with my transformation back to a human, but the shoulder especially was deep enough it was going to need to be taped up in order to heal.

"I'm sorry, Donovan. I've ruined everything. Brandon will demand satisfaction, and he'll be within his rights because of the Ja'tell bond. It was a stupid move, but I couldn't sit there and let them kill her."

Donovan shook his head as he worked.

"Master Alec, the only action worthy of you was the one you took. You could no more have watched her die than your father could have let Agony kill me. As for the Ja'tell bond, that's yet to be established. Perhaps she really is his, but even still, the old rules never would have condoned casting her off and setting his pack upon her like that. We'll weather the storm as it arrives. Doing less wouldn't allow us to remain true to ourselves."

Donovan clasped me on the arm and then limped out of the room. Rachel looked up from where she was folding Adri's old clothes. "I'm glad you saved Adri, Alec. Whatever happens as a result I think it was the right choice."

I nodded, and then looked down at Adri for the first time since Rachel had returned with the change of clothes. She was wearing a tank top and shorts, and I was struck by just how much she looked like my incomplete painting of her. The sight pulled at my chest, and left me feeling like a small boy suddenly arriving in a strange new world with no idea how anything functioned.

Rachel smiled sadly at my expression and then walked over and hugged me. "Take her to your room and lay her down on your bed. You need to be somewhere that you can keep an eye on her, and reassure her when she wakes up. She's going to be really freaked out by everything that's happened."

I nodded and then gingerly picked Adri up. She was so light it was no burden to carry her to my room. I set her down and once again was struck by her sheer beauty. Almost without conscious effort on my part I found myself back in my studio.

Somewhere along the way I changed into a new set of clothes, jeans with a shirt although I never bothered buttoning it up. The painting was too consuming to allow for such mundane things.

I painted with small, delicate strokes, stepping out into my room from time to time to study my subject once again. There was no logical reason the painting had to be finished tonight, but somehow I knew it did.

The terrible events she'd just experienced, the things she'd witnessed couldn't leave her unchanged. They hadn't had a chance to process through her mind yet, but they would; and when that happened the girl I was painting right now would in some ways cease to exist. This level of innocence, of gentle goodness couldn't possibly be sustained in the world our pack lived in.

I worked with a furious energy that pushed me for hours, but never quite succeeded in capturing her true essence. I collapsed against the wall as I realized it was time to abandon this painting. It wasn't truly complete but I didn't have the ability to complete it. I absently inscribed a simplified form of my sigil into the bottom corner and began cleaning up my paints.

I was nearly done when I heard Jasmin return to the house. The events of the last few hours came crashing back from the un-land where I'd shoved them. Moving with a quickness that threatened to tear my wounds back open, I ran to the bedroom door and pulled it closed behind me.

Even with my efforts at speed I still only managed to intercept Jasmin in the East Drawing Room. It was too close to my bedroom, and there was too much chance we'd wake Adri, but Jasmin wasn't in the mood to be maneuvered anywhere else.

"Did you wreck your bike or tangle with Vincent or what?"

"Neither. Nathanial and Simon tried to kill me."

Jasmin wasn't stupid. She started fitting the information into place very quickly and came up with the pertinent question almost immediately.

"Those two wouldn't leave a kegger for anything short of a chance to murder someone. What were you doing at the party, Alec?"

"I was worried about Adri. I was careful to make sure that nobody knew I was in the area, but then Cassie kicked Adri out of the party and the next thing I knew Nathanial and Simon were after her. I had to protect her."

Jasmin was pacing now. It wasn't a good sign. Her internal state was usually mirrored by her external being.

"You felt the need to protect Brandon's girlfriend? Do you realize you've just given Brandon the perfect pretext to come after all of us?"

I opened my mouth to respond, but Jasmin bulled right past my efforts.

"When exactly were you planning on telling the rest of us that you'd just declared war on Brandon and the others? Did it ever even cross your mind we might be in danger running about on our own after something like that?"

"Brandon isn't going to launch an attack right now, Jas, and you know it. He's got the golden chance he's been looking for to finally make the law work for him against us."

Jasmin was trembling just the slightest bit now, a preliminary sign she was starting to lose control of her beast.

"That's not the point, Alec. You never even thought about the rest of us."

Our voices had risen high enough to wake Rachel. She appeared on the other side of the drawing room still in the fuzzy pajama's Jasmin had given her last Christmas.

"Jasmin, he had to help her. He couldn't let them kill her. She's important to him. You know exactly how he feels, how..."

Whatever Rachel was about to say was cut off as Jasmin spun around and took a threatening step towards her.

Protecting Rachel had been reflex for as long as I could remember. I picked Jasmin up and slammed her onto a table, shattering a piece that had been in my family since before my father had been born.

Jasmin started to thrash about in an effort to fight me, but accessing a skill possessed by only a few moonborn, I shifted the hand holding her into my hybrid form. She calmed down almost instantly as she felt the razor-sharp claws pierce the skin of her throat.

"Don't do anything else to threaten Rachel, or you'll be very sorry..."

The rest of what I was going to say was interrupted by the sound of the garden door slamming shut.

The wash of power I'd let loose as I'd pinned Jasmin hadn't tapered off yet. I added one more command to the imperative I'd just finished issuing. "Don't leave the house, and don't call the rest of the pack here."

As soon as she nodded her acceptance of the order I spun around and headed for the same door Adri had just used to exit the house. My hand lapsed back into its human form as I skidded on newly soaked flagstones. Sometime between when I'd left the East drawing room and when I'd hit the door, the sky had cut loose with the kind of torrential downpour that wasn't usually found this far from the ocean.

The rain was so intense I could feel the scent trail washing away even as I tried to follow it. The sudden fear she'd leave without ever giving me a chance to explain all of the insanity she'd just been through pushed me to new speeds. I was just barely close enough when lightning struck to see her dart into the greenhouse.

The thunder rolled over me almost concurrent with the blast, almost as if something were riding the storm, egging it on to greater fury as the strikes got closer and closer.

I slipped into the glass-walled refuge just in time to catch Adri in the act of putting shoes onto her doubtlessly-battered feet. She was entirely soaked through. She should have looked terrible, but still somehow managed to take my breath away.

TORN

The perfect symmetry of her form pulled me towards her without any conscious thought on my part, only my step was met with horror as she stumbled back away from me. It was as if someone had reached out and slipped a knife into my chest.

I knew I hadn't been injured, that there was no physical explanation for the sudden pain, but it was there nonetheless. She'd seen the side of me never presented to the outside world and she'd been repulsed by it.

She opened her mouth, to scream in terror, or possibly to curse me, but I couldn't bear to hear it. I spun around and left at a full run. Deprived of its target when I'd entered the greenhouse, the storm's fury had abated, leaving me with nothing in which to hide from the prying eyes of men or gods.

Deprived of all other sanctuaries, I headed towards the grotto that'd served me so well in times past. Mere distance couldn't offer respite though. Somewhere along the way my interest in Adri had turned to something more substantial. Without really realizing what I was doing, I'd sacrificed everything I held dear on behalf of someone who was never going to return my feelings.

Full knowledge of what I'd done roared through me with a fury that ate away my reason. There was only hatred, loss and despair left to cushion the anger, and it wasn't enough to control the beast raging through me.

The heavy, pottery planters holding cuttings from our original Lagrimas del Angel plant caught my attention, and I stalked over and picked the closest one up in my right hand. I threw it into the unyielding stone of the grotto walls, and not even the softness of the moss and climbing ivy managed to cushion the impact enough to stop the planter from shattering into thousands of pieces.

I was on my third planter when Adri stumbled into the grotto and almost fell into the reflecting pool. I'd been so engrossed in the destruction of the roses I hadn't heard her approach. Her appearance startled me so much I froze with the heavy planter dangling from my grasp.

Faced with the very thing I'd just had denied me, I found myself unable to meet her gaze for several seconds. When I finally managed to muster the courage to fully turn and face her, my voice came out low and rough.

"Go away!"

Without meaning to I'd imbued the command with the same whip of power I'd used to give Jasmin the imperative earlier. I saw Adri's eyes go wide for a moment, heard her heartbeat spike as she struggled not to obey, but she somehow stopped herself from leaving.

I couldn't help but feel a renewed spark of respect at the strength of will required for her to do that. My next words weren't tinged with anything but my sense of loss.

"Leave. Leave now and I won't follow you."

Adri took a trembling breath and then stepped ever so slowly in my direction.

"It was you the whole time, wasn't it? The bank. The mayor. Were you responsible for the Les Misérables tickets too?"

Why now? Why did the fates choose to continue to rub my face in how amazing she was, in just how much I'd lost without ever truly owning it?

"Why? What possible difference does it make one way or the other?"

"Because I want to understand. Why me? Why would you do all of that for me?"

"You really don't understand? You saved Rachel from a beating. If for no other reason, then for that."

It wouldn't have worked with another shape shifter. It didn't work with Adri either. She was still moving with exquisite care, somehow managing to close to within a few inches of me. I felt myself tremble as she cautiously placed her hand on my arm. The planter dropped to the ground as I let her closer to me than I'd let anyone other than Rachel since I'd first shifted to a wolf.

The horror I'd seen earlier on her face had vanished, replaced with an incredible compassion, gratitude and the acceptance I'd given up hope of ever seeing on her face or the face of anyone not of the pack.

"That isn't why you did it though. Is it?"

I shook my head, imminent tears making my voice rough.

"No, I just did it for you. Maybe not so much at first, but I couldn't get you out of my mind.

You were everywhere I looked. In my class, at lunch, even in my dreams. I couldn't get away from you."

Her heart skipped a couple beats as she moved ever so slightly closer to me.

"Do you still want me to leave?"

"Do you want to leave? I won't stop you if you do. If you can convince your mom to leave town there's even a chance you'll be safe from Brandon."

She was so close now that I felt, as well as heard, the shivers that ran through her at my words.

"He's like you, isn't he?"

I laughed, but it was nothing more than an attempt to avoid breaking down as we returned to the fundamental reason she couldn't really want me.

"You mean a monster? Yes, we both feel the call of the moon. Does that scare you?"

I felt her move against me again as she shook her head. "No. I guess a little, but not like it should. You wouldn't hurt me after everything you've done for us."

"I could kill you without even meaning to. You're so fragile. All it would take is an accident, a momentary loss of control. I really am a monster."

The words burned, but she deserved the truth, not the kind of sugar-coated lie Brandon would've fed her.

"No, you're not. I don't understand what you are, but you aren't a monster. Brandon is. Vincent, Cassie. They're all monsters, but you aren't."

I finally risked looking up and fully meeting her eyes. "How can you know that when sometimes I'm not sure myself?"

She took another deep breath and then moved her hand from my arm to my stomach. She wrapped both arms around me and pressed her face into my chest as I stood paralyzed, unable to move for fear of startling her.

"Thank you for saving my life. Were those wolves some of Brandon's friends?"

"Simon and Nathanial."

She trembled slightly at the acknowledgment that someone she'd known, however slightly had been intent on killing her.

"I didn't know them that well, they mostly ignored me, but I didn't think they'd kill me."

I felt another surge of elation wash through me as I carefully returned her hug. It was hard to know how much of the truth she was ready for, but it was only fair that she know who and what she'd really been dealing with.

"Maybe they weren't going to kill you. I can't say for sure, but they've both killed people before. I couldn't take the chance that they weren't just playing around. I had to stop them."

Her delicate fingers reached up and traced the periphery of Donovan's handiwork on my shoulder. The gauze rustled quietly as she sought for the right words.

"They could've killed you?"

"I came out okay all things considered."

Her face had long since dropped the emotionless mask she used most of the time. Her expression momentarily took on an unsatisfied cast at the same time her scent peaked slightly. Part of me spared a thought to wonder what had caused her disquiet, but the rest of me was overcome by the sudden realization that for the first time since I'd first seen her at school she smelled whole and healthy.

Her studied response distracted me before I could finish the thought.

"Well, I'm glad things turned out the way they did. Otherwise we'd both be dead."

Dead. I felt myself tense up as I contemplated our coming destruction. I'd just killed two people, but somehow that didn't bother me as much as the fate I knew awaited everyone that mattered to me.

"I suppose I'd better clean this up or Donovan is going to be very unhappy with me."

Adri looked around at the shattered pottery and shook her head slightly in amazement.

"Who's Don..." She stumbled slightly as some realization struck her. "I've been here before. In my dream. Then I drew it, which I didn't understand because I only ever draw real places, and this was imaginary. Only it wasn't, but there wasn't any way for me to know..."

She turned back towards me with astonishment written all over her face, only to look confused when I didn't comment.

"Isn't that odd? Doesn't that make you want to know what's going on?"

I wanted to tell her the truth about this too, but there was just too much that it wasn't safe for her to know. The Coun'hij was lax about many things, but they were absolutely rabid about ensuring our kind remained a secret from the world at large. It wasn't just the humans who could become a danger to us. The humans had numbers and effectively unlimited resources at their disposal, but there were other, darker things that we'd managed to hide from nearly since the dawn of time.

I opened my mouth to tell her *something*, but she cut me off.

"Don't lie to me."

"I'm not sure what to tell you. There's so much you don't know, and most of it I can't tell you. More importantly, you're better off not knowing."

Despite my having just told her I couldn't tell her all of the things she'd just asked about, she seemed to be waiting for me to go on.

"Hold on there. You can't just leave me in the dark about all of this. I'm in up to my neck; you have to at least let me know what I've fallen into."

"I'm sorry, I know this has to be hard, but you don't belong in this world. You admitted yourself that you don't know anything about us. It was a mistake for me to let you get involved."

It was surprising just how hard the next piece was to get out.

"I'm going to remedy that right now. We'll get you home, and then your mom is going to get an offer that's too good to pass up. With any luck you'll both be out of town within a couple days. I think I can arrange it so neither of you will be back for a year or two. That should be more than enough time for this all to resolve itself one way or another."

Adri's pulse shot up like a heart-attack victim. "Wait. No. You can't do that."

I was already headed out of the grotto, but the sound pulled me back around in time to see her collapse. I just managed to catch her before she hit the ground. I picked her up and waited anxiously for her eyes to flutter back open.

"Are you okay?"

I tried to set her back down as I spoke, but she grabbed onto me with surprising strength for someone so delicate.

"Don't leave me. Please don't make me go."

The tears seemed to tear at things that were still raw, things that hadn't had a chance to fully come to term with the idea that she didn't hate me. I wanted to give in, to promise her anything, but duty compelled me to do what was right for her, even if she didn't know it yet.

"Adri, you don't understand. This is the only way to keep you safe. I can't protect you here. I can't even protect my own family."

"No, *you* don't understand. This whole time I thought I was in love with Brandon, I didn't even know him. You did so much for us and didn't even hate me when I was so rude. I've been so stupid, please don't send me away."

TORN

She was building up to another attack, and I didn't have the heart to put her through that again, not so close to the last one. I placed a finger on her lips to silence her and then said the last thing I should have been saying.

"Very well. I should send you away for your own protection, but I'm too selfish to do what's best for you. Maybe later I'll be able to do what's right, but not right now, not so soon."

Chapter 21

Rachel was waiting for us, happiness and concern warring with each other on her expression. I knew what was bothering her as soon as I got close enough to feel the energy surging out from the rest of the pack. I gently put Adri down as I prepared for the coming battle.

I vaguely heard the girls apologize to each other, but couldn't focus on anything other than keeping my beast from tearing free into my hybrid form and going for blood. A tiny fraction of me wondered at how much stronger my protective instinct had gotten when both Rachel and Adri were involved, but there wasn't time to explore the change.

I pulled the door open, only to have Rachel place a hand on my arm to stop me.

"The rest of the pack is back. Jasmin already told them what happened. It doesn't look good."

It was a confirmation of what I'd already known was coming, and I felt a growing distance settle on me as my power surged out in challenge. I turned towards Adri and offered her the best comfort I was able with my beast riding me.

"I realize it's unreasonable to ask you to trust me right now, but I'm going to need you to do so. Can you remain quiet for the next few minutes?"

The words she responded with were unimportant, I could smell her agreement, feel acquiescence in her heartbeat. Rachel shook her head at me, but my heightened senses knew she was agreeing with me whatever her body language might be indicating. I stalked inside the house and went directly to the East Drawing Room. I heard the girls follow behind me, but my attention was on Jasmin.

The rest of the pack was clustered around her, James and Jess on either side, with Isaac and Dom further back. I only just managed to focus on Jasmin's words. I had to. If there was a chance to head this off without bloodshed, then it was my duty to find it.

"She goes back to Brandon tonight. It's a long shot, but it's better than nothing. She brought it on herself so there isn't any reason to cry over what might happen."

"Unacceptable. She wasn't properly his. There was no bond of Ja'tell, and consequently we have no obligation to return her to him."

My voice already sounded like the transformation to hybrid had begun. It was enough to give Jasmin pause, but not Jess.

"Alec, we have to do this. None of us are stupid; we know what's going to happen. You killed two members of his pack."

"Still unacceptable. You've all aired your opinions; you can retire to your beds now."

James looked up. He was shaking so badly it was obvious he was even further gone along the process of losing control than I was. Dom tried to calm him down, but he shook her off with a roughness that was uncharacteristic directed at her. His voice came out as a near growl.

"You selfish jerk. You've been mooning over her for weeks. You've got her now, but at what cost? This isn't open to discussion. We're taking her back to Brandon and asking for leniency."

The girls had shifted slightly, angling for a better view probably, but I reached back and gently moved them so they were directly behind me. The last thing we needed right now was to give anyone an actual visual target.

I was trembling now too. It was becoming harder and harder to talk when so much effort was being consumed in not going for James' throat.

"There's only one way you're going to touch her, James. Are you really ready to take that step?"

James replied with a wordless but unequivocal pulse of power. Jess and Jasmin joined in with their own metaphysical wind as they too began shaking. A growl brought my attention back to James, and when he looked up at me the brown of his human eyes had been replaced by the hot yellow of a predator that'd owned the planet since before the last ice age. Mine were already the ice blue of a royal hybrid, and as my control slipped ever so slightly my hands transformed to hybrid claws.

They were moving forward now. If I'd been inclined to back down now was the time to do it, before they edged into pouncing range, but the thought never gained any traction in my mind. Two of the most important people in my world were behind me, and I would kill for them even if it meant laying down my own life.

Adri's pulse was hammering away behind me, but Rachel's oddly maintained a near-resting rhythm. She murmured something nearly inaudible but strangely comforting to Adri and then shifted slightly behind me.

"Jasmin, please don't do this. I'm not going to move. She doesn't mean anything to you. What about me?"

Jasmin stopped her stalk as Rachel's words hit her. Jasmin and I had been best friends for nearly my entire life, but she shared a bond with Rachel I didn't really understand. That relationship did what even the threat of death couldn't.

With an effort no human could ever appreciate, Jasmin brought herself back under control. As soon as she stopped trembling she turned and left the room, moving at something more than normal speed in an effort to leave before temptation overcame her again.

The odds against me had just noticeably improved, but James and Jess were still stalking, moving forward in imperceptible increments in an effort to reach attack range.

Dom had shown her bravery on more occasions than I could count, but I was still surprised when she carefully moved forward and placed a hand on James' arm. She leaned in and whispered into his ear. It was too quiet even for my ears to pick up at this range, but it cut the anger that had been fueling him into something tamer, something that could be reasoned with by the portion of him not completely consumed by his mother's fears and goals.

His expression said he wasn't done, that at some point he'd demand an accounting of me, but he left the room trailed by Dom and then there was only Jess. It was complete foolishness for her to continue unsupported, but Jess had suffered at Brandon and Vincent's hands more than anyone else in the pack. She wasn't entirely sane anymore where they were concerned.

Desperate to stop her without being forced to hurt her, I found new levels of energy inside me and threw them at her with all the force I could muster. Faced with such an inarguable demonstration of just how out of her depth she was, not even Jess could continue. She spun away and left the room.

Isaac met my gaze for several seconds. The look conveyed gratitude for not hurting Jess, combined with a request to be released to follow her. I nodded, and he left, no doubt hoping to catch her and calm her down before she made it back to her father.

Adri's breathing changed alarmingly, and I spun around as Rachel squeaked. I only just managed to get my hands back to normal before I caught her.

"There isn't anything to worry about now. Go ahead and catch your breath."

It seemed odd to be talking of something so mundane after everything that'd just happened. Even among the perennially violent moonborn it wasn't every day that half the pack nearly attempted a coup.

Adri understandably had questions, but my full attention wasn't on her immediate needs. Donovan and Mallory had spent nearly two decades molding my mind into something that didn't lock up in an emergency. They'd succeeded and I was already looking ahead to what was going to happen next.

Brandon wouldn't move against us directly, not until after he'd felt out his contact on the Coun'hij. The real danger was the indirect actions he might take. He was as vindictive as they come, and the easiest person for him to cause problems for was Adri.

I shook my head to clear it and then met Adri's eyes.

"This isn't the time; we need to get you back home to your mom. It would be most unfortunate if she were to arrive and find you gone."

"No. She's not going to be home until Sunday. There isn't any reason to go back there yet."

"You mean she wasn't planning on coming back until Sunday. Once Brandon gets involved in things, they tend not to go as expected."

Rachel reappeared just in time to bolster my case.

"He's right, Adriana. You need to be home in case your mom returns sooner than expected. Things are going to get plenty weird enough over the next couple of weeks. You don't want to start out with your mom already mad at you."

She nodded, but I could taste her fear. She thought I was going to send her back by herself.

"Don't worry; I'm not going to send you back alone. We'll make sure nothing happens to you."

The timing wasn't optimal considering that I'd just pissed Jasmin off, but there wasn't any choice. I pulled my cell phone out of my pocket and dialed Isaac's number, automatically lapsing back into the hushed whisper the pack used over the phone.

"Isaac, I'm sorry to pull you away from Jess, but I need you and your toys. We're going to need to set up a call forwarding station. I know, but it's necessary. Assume that they've got a standard landline and grab one of the backup cell phones."

Jasmin almost let it ring through to her voice mail.

"What do you want?"

"I need your help. We're going to provide security for Adri's house until I can get her mom out of the country."

"And who's going to supply overwatch for Donovan and the others while you take the pack out to babysit?"

"This isn't open to discussion, Jas. I'll see you in the garage in five."

Dom answered on the second ring.

"Yes, Alec?"

"Dom, I'm sorry. I know it isn't the best time to ask this of you, but I need you to come play wheels for twenty minutes."

I heard her sigh in unhappiness, but with Dom it was never a sign of defiance. She would do whatever the pack required of her; she just wasn't looking forward to the fight with James and his mother later.

"Si, Alec. I'll be there as soon as I'm able."

Either Dom was becoming more assertive, or she had James even more tightly wrapped around her finger than I'd realized. She was standing outside her Toyota waiting for us when Adri and I finally made it out to the garage.

Chapter 22

Dom drove with a shadow of James' normal aggressiveness behind the wheel, managing to get us to Adri's almost a minute quicker than I'd expected. As we came around the last corner to Adri's house Dom dropped down to thirty miles per hour and Jasmin, Isaac and I piled out of the car.

It was a tricky maneuver, but we'd practiced it several times over the last few years. Donovan and Mallory disagreed in a few areas regarding what had made my father an effective leader, but they were completely united on one thing. My father's unyielding resolve to game out every possible scenario he could think of with his most trusted warriors had saved them on more than one occasion.

I'd attempted to follow in his footsteps, and high-speed dismounts and entrances into vehicles seemed like something we might need at some point. Besides once you got over the bruises and road rash of your first few tries it was extremely fun.

As Dom turned down Adri's gravel lane the other three of us fanned out around the car. We stayed close enough to support each other, but tried to ensure we were scattered enough to pick up any scent traces if Brandon's people were hiding from us.

Adri exited the car after a few quiet words with Dom, and then looked up at her house. I joined her at the porch only to see her jump as she realized I was there.

"I'm sorry, I didn't mean to scare you."

"It's okay. Where were you?"

Watching you; wishing there was some way I could spend more than just the next few hours with you. Wishing I didn't have to send you away with your mother. I settled for a half truth.

"Scouting. We had to make sure Brandon's pack wasn't waiting for us."

"How can you be sure? They could be hidden anywhere."

She'd apparently shared my dreams and some of my enhanced senses, but hadn't really grasped the implications for those of us who really possessed them.

"No, if they were hanging around outside we'd be able to smell them."

"So not only are you faster and stronger than normal people, you've also got noses like real wolves?"

"Of a sort. That's not really important though. Let's get you inside."

She nodded and started towards her door. I was once again struck by the sheer bravery wrapped inside that fragile, human package. I moved up to her side and placed my hand on the doorknob before she could open it.

"May I have permission to enter and make sure it's safe inside?"

"I thought you said you'd be able to smell them if they were here."

"If they were outside, yes. Under normal circumstances we'd be able to determine whether or not they'd been here in the last few days, but the rainstorm last night was strong enough to wash away all of that."

She marshaled her courage and then nodded. I slipped inside and quickly went through the entire house. There wasn't any real need. The rain storm wouldn't have impacted the scent trail indoors. Still, I followed Adri's rich scent upstairs, stuck my head inside her room and breathed it in.

This was a piece of normality, a part of her life I'd never share. Sure that nobody had intruded on their home since Brandon had picked her up for the party, I headed back downstairs. If I somehow survived what was coming, maybe I should buy this house. It smacked of insanity, but if I wasn't going to be allowed to have her, it would at least allow me to be surrounded by her scent.

She looked up at me with such trust that my heart skipped. It was a good thing both Jasmin and Isaac were so far away. I couldn't afford to appear weak right now.

"It's safe; there's no trace of them."

I held the door for her and then crossed back outside.

"You need to erase any evidence that you weren't here all night. Take a shower, change into some of your own clothes, and then go to sleep. We'll keep watch outside until your mom gets back."

I pulled the door closed behind me and took up my station at one end of the triangle we'd created around her house. I pulled out my phone, checked the clock and then mentally advanced it eight hours to Italian time. It was about time for Isabel to be taking her mid-morning coffee, but she probably wouldn't resent me too much for interrupting her daily ritual. She'd been an aging model when my father had first met her, but her love of fashion and the amount she'd saved over the years in the hopes of starting her own business had impressed him so much he'd helped her get started.

She'd long ago bought out the family interest in her business, but she and Donovan remained on cordial terms and we were careful to steer relevant business her direction.

"Buongiorno."

"Isabel, it's Alec Graves."

"Oh, Alec. How are you this morning?"

"I'm doing well, thanks. How's business?"

"You know how things go. Sometimes the rich, they spend, sometimes they get nervous and don't spend. The lean times, they come and go. We've got the show in Paris this week and then another in Milan after that."

It was exactly the opportunity I needed.

"I've got someone I need to move out of the country for a few weeks, preferably without them realizing they've been managed. Do you think you could find a spot for another photographer?"

She paused as if considering the question and then sighed. "That is difficult, Alec. Francisco, he is very good, and very touchy. He will not like it if he feels as though I'm grooming his replacement and I cannot afford to lose him right now."

"I'll cover your costs to bring her on board and throw in a fifty percent markup. If you think it would help, you can offer Francisco a healthy bonus to train this friend of a friend, and I'll cover any losses that result if things do blow up in your face."

"Oh, Alec. You're just like your father. Money truly doesn't mean anything to you. Very well. Francisco, he loves intrigue as much as any artist; I think I can present it to him in such a way as to win his support."

"Thanks, Isabel. I owe you one for this. I'll have Donovan wire the money over first thing this morning."

"There is no rush. I know that you are good for it."

I almost didn't tell her, but she was the closest thing to a family friend we had outside the moonborn.

"It would be best if I had him take care of it sooner rather than later. Things have deteriorated somewhat over the last few weeks and I wouldn't want to leave you with no recourse in the event that Donovan and I aren't around to satisfy the debt. In fact, maybe you should put together a generous estimate of what your losses may run if Francisco doesn't cooperate and I'll send that over as well. I'll call later with the phone number so you can extend the offer."

There were several seconds of silence and then Isabel sighed in sorrow.

"I won't press you for details, Alec, but I'm very aware that Donovan was more than usually vague when it came to the details surrounding your father's death. My daughter thinks you're all drug runners or some such, but I do not believe it. You've all been nothing but honorable to me, and I mourn whatever business it is that brought an early death to him and now threatens the young man who is the closest thing to a son I've ever had."

"Thanks, Isabel. That means a lot. Both the sentiment and your not asking questions I can't answer."

We made our goodbyes and then I called and discussed the arrangements with Donovan. He promised to see to the details and then there was nothing left but to wait for Adri's mother to return or for us to be overrun by Brandon's people. We were all praying for the former but Jasmin at least was convinced Brandon would arrive first.

I listened to her grumbles for nearly an hour as the price of her cooperation so soon after being forced to back down over the whole Adri issue.

I was just close enough to the house to hear Adri as she came downstairs and hesitantly opened the front door. I was so excited to see her that I moved towards her too quickly. She emitted a startled gasp at my sudden appearance.

"I'm sorry, I didn't mean to frighten you."

I was usually much better than this at maintaining appearances. Something about her made me forget myself, or maybe it was that she brushed aside the illusions and somehow brought out the real me.

"It's okay, it must be really limiting to always have to pretend you're slow and normal."

Once again she'd all but read my thoughts. It was uncanny how easily she did that. I managed a casual shrug and hoped the ability was intermittent.

"Actually I've spent so much of my life trying to hide the unusual aspects of my nature, it's usually effortless. For some reason, I forget myself around you."

Her pulse peaked slightly. She was obviously in the grip of some emotion, and based on the tentative way she was looking out at the darkness, it wasn't joy.

"Are they out there waiting now?"

I shook my head, wishing that the truth was capable of consoling her.

"No, I'd already have come and carried you away if any of Brandon's people were around. Barring that, you'd hear us fighting. Mere doors and windows wouldn't do much to muffle the sound."

"You'd be fighting, because of me."

Even on what had to be the most terrifying night of her life, she was still worried about the impact to the pack, the impact to me. It was stupid, I'd already touched her too much tonight, but I reached out and took her shoulders in my hands.

"Please don't try and take the blame for this. We've been on a collision course with Brandon's pack for years."

Apparently my touch had made her uncomfortable. We stood in silence for several seconds and then she finally found something to break the awkwardness.

"I can't sleep. I've been trying, but I'm too wound up to do anything but just lie there. I thought I'd come downstairs and talk to you instead. I mean, unless it's bothering you. You know, keeping you from patrolling or something."

Bothering me indeed. It was good she didn't realize just how far gone I was. Earlier words notwithstanding, she'd have been repulsed if she'd realized just how badly I wanted to be with her.

"No, you're not bothering me in the slightest. Jasmin or Isaac either one could easily keep watch. Our sense of smell and hearing are good enough that it's all but impossible for even other wolves to catch us unawares. They're here more in the role of bodyguards. If Brandon's people do show up, it'll likely take all three of us to get you away safely."

"So you don't mind? You'll stay here and talk to me?"

Now that she'd actually made the offer I found my sense of duty kicking back in. She didn't understand what she was asking. I cast about for an excuse.

"I'm not sure that's the best idea. You really need your sleep. The whole purpose of this little exercise is to convince your mom you've been safely home this entire time. If you crash later in the day, she's going to know you didn't sleep tonight."

"Maybe if you stayed with me it would help me sleep."

"That doesn't strike me as being a much better solution."

The words came out harsher than I'd meant them to. She backed away in embarrassment and despite the fact it would increase my agony when I finally sent her away, I did the only thing I could think of to ease her discomfort.

"I'm sorry; that didn't come out as intended. If it would help you sleep, of course I'll come upstairs and sit with you. It's the least I can do after allowing you to be dragged into this mess."

I followed her upstairs, let her get comfortable in her bed and then sat on the floor as I turned off the lights. If I had to be teased with her presence, at least I could put some physical distance between us.

We exchanged some small talk, and then she got to what I expected was the real reason she'd invited me up.

"What...I mean, you're all so different..."

She'd almost recovered, but when the most effective way of lying remaining to your kind was to allow someone to believe you'd said something other than you really had, a person got very good at listening to exactly what had been said.

"I think you meant to ask what I am."

She nodded, barely visible in the darkness, and my heart sped up slightly at just how beautiful she was. There was so much she couldn't know, but apparently I was willing to sell my soul in this as well. Anything to spend a few more minutes with her. Even if the knowledge I was imparting potentially put her in even greater danger.

"We share a little in common with a bunch of different legends, but none get it quite right. In short, we're shape shifters, people who can take the form of animals."

"You mean like werewolves?"

Even the full knowledge her question came from ignorance didn't save me from the surge of anger as she used the most ancient insult known to my people. She had no way of knowing how different we were from the mindless killing machines that we'd spent millennia trying to exterminate.

I brought myself back under control just enough to answer her.

"No, not like werewolves."

"Did I say something wrong?"

The uncertainty, the near-hurt in her voice brought my humanity back to the fore. The rage dissolved, allowing me to answer her with more gentleness.

"No, you've nothing to feel sorry about. I should tell you though that calling a shape shifter a werewolf is the kind of insult that nearly always results in a fight, and often even a death."

She gasped. It was so hard to remember that she wasn't part of my terrible world. It felt like she was the missing piece of my life, but that didn't mean she felt the same way, that she truly belonged with me.

"I'm sorry; I didn't mean to scare you. I forget sometimes how much more violent my world is."

Her face broke into a smile again, and I wished I had my paints with me. It would be a very long time, if ever before I found myself painting anything that didn't include her as its subject, but another image needed started before I could think of recording this part of the night.

"That's better; I much prefer the happy Adri face to the scared Adri."

"Wait, you could see me smile? I guess that all follows, better hearing, better sense of smell. Of course you'd have better vision too."

She paused for just a moment and then launched into one of the things that I shouldn't tell her about.

"Sorry, it's just that this all makes me think of these amazing dreams I've been having since I arrived. I'm transported to various places, but in every case I can hear and smell better than I can in real life. Not only that, everything is glowing. Only that isn't the right word for it. Mostly there's just light coming out of the people and the plants and animals. It's so beautiful. Funny your having more acute senses would make me think of that."

How would she feel about knowing that we'd been sharing our dreams? Would it lend itself to her feeling the same kind of bond I felt, or would she feel intruded upon?

"It's bordering on stuff I shouldn't tell you, but you deserve to know. You've just described exactly how we perceive the world. The colors are all more vibrant, the breeze is more alive with scents than anyone could ever know."

Her breathing had just sped up. Did she understand what I was implying?

"Your paintings. That explains them. You were superimposing what you see over top of what someone like me would see. Only how would you know what things look like to us?"

Had I covered the painting I'd done of her before I'd left to confront Jasmin? Was she trying to give me the chance to come clean? I forced a false measure of gaiety into my voice.

"You are amazing. Anyone else waking up in a strange place would've run away as soon as they regained consciousness. At the very least, you should have started screaming. Instead you wander around, take in some rather feeble attempts at art, and then sneak out without saying a word."

She stuck out her tongue at me and I felt myself breathe a little easier.

"Hey, my survival instincts, or lack thereof aren't the point. Stop trying to distract me."

"I suppose I deserved that. It's just more than a little unsettling how quickly you're putting pieces together. There really are things that aren't safe for you to know. Among them, the reason why it isn't safe for you to know them. To answer your question, I wasn't always like this. When I was younger I saw exactly the way that you do. Even now, my vision is more like yours when I'm in this form. I still see incredibly well, and there's just the slightest hint of light from living things, but nothing like what you saw in the dreams."

She nodded once more in the darkness as the pieces continued to snap into place for her.

"So you work from memory mostly then? That and trying to make what you see when you're in human form even more drab than what you really see?"

"That about sums it up, although I didn't really expect you to pick up on that last part so quickly. You're remarkably perceptive."

She blushed at the compliment and then retreated to more mundane subjects.

"So what does a seventeen-year-old shape shifter spend his time doing?"

Finally something safe. Something I could reveal without binding myself even more tightly to her.

"Well, I spend a ridiculous amount of time trying to keep my friends away from each other's throats. We've got some pretty strong personalities, and it's nearly a full-time job stopping minor disagreements from boiling over into something bigger. Apart from that, I spend an hour or two every day vetting Donovan's management of the family assets. He does an incredible job with everything, but even so, there are certain things I have to approve myself."

"Who's Donovan?"

I laughed at the absurdity of trying to answer that question. How could I explain a man who I didn't completely understand myself? The man who'd raised me, who'd found a love even more forbidden and impossible than mine.

"That's one of the most difficult questions you've asked so far. He likes to call himself our butler, but that doesn't even begin to describe him. He does take care of most of the duties a typical butler would assume, but he's also our financial manager and long-time family friend. I'm excited for you to meet him tomorrow. I think you'll like him."

"Yeah, but will he like me?"

She sat up and I felt a stab of pain as I realized I'd misspoken. She couldn't meet Donovan because she needed to leave. I couldn't begin planning my life around her because it wasn't safe for her here. I'd just cause myself additional pain by pretending otherwise.

"Please lie back down. You have to at least be trying to sleep. Otherwise I'm heading back downstairs. And don't pout. It won't influence me in the slightest."

"It's just *sooo* hard for my merely human ears to hear you from so far away. Maybe if you were to move over here I wouldn't have to strain to catch every word."

She dangled the promise of closeness before me like the most expert hunter ever, but I couldn't resent her. Not when I wanted so badly to touch her. It was almost as though the Ja'tell bond had been reversed.

"All right, I'll come over and lean against your bed, but you really need to try and sleep. You've got to be nearly exhausted."

"What about you, mister superhero shape shifter? You've been up longer than I have. I'm not the only one who needs to sleep."

There it was, the chance to try and tell her about the loneliness. I took the coward's way as I so often did these days.

"That's actually one of the benefits of my condition. I don't actually need normal amounts of sleep. An hour or two per night is usually more than enough."

"So you don't need to sleep. What do you do with all the rest of your time?"

It was wrong for me to want to kiss her, to imagine the feel of her skin against mine. I shook my head to clear it.

"Well, I do spend a fairly significant amount of time each day sitting in class. Kind of like someone else I know."

"Unacceptable. I've added that up in my head, and you've still got several hours each day that you haven't accounted for."

She was finally starting to fall asleep. Her voice had taken on the breathy, mumbled quality of the truly tired. I let my voice creep down in volume, hoping to coax her to sleep, praying the respite would give me strength to do the right thing.

"I'm afraid that really is the balance of my time. I spend time with Rachel of course. Then there are a few odd minutes where I squeeze in some reading, or a bit of painting."

"They're beautiful. Best I've seen. Ever."

I smiled at the compliment. It somehow meant more than the rest of the praise my work had ever received.

"Thank you. I'm afraid mostly all I see is the flaws. Even with the most perfect subjects, I still generally fail to capture their true essence."

"But not all?"

"No, not all of them."

Her breathing had deepened and slowed. I waited several seconds, but she finally mustered another sentence.

"Sounds fulfilling. Busy, but fulfilling."

"It's always seemed fulfilling. At least until recently."

She trailed off into insensibility and I felt something inside me relax as I was finally safe to be myself without fear of driving her away. I reached out and gently ran my finger along the perfect line of her cheek, and then told her sleeping form the truth.

"Somehow that all changed after you arrived. Little by little I started to realize just how empty my life really was. I wish I could come right out and say it while you're awake. I don't want that life anymore. I don't really want any life that doesn't involve you. The truth is, I've fallen well and truly in love with you."

Chapter 23

I passed the next several hours in an odd combination of joy and torment. I was exactly where I wanted to be, but watching the slow rise and fall of Adri's chest only served to remind me that my world would just destroy the sweet perfection dreaming only a few feet from me. I slowly moved further and further away in an effort to wean myself off her presence.

My phone vibrated as Jasmin texted to warn me that Adri's mother had just turned onto their lane. I stood and walked back over to Adri's bed.

"Adriana, it's time to wake up now."

She made a tired, satisfied sound, but obviously wasn't ready to wake yet. I sat down on the edge of the bed and tucked a stray hair behind her ear and tried again.

"Adriana Paige, your mother's on her way."

I was on my fourth iteration when she abruptly sat up, nearly knocking me off of the bed.

"You're still here."

I'd hoped that her racing pulse had been excitement, or at least adrenaline from being woken before she'd fully rested. I hadn't realized it was unhappiness. I forced lightness into my words as I responded to her.

"You sound disappointed. Do you want me to leave?"

"No, not disappointed, just surprised. I figured I'd wake up and find everything had just been one amazing, crazy dream."

I wasn't going to get a better opening than that. I took a deep breath and forced the words out.

"Would you prefer things to take that course?"

She looked too crestfallen for it to be an act, and I felt another selfish ray of hope that she might come to reciprocate some of what I felt for her.

"No, how could you think that? Why would I possibly want to have you vanish when I've just now finally found out it's you who's been watching over my mom and me since we got here?"

It was nothing more than gratitude. I looked away to hide my disappointment. When I still wasn't able to control my expression I stood and walked over to the window.

"It would be for the best, you know. I could arrange for you both to leave the state, and never have to come back to Sanctuary again. You'd be safer."

I heard her breath catch at my words, but couldn't bring myself to turn around and look at her face.

"Is that what you want? Not what's best for me, or what you think is best for me, but what you really want?"

Everything good and wholesome inside me demanded that I nod, that I drive her away to safety regardless of the price, but I couldn't do it if her hating me was the cost of the bargain. I stood motionless for several seconds and then finally shook my head.

"Good, because I don't want to leave. You said last night that your life felt meaningless before I came here, well, mine was even worse. The only thing that's kept me sane has been your behind-the-scenes help. I want to stay with you. I want to be with you."

I felt like I was sealing her death warrant, but I told myself I'd convince her to leave in a couple of days. I just needed a chance to spend more time with her.

"Very well then. It's just after ten o'clock. Your mom is about to pull into the driveway. Do your best to convince her you spent the night safely at home. We'll stay here and watch over the two of you. Also, if you can convince her it's safe to leave on an extended trip, that would be very helpful. Once she's gone, I'll come back for you."

The Jeep had pulled up to the house now. I had only seconds in which to leave. I looked back at Adri one more time.

"You're sure this is what you want?"

Her nod freed me to act, and I sprang from her window, easily landing down on the ground, nearly twenty feet below. I sprinted directly away from the house, aiming for a stand of scrubby trees that should be more than sufficient to hide me from Adri's mother.

"Nice of you to rejoin us plebes down among the bugs and dirt."

"Can it, Jasmin, I've only got a few minutes to do this."

I pulled my phone out as I was speaking and dialed Isabel's number.

"Buongiorno, Alec. Is it time?"

"Yes, did Donovan get you the number?"

"Of course he did. He's a wonderfully productive man, that one. Alec, are you sure there isn't anything else I can do to help from over here?"

"Thanks, Isabel. You're already doing more than enough."

Donovan picked up on the first ring. "Yes, Master Alec?"

"It's time. Please set everything in motion, Donovan."

"Yes, Master Alec. Mrs. Paige should get the call from the bank only minutes after she finishes with Isabel."

"Thank you, Donovan. Everything's still okay there at the house?"

"Yes, sir. James hasn't reported any kind of activity along the perimeter yet."

After finishing with Donovan I slipped over to Isaac's position. He patted his backpack as soon as I came within sight.

"I've taken care of everything I can without physically touching the hardware. As soon as her mom leaves the house I can have a redirect up and running. Shouldn't be anything more than just plug and play."

I nodded my thanks and then settled back to wait out Adri's mother while Jasmin kept up a running commentary on just how stupid she thought the entire exercise was.

"You realize that none of us have had any sleep yet? If Brandon's pack does happen to come strolling around the bend we're going to be outnumbered and fighting like drunks. Not to mention the fact we've got two noncombatants, one of which doesn't know anything about the moonborn."

The monologue quickly turned into something that I could tune out completely. I was so far gone into my own thoughts that I almost didn't hear her expletive.

"What happened?"

"I just saw movement up on the ridge. I'm pretty sure it was one of Brandon's wolves."

I could hear her dropping down to shift, but there was no way she could catch another wolf who had that kind of a headstart.

"Hold your position, Jas, it could be an ambush."

"We can't just let him go or we'll be neck deep in wolves inside ten minutes, fifteen at the outside."

"I know that, but you running off and getting killed won't help matters any. We've got ten minutes, hopefully that will be enough."

I pulled my phone back out and dialed James' number.

"What do you want?"

"I need you here right now. Jasmin thinks she just saw one of Brandon's pack and we're going to need an extraction."

James was already moving towards his car by the time I hung up. He hadn't protested the order, but we both knew even on his best day the odds of him getting here before Brandon's people were slim.

Isaac remained calm to all outward appearances, but Jasmin was bouncing around so much that I could clearly hear her even with the house between us.

"We need to go, Alec. We need to go."

Her mantra mirrored almost exactly the one inside my head, but there wasn't anything we could do but hope Adri was able to hurry her mother along.

I watched our ten minutes slip away all too quickly, and was nearly ready to try something crazy when Adri's mother finally came outside with an impressive amount of luggage and photography equipment. We moved forward to the extreme edge of our various bits of cover and crouched impatiently while the gear was loaded up and Adri's mother hugged her goodbye two or three times.

By the time the Jeep was finally headed down the lane eleven minutes had passed from Jasmin's sighting. There wasn't time to wait and make sure Mrs. Paige hadn't forgotten anything. I sprang from my cover as soon as she was out of sight and sprinted up to Adri.

"We need to go. One of Brandon's people just got close enough to smell us. They left before we could tell for sure who it was, but the odds of them coming back with lots of help just went through the roof. If we're still around when they do, things will get ugly."

I expected Adri to freeze, or maybe collapse, but instead she nodded calmly and turned as if to head back up to her room as Isaac ran into the house, already unzipping his backpack. I gently grabbed her shoulder and pulled her back around.

"There isn't time. We have to go now."

There wasn't time to wait for James to arrive, we were going to have to try and meet up with him on the road. I got Adri situated on my back and then took off at a pace that was only slightly reduced by my passenger.

I could hear and smell Jasmin off to the left, playing free agent in an effort to cover both me and Isaac, but as I turned off of the lane and began paralleling the road, I heard Isaac exit the house. Things were starting to look up. I'd even begun wondering if Brandon hadn't sent anyone back to investigate when the first howl sounded behind us.

Isaac had caught up to us. He and Jasmin paced me on either side in an effort to provide some security, but we could already hear our pursuit, and there were at least five of them. Even under normal circumstances, even if all five of our pursuers were just wolves there was no guarantee that we could take them in a stand up fight. Given that one or both of the other pack's hybrids might be back there, we simply couldn't allow them to pull us into a fight. Especially not with Adri present, she was just too fragile to risk it.

All it would take would be one wolf slipping past us for her to become nothing more than a lifeless corpse.

My human body was too close of a copy to the real thing. Parts of me were capable of greater speed, but it wasn't a form truly designed for covering distances. They were gaining on us, but as we rounded the first corner I heard the whine of a twin-turbo engine under hard acceleration. It was going to be close. Jasmin and Isaac had fallen back slightly, I veered up onto the road, dodging branches and roots with a speed the human mind simply wasn't capable of processing.

James saw me and brought his heavily modded Accord screaming around in a blue and white one-eighty skid. There wasn't going to be time for all of us to pile into the car while it sat motionless, so I continued to sprint down the road. James correctly read my intentions and was already in motion towards us, overtaking with a speed that nothing living could have matched.

As the Accord pulled up even with us I reached over and pried the passenger door open. Buffeting winds tried to slam it shut, but I held it firm and then reached back with my left arm and pulled Adri off of my back. She yelped a little as I slid her into the car, but the handoff was so quick there almost wasn't time for her to get scared before it was over.

I looked back at Isaac and Jasmin and found that the latter was halfway to us already, but that Isaac had hung back far enough to serve as bait. Even as I turned back to call him forward one of Brandon's wolves appeared behind him and lunged.

Demonstrating the grace and skill that had made him the pack's second most dominant member, Isaac reached out with his bare hands, plucked the wolf out of the air, and then spun around like a discus thrower and hurled it back into the rest of the wolves that had just come into view.

I held the door open for Jasmin and then piled into the car as Isaac caught up and jumped into the other side. As soon as both doors clicked shut James wound the car up into triple digits before braking just enough to sling it around the first curve in the road. Adri went pale as she looked into the passenger mirror and saw the darting shapes of Brandon's wolves falling steadily behind.

She looked back at me and I tried to reassure her with my expression, but found the truth slipping out despite my intentions.

"They were pretty close. There weren't that many of them, but they could've decided to push the issue regardless."

It wasn't until we were almost home that the adrenaline finally flushed its way completely out of my system. It had been a lot closer even than she realized. If Isaac had been one bit less graceful they would have ripped him apart and there wouldn't have been anything the rest of us could have done about it.

We returned and I introduced Adri to Donovan. He was just as charming as always, which freed me for a moment to worry about all of the other things that could potentially be crumbling right now. Rachel's arrival heralded another duty.

"Mother's been asking for you, Alec. I told her you'd be back soon, but she's worried."

"I suppose this is a good opportunity to introduce Adriana."

Rachel suddenly looked torn. Apparently she hadn't realized I would have to present Adri to Mother.

"Are you sure, Alec? I could go help her get settled into the Lilac Room."

My heart went out to Rachel but sooner or later Adri was going to meet Mother and if we didn't take care of it, Donovan was more than capable of making it happen when we weren't around.

TORN

It was always best to control those types of things rather than let them develop in ways you weren't prepared for. It seemed inconceivable that Adri would hold our mother against Rachel, but as with so many things of the heart, her fear wasn't something mere logic could overcome.

"No, Mother's still the mistress of this house. We've waited too long as it is. If we don't take care of it now it may be another week or two before we have a chance, and Donovan will be severely disappointed in both of us."

Rachel grinned at the reminder of the way Donovan managed us despite supposedly being 'mere hired help' and I found myself returning her smile. Still, it was with a measure of apprehension that I knocked on Mother's door once we arrived.

"Come in."

I looked at Rachel but she obviously wasn't going to join us. It was a tough call. Be completely ignored or listen to Mother disparage her.

Mother's rooms were spotless as always. Much as I might hate what James' mother did to him, I couldn't fault her care of my mother. Most of the pack hadn't particularly approved of Father marrying a human, but Addison had been one of my mother's two, surprisingly vocal supporters. Everyone in the pack had duties—Addison's revolved principally around caring for my mother.

The suite was part of an addition my father had ordered constructed just after marrying Mother. The main room was principally encased in glass, providing excellent lighting and an incredibly open space.

Mother loved caring for plants nearly as much as she loved her music. She'd quickly covered every shelf and stand with some plant or another. Donovan said my father had just chuckled and created more stands.

I gently guided Adri over to the alcove that contained Mother's piano. As always she was seated at it, humming to herself in preparation for the next attempt at whatever piece she was working on.

"Alec. I'm so glad you're safe. Rachel was going on and on about some kind of problem with the pack. She's so excitable. I told her everything would be fine, but she worries so. Your dad was the same way. Always going on and on about some crisis or another, but nothing ever really materialized."

She'd lost weight again. There was only so much Addison could do there. I needed to find a way to spend more time with her and see what I could do to remedy the situation.

I smiled at the cheery sun dress she was wearing and then nodded.

"We're experiencing a time of more than usual difficulty, Mother, but that isn't why I've come by. I wanted to present my friend Adriana to you. She'll be staying with us for the next few weeks."

She was already somewhere else. The smile she managed was extremely distracted. "That's nice, dear. You remind me so much of your father. So serious and worried all the time. Oh, how I miss him."

"I know you do, Mother. Rachel and I miss him too."

I winced even as the statement came out. It was one guaranteed to cause problems.

"You barely remember him. Rachel's a good girl, but she was so young when he died. She can't really miss him. Not like I miss him."

I wanted to argue, for Rachel's sake if nothing else, but there wasn't any point.

"Will you play something for us, Mother? Adriana hasn't had the pleasure of listening to your songs."

"No. You know it isn't ready. I'll tell you when I've perfected it. Yes, you can bring Rachel, but I can't let anyone listen to it before it's ready."

The demands of propriety fulfilled, I bowed my head and then turned to leave. Mother grabbed my arm, attempting to stop me.

"Don't be angry with me, Alec. You're all I have left."

"I'm not angry, Mother, but you're wrong. You have much more left than just me."

She shook her head with a youthful smile. "Such a good boy."

I pulled Adri along behind me. Rachel was already crying by the time we exited the suite. She ran off as soon as she saw us. Adri started to follow, but I recaptured her hand and shook my head.

"She just needs a little time. Donovan will alert Jasmin."

Adri obviously wasn't convinced. It wasn't necessarily my business, and Jasmin had been nearly ready to send her back to Brandon, but I didn't want her to continue to think of Jasmin as some kind of loose warhead.

"There's still a lot you don't know about all of the others. There's much I could tell you about Jasmin, but it isn't my story to share. Suffice it to say only Dominic has a greater capacity for empathy."

We walked in silence to the Lilac Room, which was really a suite of rooms, and found Donovan finishing preparations for Adri's stay.

"I trust your mother was well, sir?"

My response was cut off by the sound of a cell phone. Knowing Isaac's usual efficiency there was no question but that the phone located on the bedside table was the one used to forward their landline. I handed it to Adri.

"It's for you, probably your mom. Pretend you're home, I'll explain once you're finished."

A split second later my phone started vibrating. I picked it up and stepped far enough away that I wouldn't disturb Adri.

"Yeah?"

"Alec, we need you over in my father's suite right now. He's reverted to his wolf shape and it's all Isaac can do to stop him from hurting himself."

Jessica's normal dislike of me had been replaced by fear for her father.

"I'll be there as soon as I can."

"Please hurry."

Adri was just finishing up her conversation as I hung up. She looked up from her phone with surprise.

"You redirected our calls?"

"Correct. That's what Isaac was doing in the kitchen after your mom left. I thought it might come to this, so I had him bring along some of his toys. You'll want to change the message sometime tonight, so you can let it roll to the voice mail if she calls while you're at school."

"You really do think of everything, don't you?"

It was hard not to smile as her praise warmed me from the center out. "I don't think you can go that far, but I try to anticipate most eventualities."

Even as I made the statement I was reminded of all the times I hadn't seen problems coming and suddenly I felt every single hour since I'd last been asleep nearly thirty-six hours ago.

"For most of my life, there's been quite a bit riding on my ability to do so."

She again displayed her uncanny ability to read me, and chose not to pursue a painful line of questioning. I was already realizing just how hard it was to deny her anything she really wanted to know.

"You got a call too?"

I felt a spark of guilt as I realized I'd nearly forgotten about Jess already.

"Yes. I'm afraid something has come up. Will you be okay here for a few hours?"

Her shrug was perfectly nonchalant, but her heart and breathing didn't match it.

"I rather suspect whatever 'came up' is important enough I'll just have to be okay."

I flinched as I realized she'd already begun figuring out just how many demands there were on me, just how many different ways there were for me to disappoint her. I opened my mouth to try and make things better, but my phone started buzzing. I nodded regretfully and hurried out of the room.

I was almost at a full run, but even so it took me five minutes to get to Andrew's suite. I burst into the central room and found furniture scattered everywhere. Jess was curled up in one corner crying while Isaac and Andrew were a rolling, writhing ball on the floor.

Andrew was indeed in his wolf form, attempting to break away from Isaac despite the mangled back legs that were Agony's legacy. In a straight-up fight, even in his prime, Andrew wouldn't have been a match for Isaac, but the latter had remained in his human form with all of its inherent limitations to avoid hurting his adopted father.

Andrew looked up at me with hatred in his yellow eyes and almost broke free of Isaac as he threw himself in my direction. Isaac had flooded the room with power, but in the age-old manner of parents, Andrew was refusing to heed the imperative.

I took a deep breath and then unleashed my beast. My hybrid form roared out with even greater than usual violence, shredding my clothes and blasting all three of the others with a torrent of power that washed away everyone else's metaphysical presence.

I didn't plan on hurting Andrew, but his beast was more likely to respect my hybrid form than my other two.

"BOW, ANDREW!"

The imperative roared out from me with all of the authority of Andrew's alpha, and his struggles suddenly ceased. The hatred was still there, but it was bridled by fear once again.

As Isaac carefully released Andrew, I picked up a blanket from the back of the couch and threw it over Jess' father.

"Change back to your normal form."

He wasn't cushioned by his rage anymore and the transformation pulled at ancient wounds with such force that he screamed as his body folded in on itself. I expected him to take a few minutes to regain his composure after the change, but he started yelling at me as soon as he'd reformed his vocal cords.

"You could have gotten him killed, Alec."

"I'm aware of that, Andrew. Nobody is more relieved than me that we all made it through."

The hatred was bubbling back to primacy so I sent out another pulse of power. It helped. Andrew didn't really want to throw his life away by attacking me, but he was an angry parent.

"It's bad enough the risks you make them run on a daily basis, but things are getting worse and this was all because of this new girl. It's not right for you to place her above your pack mates."

He'd said too much, and suddenly it was me that was trying to keep my furious beast in check. Jess had no business running back to her father and complaining that I'd stopped her from killing Adri.

"She didn't do anything to deserve to die, and everyone seems to be quickly forgetting that part of our reason for existence is to protect innocent humans. Did Jess tell you she was ready to kill Adri herself?"

He flinched. She'd told him, but he'd made excuses for her.

"I'm not courting danger casually, but I'm through sitting back and letting Brandon's people slaughter innocents."

Andrew shook his head. "We all know that's not why you did it, Alec. Of all the things to breed true from your father, why did his unnatural fascination with the humans have to be the one trait he passed on?"

I left before I could lose control and kill him, but even after I'd put distance between us, it was all I could do not to turn around and head back to his suite. I wanted to go find Adri, but feared she'd pull back in horror. I was too angry to shift out of my hybrid form and she'd fainted the last time I'd approached her looking like this.

I angrily made my way out to my father's shop and strapped myself into the machine. Donovan found me near the planned end of my sets. He entered the shop and then stopped well beyond striking range, once again displaying his usual ability to sense the mood of those around him.

"What is it, Donovan? Something wrong?"

He shook his head slowly, but a slight uptick in his pulse gave lie to the calmness.

"No, sir. There was an item I'd planned on discussing with you, but I think it best I wait for a few days. The business side of things is going as planned, and there isn't anything I can't handle for a day or two."

The beast inside of me wanted an answer now, wanted to be faced with whatever Donovan didn't want to talk about, but I knew better. I was trembling with exhaustion but still entirely too dangerous. I'd take even the most gentle of criticism poorly in my current state and Donovan was correct to want to avoid me until that changed.

Rachel appeared as Donovan was leaving.

"Alec, can I take Adri shopping tomorrow? Not in Sanctuary, some place further away, like Vegas. She needs clothes and stuff since she didn't get a chance to pack before you guys left."

Rachel was normally able to calm my beast, but it was all I could do not to snap at her. I took a deep breath and then nodded. "You have my permission as long as you can convince Dom and Jasmin to go with you. Even all the way down there I want you to have some protection."

"Thanks, Alec. I'll pick you up some new stuff too. Lately you've been tearing through clothes even more often than normal."

Her impish grin brought a smile to my face, but it still wasn't enough to truly make me safe to be around. As she left I attacked the weight stack with renewed determination, forcing my muscles further and harder than I'd ever done before. Even past the clang of iron striking iron I was able to hear the house slowly quiet down as everyone went to bed.

Finally it was only Donovan who remained, working away in his office. I was long past the point of exhaustion, so I headed back to my room, relieved to have been able to avoid terrorizing Adri with my inability to control my rage.

The lights were all off, but it might as well have been high noon to my hybrid eyes. I easily navigated the familiar halls of the house, silently slipping into my room and then pulling up short as I found Adri sound asleep on my bed.

The sight of her peaceful slumber did what even multiple hours of weightlifting hadn't managed. My anger evaporated and my form shrank back down to the one I presented to the outside world.

The sudden exhaustion of the last forty-eight hours struck with such force I nearly fell to the floor. I was just able to make it to the bed, where I lay down next to Adri. I needed a few seconds to rest or I'd drop her before making it even halfway to the Lilac Room.

Adri's violent thrashing pulled me out of unintended slumber. She was breathing heavily and trying to push herself into the wall with such force I was afraid she'd hurt herself.

Without thinking I reached out and clamped my arms around her, restraining her as I called her name in an effort to wake her up.

The struggles abruptly cut off as she finally came awake. She looked nearly as terrified of me as she'd been of whatever she'd been dreaming about.

"Are you okay? I'm sorry about that, I was afraid you were going to hurt yourself."

Adri blushed as she finally realized she'd been dreaming.

"I'm sorry. It was a nightmare."

She seemed at the point of telling me about the dream, but suddenly gasped as she took in her surroundings.

"I'm so sorry, Alec. Donovan and Rachel told me you had copies of our textbooks in here. I was studying and must have fallen asleep. Please don't think…"

She looked as if she might cry. I wondered how her parents ever had the heart to discipline her. One look at those tear-filled eyes made me want to give her anything she asked for. My words almost tripped over each other as I hastened to reassure her. I reached out and hugged her against me.

"It was all just a dream, and you don't have anything to be sorry about. I don't mind you being here. I'm sorry I had to leave you alone for so long, it was inexcusable."

If I'd had even a shadow of my normal self-control I could have spent the last few hours with her instead of locked away where I couldn't hurt anyone. I banished the thought and tried to make my words light.

"Actually, I owe you another apology. When I returned and found you here I meant to carry you to your room. I was only going to sit down for a second, but apparently I was more exhausted than I realized. I hope you don't think my actions are inappropriate."

She'd calmed down completely now. If she'd been a cat she'd have been purring. I wanted to stay with her pressed up against me, but didn't want to give her another chance to reject me. I was already much too deeply in her power. I warred with myself for several seconds and then sighed.

"Well, I suppose I'd better get you off to bed."

Adri didn't respond until I slid my arm out from underneath her and stood up, but then she fell apart with all of the speed normally reserved for her panic attacks. I heard her pulse skyrocket at the same time the rest of her froze into immobility. I turned back towards her and found panic written in every nuance of her expression and body language.

"You stopped breathing. What's wrong?"

When she finally pulled herself up onto her knees, tears were heavy in her eyes and her voice was a shadow of its normal, confident tone.

"Please don't send me there. Not after my dream."

It was like she'd reached into my being and read the desires there. I wanted nothing more than to spend every waking and even sleeping moment with her, but there was a limit to how much of that she could be exposed to without becoming addicted to my touch. I forced my face into impassivity, praying it wouldn't give lie to my words.

"I'm not sure that's the best idea."

She collapsed back onto the bed, tears flowing freely even as she tried to crawl to the edge despite the sobs wracking her body.

"You're right. I'm so sorry to be such a bother."

Her desolation destroyed my resolve and I reached out to her. She rolled away as my hand touched her shoulder. She continued to try and flee me, but I stopped her by pulling her around and carefully pulling her face up so our eyes could meet.

"Adriana Paige, it isn't that I don't want to be with you. I want it more than anything else right now. *That's* why I'm not sure it's such a good idea."

She was so beautiful it was all I could do not to lean in and capture her lips in mine. It was completely inappropriate but only a decade of practice denying my wants allowed me to forgo the pleasure.

She finally nodded, burying her face against my chest and letting the tears run their course. Several minutes later she was able to speak once again.

"You're so ready to send me away it's hard to believe sometimes that you really want me here."

Her words took me by complete surprise. She seemed so able to read me. It defied logic that she wouldn't know exactly how I felt about her. Ignoring my earlier worries about the Ja'tell bond, I reached out and touched the side of her face.

"I really want nothing as badly as I want you here. If I were to be completely selfish I'd never have even made the offer, but that wouldn't have been fair to you."

She moved in closer to me, leaning against my body.

"Well, I just want to log my vote for you to be more selfish."

Her gay tone was completely at odds with her earlier hurt. It was amazing that someone could be so mercurial. It was like she lived completely in the moment.

"According to my father, we shape shifters were created specifically for the purpose of not being selfish, of watching out for the dayborn even at the expense of our own desires."

Now she was serious once again.

"You miss your dad. I can tell it in your voice."

I shrugged, attempting to hide how much hurt the thought of my father caused me.

"I do. I don't really remember him, but I've read through his journals dozens of times. It seems crazy to miss what you never knew, but there are days when I really wish he were still around to give me advice. I think that's what I missed the most. That and his stories."

Adri's smile was at odds with the pain scent she emitted as she talked about her father.

"That sounds nice. We never got stories at my house. Dad played with us plenty, but bedtime was bedtime."

"Donovan said Dad used to tell me stories every night. After Dad died, Donovan took over telling them to both Rachel and me. It wasn't until after I grew up that I found out they were legends about where we came from. That we weren't normal like everyone else."

"Like the...dayborn? What did you mean earlier?"

I shouldn't tell her. Despite everything, a part of me was still convinced I'd eventually send her away to protect her. Once that happened, the less she knew the better off she'd be.

"That touches on the things you shouldn't know."

"Please. It will help me go to sleep. I need something else to think about."

I paused again, but finally launched into the first Tale of Adjam and Inock. It was a story I hadn't heard for years, but I was surprised at how easily it rolled off of my tongue. It should have caused me pain, but instead I found it relieved some of the conflict inside me.

By the time Adri finally nodded off to sleep I wasn't worrying about the future. I curled up next to her and fell asleep a short time later.

Chapter 24

There'd been more than one reason I'd told Rachel she had to take Dom on the shopping trip. It was past time to see just exactly how far I could push James, and I needed to do it when Dom wasn't around to calm him down.

The coming storm was likely to be something I could keep just between Brandon and me, but if it wasn't, if things were going to leak over onto the rest of the pack, I needed to know the true strength of the weapon I was taking into battle.

I'd considered sending Isaac with them, but if things went as badly south as I was afraid they would, then I might need Isaac's help to restrain James without killing him.

Jess was another concern, but when it came right down to it she was the weakest fighter in the pack. Her standing with us, or even against us, wouldn't make all that great of a difference.

I spent the morning with Donovan and then with my books. We covered nearly every aspect of the family business and discussed Brandon's probable responses to everything that'd happened, both economic and otherwise, but he never brought anything up that could account for the level of concern he'd evidenced the day before. I briefly contemplated forcing the issue, but Donovan sometimes knew me even better than I knew myself. He probably had a good reason for not saying anything yet. He'd tell me if I demanded an answer, but doing so would be devaluing his judgment.

I'd been deeply involved in working through a chemistry assignment when Addison's knock had pulled me out of the world of covalent bonds, moles, and periodic tables.

The idea of Addison seeking me out was so foreign that I nearly did a double-take.

"To what do I owe this pleasure?"

"Don't push James today, Alec."

"I beg your pardon?"

Addison's smirk was one of the most infuriating things about her. She tended to think she knew much more than she actually did, which was made even worse by the way she acted when she was right.

"With everything that's happened, you've got to be worried about what's coming down the pipeline with the Coun'hij. You sent Dominic away because you want to see if James will stand with you when you really push him. It's exactly the kind of thing Donovan's been teaching you all these years."

I leaned back in my desk and studied the woman who'd had the greatest influence into shaping James into the willful, obstinate man he was becoming. She'd fought me on almost everything for as long as I could remember.

"Assuming you're right about what I'm planning, why should I listen to you? You're hardly without ulterior motives."

Addison shrugged, a painful movement that demonstrated just how much she'd lost the night her husband had been killed.

"I'm not going to pretend I like you, Alec. You've held my boy back. He could have led his own pack, but you favor even Jasmin over him. Your father never would have allowed that kind of imbalance in power to exist inside his pack."

"You could have left at any time, Addison."

"I thought about it, but I swore an oath to your father, and thereby your mother. I'm not abandoning her. Once she dies I'll have James gone so fast you'll never even see it coming, but until then he and I will defend her even if it means defending your worthless hide."

"Again, why should I listen to you?"

"Because young Dominic's convinced me that your primary motivation in helping the girl was selfless. For the first time since you were born you're actually living up to your father's legacy instead of Donovan's cowardly fears. I'll make sure James stands with you, but if you bully him right now you'll reinforce everything I've told him about you."

I stared at the spot where Addison's wheelchair had sat for several minutes after she left. Believe what she might, she'd done more to contribute to James' unhappiness than any other factor. She'd made him a dominant by encouraging willfulness and a misplaced sense of entitlement.

In the end though I decided to follow her advice. She might or might not be lying, but it all boiled down to the fact that James was my friend, and if there was a reason not to bully him I'd take it.

The afternoon found James, Jess, Isaac and I up in the north end of the valley. It was always a bit of a risk to let any shape shifter lock with another. Even what was supposed to be nothing more than a sparring match could easily turn bloody and lethal if the wolves involved lost control of their beasts.

We started with Isaac and Jess and then worked our way up to the rest of us. As always Isaac's incredible control was a godsend. It was almost impossible to make him lose control, which meant I could concentrate on holding James off until he calmed down instead of jumping between two full-grown hybrids who both wanted to tear into each other.

By the time the sun started setting and it was time to call it a night we were all bloody and exhausted. We ran a quick circuit of our territory, returning to the house a few minutes after the girls returned from shopping.

TORN

I'd helped Donovan transport Adri's portion of the day's haul to the Lilac Room and then joined everyone for a late dinner. Between the nine of us we polished off an incredible amount of food and then it was time to go to bed. It had seemed as though Adri wasn't finished eating, so I'd planned on returning to conduct her back to the Lilac Room, but she followed me to my room and quietly asked if she could sleep with me again.

Once again I couldn't deny her. It should have been a restless night. Sleeping next to another person was hardly the kind of thing that engendered uninterrupted rest, but it was as if her presence calmed me on levels I hadn't known were anxious.

All of us shape shifters woke several hours before either Rachel or Adri, so I gathered everyone together and informed them we needed to come up with a revised set of schedules for everyone that would allow us to have someone from the pack with Rachel and Adri at all times.

I half expected arguments from Jess and James with some muttered protestations from Jasmin, but everyone had simply nodded like they'd been expecting my announcement and sat down to figure out how best to make it happen.

Donovan provided us with a complete class listing and makeup for each teacher in the school, doubtlessly hacked from the school's mainframe, and a relatively short time later we were finished.

I was unaccountably anxious to be there when Adri awoke, but I detoured past the Lilac Room on my way back and retrieved most of the clothes they'd bought in Vegas.

I made it back just in time to see her awake and tease her into a semblance of normality. It was apparent she didn't really believe me when I told her we'd need to rearrange everyone's class schedules to provide her and Rachel with bodyguards. I half thought she was going to gasp when we all filed into the office half an hour before school started.

I asked Mrs. Pendely to speak to Principal Gossil and was conducted into his office in short order.

I received a frown as I entered the office and pulled the blinds closed, but apparently Principal Gossil was still smarting from our last confrontation.

"What do you want, Graves? You can't just show up here every time you have your eye on some skirt who hasn't become immediately overwhelmed by your family's wealth."

He was fishing. He thought he had something on me now, but he was about to face a rather rude awakening.

"I assure you I'm no more anxious to continue our conversations than you are, Principal Gossil. Unfortunately I'm going to need your approval with regards to some class changes."

I thought for a second the vein in his forehead was going to explode. It was petty, but I took some satisfaction in seeing his blood pressure rise.

"That's ridiculous. There's absolutely no way that I'm going to approve anything of the kind. Do you have any idea how pissed the faculty would be if I let you change your classes around this late in the semester? I don't care what kind of dirt you think you've got on me, you're not getting your way."

I let him yell for another ten minutes and then let my beast flood the room with power. It wasn't elegant, and it wouldn't work long-term, but Principal Gossil folded like a pinata when the first burst of energy flowed over him. I hadn't done his heart any favors, but once he stopped jumping at shadows in a day or two he'd probably be okay.

Donovan had prepared notes for Principal Gossil to sign, which he did somewhat shakily. We informed the recently-arrived school counselor of the changes and then everyone split up to go to class.

Adri had obviously been fuming at being one of only two people not changing their schedules around, but managed to keep her dissatisfaction inside until we were nearly to her Biology class.

"You should have had me change some of my classes. Everyone is already bent out of shape over what you've done for me, I don't want the rest of the...your friends even more mad at me."

I shook my head and pulled her along behind me.

"You and Rachel are the ones who need the most sleep, ergo you don't change classes."

"That's crazy."

She tried to stop, but I had a pretty good feeling that would lead to an argument.

"It's not crazy. Everyone who swaps classes is going to be doing double homework for the duration. Assignments for their old class, which they presumably still want to get credit for, and assignments for the new class so as not to make any more waves than necessary with their temporary teacher. It only makes sense to place that burden on the ones who can most easily deal with it."

The entire conversation had been conducted in a whisper, but she lost a little volume as we finally did stop just outside her Biology class.

"I can help. I could switch at least one class and still keep up."

Donovan's hacking skills ranged to more than just getting us scheduling information from the school computer. I hadn't wanted to bring it up, almost hadn't wanted to believe it, but I'd seen the unofficial notes her teachers had been leaving.

"Adriana, you're struggling in two classes already. How do you propose to handle yet another set of homework?"

Her mouth abruptly slammed shut. For a second I worried she'd bitten her tongue. It'd been a low blow but we had to get into class before the bell rang or we'd just end up with more of a fight on our hands when we told Mrs. Sorenson she was going to have to accept me into the class.

"But they'll hate me even more."

I'd thought she'd just been looking for fodder for her argument earlier. I hadn't realized she really thought Jasmin and the others hated her.

"They don't hate you. A few of them are scared almost senseless, but nobody hates you."

Her voice dropped to something even fainter than a whisper. It was possible she didn't even mean to say the words out loud, but I was still able to hear them.

"They were willing to kill me. They wanted to trade me back to Brandon."

I pulled her into a hug, ignoring the scattered gasps from inside the room and a couple of wide eyes among the students walking past us. Leaning my face up against hers, I whispered into her ear.

"I'm not going to let anything happen to you. If there's a way to keep you safe I'll find it."

She pulled back and offered me a brave smile. It was unlikely I'd really convinced her, but some fears could only be defeated with time.

I walked into class and handed Mrs. Sorenson the signed note from Principal Gossil. I had some suspicions already about her based on the fact she was one of only two teachers to be giving Adri less than an 'A', so it gave me the slightest tingle of satisfaction to see her eyebrows rise halfway to her hairline at the bold, uncompromising language of Donovan's note. It had to suck when the administration essentially told you to suck it up and let two of your students do pretty much whatever they wanted.

"This is highly irregular, Mr. Graves. In fact I don't believe the administration can legitimately expect me to comply."

I gave her a bland smile and held my hand back out for the note.

"I promise not to get in the way. In fact if you could just find us a couple of desks in the back corner you'll hardly know we're here."

She shot Adri a look that didn't bode well for Adri's continued enjoyment of her class.

"Ms. Paige has an assigned seat towards the front of the class. Based on her scholastic performance to date it would be highly irresponsible of me as an educator to allow her to change seats."

Half the secret to getting what you want out of people when you have the upper hand is letting silence work on them. I looked rather pointedly at the note and then waited for her to run down the logic tree and realize she didn't really have any other choice.

"Ms. Bellarose, please move up to Ms. Paige's old seat."

I collected the note and then led Adri back to the far corner of the room. Mrs. Sorenson proceeded to deliver on the unpleasantness her earlier look had promised. I'd had her for Biology the year before and enjoyed the subject enough, despite her efforts, that I'd spent some time in a couple of college texts.

It didn't take a doctoral student to see she was singling Adri out for a fairly humiliating session of question-and-answer. Even when Adri couldn't answer her unreasonable questions she didn't stop badgering her. I felt my beast bubble to the surface with all of the rage that normally accompanied it.

Adri had demonstrated a better understanding of the subject than anyone in my class last year had possessed, but was still being wrung out and left looking stupid. I kept the anger off of my face, but was already planning ways to improve the situation.

I trailed along behind Adri, letting the last few pieces snap into place as she reached her locker.

"Is that normal for her?"

Adri's laugh was slightly hysterical. She cut the sound short, nodding as she slammed her locker shut.

James was already nearly to us. There wasn't time to do anything about Mrs. Sorenson right now, but that would change.

"We'd better get you to your next class. Dealing with that will have to wait until later."

I watched James and Adri disappear around the corner and then slipped off to History. I stayed out in the hall just long enough to text a question to Donovan, and then went in and suffered through another hour of Mr. Simms doing absolutely nothing to teach anyone anything.

If it had been Jess or James that'd been assigned to take Adri to her third hour class I probably would have made sure they didn't conveniently forget to pick her up, but I had faith

Jasmin would keep her promise to me. She occasionally went off half-cocked when it came to the other pack, but she never failed to do the things she'd committed to.

I was busy confirming my earlier hypothesis with Donovan when I felt twin rushes of power from the other side of the school. I took off at a brisk pace, something that would have been a near run for a human.

The halls had already started to clear out, but it was still all I could do to avoid running into the scattered students. I brushed past people with more force than was polite, ignoring their angry gasps.

Jasmin's familiar power was so quiet as to be non-existent. I broke out into a full run as I heard Isaac come up behind me. We came around a corner just in time to see Brandon come into view on the other end of the hall.

Vincent and Cassie were already mere inches away from Jasmin, and their power sparked higher with Brandon's presence to back them up.

I let an answering roar of power surge from me as I closed the remaining distance to Jasmin. I could only assume that Adri was safely inside the classroom surrounded by witnesses.

"We could kill all three of you right now."

Vincent's subvocalized taunt was designed to egg Jasmin on, but she kept her calm with surprising restraint considering just how irrational she'd been with regards to Vincent lately.

"If you attack now, with so many humans around, the Coun'hij will crucify you."

My voice came out more even than I'd expected, but Brandon laughed off the threat.

"Please, you've finally played right into my hands. We meet at lunch to resolve this or we'll create the kind of ruckus that'll have people wondering how you managed to survive being thrown through cinder block walls."

It wasn't something we had to do. I'd be within my rights to refuse to talk to him, but it wasn't a practical solution. Besides, the Coun'hij tended towards extremism when it came to punishing both sides of any confrontation that risked disclosure of our secret to the public.

"We'll be there, now get lost."

Brandon's lazy smile seemed to say he knew exactly what I was thinking, but Mr. Rindell, the assistant principal, chose that moment to arrive and break up the impending fight.

"Class is about to start, and if every one of you isn't where you're supposed to be before the bell rings, you'll have detention for the next month."

Vincent's hiss was just loud enough to carry into the classroom.

"This isn't over."

I wanted to check on Adri, but there wasn't time. Mr. Rindell was singularly incorruptible, and I couldn't afford to push him any further than I already had lately. He was capable of creating all kinds of problems for us.

I headed up to my art class at something less than a dead run, but at a quick enough clip to satisfy Mr. Rindell that I took him seriously. A quick text as I ducked through the door ordered the entire pack to meet at Adri's locker during lunch and then I was forced to sit through another hour of class before I could hurry down and breathe a sigh of relief at the fact that Adri was unhurt.

I took her hand as soon as I was close enough to touch her.

"Are you okay?"

She shook her head, presumably out of shock over everything that had just happened.

"This is going to be really bad, isn't it?"

It felt odd to be talking of such things around the pack. I paused for a second and then tried to parry her questions.

"I'd...we'd...spare you it if we could."

"No, this is my fault. I belong here, not cowering in a corner somewhere."

Rachel and Dominic closed ranks around Adri, and then we all walked outside. Brandon's entire pack, less Nathanial and Simon, was waiting for us already. I faced off against him as the two packs fanned out at our backs.

"I demand satisfaction on behalf of my pack for the two of our number that you brutally murdered. This is within my rights under the laws that bind us. I demand two lives for the two lives robbed me."

TORN

As always Brandon ignored the actual law, instead twisting it into something that served his purposes. Still, his demand was exactly as expected. He'd gone after something that would destroy my pack.

"Your wolves were lawbreakers who were executed before they could break further laws. The protection of the people, of the secrets that guard our nature from the dayborn, represents a law that supersedes any question of territory or dominance."

Brandon's pack tried to batter us to our knees with a surge of power, but we collectively answered with a blast of energy that was equal to theirs. I felt Rachel and Adri shaking from being on the fringes of the exchange, but there wasn't any time to worry further about them. I continued with my prepared defense.

"By their actions Adriana Paige learned of our nature, and it was only by the grace of the Maker that I was able to stop them from killing her. Their deaths were an unavoidable price to save an innocent."

Three of Brandon's wolves flinched at my words. I had a second to realize that it was Jack, Sam and Alison, and then Brandon laughed.

"Her life belonged to me, it was mine to dispose of as I saw fit."

It was a gross corruption of the ancient code. It was the kind of thing the southern shape shifters believed, but not us wolves.

"The ancient laws don't support her life being a disposable commodity, extinguished at your whim. Not even the bond of Ja'tell provides you with that right."

Brandon's grin was sarcastic.

"Ah, but those aren't the laws under which we labor now, are they? She's mine, and I have every right to do whatever I wish to her. Her presence among your pack is a direct affront to my rights and honor. I could demand your life, be glad I'm only requiring two of your pack."

I felt my face go wooden as I realized there wasn't any way to save the pack. The Coun'hij currently treated any human a shape shifter took an interest in as Ja'tell. They would support his position that no mere human was worth the lives of two shape shifters.

I shook my head and invoked the ritual words.

"By the same laws set down by Adjam and Inock when they first took mates from among the dayborn, I challenge your bond of Ja'tell. I challenge your standing among the people, and your personal honor. The dispute between us is such as can only be settled by blood."

Brandon's expression flickered slightly, but it couldn't be true surprise. He'd been maneuvering for exactly this day ever since he'd manifested his power and become confident he could kill me. Maybe he was just surprised he'd finally succeeded in backing us against a wall.

TORN

Brandon abruptly closed the distance between us and growled at me. "Too bad your pack has such an idiot for a leader. You're going to die, and then they'll finally be exposed and helpless. It may take a few months, but eventually they'll fall and then I'll absorb whoever I don't kill. All for a skirt."

His barb, intended more for the rest of the pack than it was for me, safely delivered, Brandon backed away, turned and left.

Chapter 25

After the faceoff with Brandon we'd all gone back to the cafeteria. Nobody was really in the mood to eat, but we'd all learned a while ago not to skip meals. Whatever supernatural forces stoked our abilities and strength, there was still a hefty need for food to help fuel the fires.

I could see the fear and worry on everyone's face, but now wasn't the time to tell them about the backup plan.

I gave Adri's hand a squeeze and then turned her over to Isaac. She was off to History, while I had to go sit through English. I caused quite a stir when I walked into class and handed Mr. Whethers my note. He'd apparently seen more than one of them over the course of the day. He didn't bother reading it but shot me an unhappy look as he sent me to the back of the class.

A couple of the other students looked like they wanted to ask me questions, but I was saved having to ignore them by Mr. Whethers, who kept a much tighter rein on the class than normal. I endured the time, barely able to focus on what was being said, and then fled back to the lockers and met up with Adri.

Isaac gave me a respectful nod and then disappeared off to his next class. Adri on the other hand had a considering look about her as I led her towards Physics. I could smell a new person as we got down to the end of the hall.

It took only the briefest look inside the room to verify that we did indeed have a substitute. Under other circumstances I probably wouldn't have skipped, but that considering look combined with my own restlessness to convince me otherwise.

I convinced Adri I'd be able to persuade the secretaries to make our absences go away, and then we headed out to a cluster of trees roughly fifty feet from the school.

Once we'd sat down with our backs to a tree Adri looked up at me with a grin.

"So is this nearly complete disregard for consequences typical?"

I stared at her for several seconds, attempting to divine just how much of her gaiety was assumed. She looked away from me and tried to let go of my hand, but I maintained my grasp on it, stopping her from moving further away.

"Please don't. I didn't mean to make you nervous. It's just that you continue to surprise me."

"It's more than a little creepy how you all can do that. Are all shape shifters born with the ability to read people's minds?"

I found myself smiling at her.

"Minds no, scents yes. The human body is quite marvelous in how many different systems it recruits to match its mood."

She was thoughtful for a moment and I wondered if she was going to drop whatever bomb she was holding in reserve. I finally broke the silence.

"Actually, none of us are born with any unusual abilities. All of the changes tend to show up more or less around puberty. And no, disregard for the consequences of my actions isn't typical. In fact I've spent nearly a decade weighing almost every word."

"So dashing off to rescue an admittedly stupid teenage girl and landing yourself in a fight to the death that you probably can't win isn't how you normally run your life. Why did you do it then?"

I felt my beast try to surge to the top of my consciousness, but I clamped down on it. Isaac hadn't quite been violating orders as long as he hadn't told her anything the Coun'hij could come after her for.

"Apparently Isaac's decided there are a few things you should know. Don't try and tell me it wasn't him, you didn't know that particular piece of information an hour ago, and nobody else has had the opportunity to tell secrets."

She tensed up with worry but I waved her concerns away.

"In answer to the core of your question, Jasmin thinks it's because I've finally gone over the edge, that in essence I've snapped due to the stress, and this, 'obsession,' as she terms it, is merely a novel way of committing suicide."

She gasped ever so slightly at the word suicide, but I didn't give her a chance to interrupt.

"The other school of thought is that I'm more of a healer than anyone realized, and that I couldn't resist your obvious need."

I'd obviously lost her. It was nice that Isaac hadn't entirely spilled his guts.

"Wait, what do you mean?"

I felt myself settle down a little as it became evident she didn't know too much yet. She gave me an expectant look and I realized I hadn't answered her questions.

"You glow. All of the time. Until now we always thought someone had to be a shape shifter to do that."

"But I'm just a normal person. Why would I appear different than anyone else?"

"With shape shifters, we believe it's because the animating energy, the soul if you will, burns more brightly than normal. I think it's tied in with what allows us to shift forms. With you, there isn't any obvious reason, but I think that Dominic has probably hit upon the root of the matter."

I'd entered lecture mode without really pausing to think about how the information was going to strike her. As that understanding finally made its way through my unusually slow brain, I paused and cast about for a different way to say it all. A subtle tightening of her eyes warned me that her lie detector was starting to go off, so I finally just answered her.

"You know that our legends indicate a belief we were created in order to watch over and protect humans? Well, Dominic believes that your light represents a defense mechanism. We don't know of any accounts where humans have burned so brightly, but it's possible the primitive parts of you, the ones that remember what it was like to be watched over by our kind, hit upon a way to call for help from us, while not admitting a problem to your own kind."

She seemed to contemplate the implications of what I'd just told her and then nodded slowly.

"So you're saying that I was, am, so broken I glow so your people would be able to pull me aside and fix me."

Her smile was a little tremulous, but it was enough still to loosen the sudden knot in my chest.

"I guess that makes sense. Nobody likes to be told there's something wrong with them, but I can't exactly say everything is just Jim Dandy. Not when I still collapse at the mere mention of what I've lost."

I hadn't meant to bring the conversation around to her father and sister, but there it was.

I'd avoided prodding the open wound but that hadn't stopped Donovan or I from continuing to try and dig up information about what had happened. We'd found nothing, which was incredibly maddening, but I'd forbidden anyone from asking her about it. She could volunteer whatever she wished, but I wouldn't contribute to her pain.

I waited expectantly and she finally offered another brave smile.

"So you're just one of those guys that can't resist trying to help the broken girls, huh?"

"No. That's Dominic's theory, I didn't say it was mine. I did what I did because when I close my eyes I still see you there."

Her pulse and breathing sped up, but I took it as a good sign. It was an unfair advantage to be able to know her mood, but it gave me the courage to continue.

"I don't know why, not really. Your incredible, unearthly beauty helps, as does your stubborn determination to continue soldiering on, despite how badly you've been hurt. That doesn't explain it all though. Neither does the fact that you stepped in and saved Rachel from a beating I couldn't stop."

I'd faced death at Brandon's hands multiple times and was going to die in just a week's time, but I was too scared to do what I really wanted to do. Instead of leaning in, I remained where I was and just brushed a stray strand of hair behind her ear.

"Whatever the reason, since your arrival here, I just feel like parts of me that were missing have come back home. Even when I thought you were some kind of...rogue...shape shifter come to destroy my pack, I was still drawn to you."

The glimmer of tears should have warned me she wasn't quite on the same page as me. If I'd been thinking rationally I wouldn't have assumed the emotions she was feeling were necessarily positive. I shouldn't have been so quick to assume that all of her revelations had been made. She looked up with the emotionless mask that had been gone for the last few days and shattered me.

"Alec, what if I were to go back to Brandon? Would that stop everything from going wrong? I mean, then you wouldn't have been poaching his property or whatever you call it."

It was so unexpected I nearly lost control of my beast. There was a reason Rachel, for all that she loved and trusted me, was careful with what she said around me.

In some ways I wasn't really just one person, and the primitive, powerful side of me wasn't governed by the modern, cosmopolitan rules that the rest of the world functioned on. Concepts like right and wrong, property and ownership were recognized beyond almost anything else.

It was that simple fact that gave Brandon the right to demand my death, but in that moment I knew he'd never really cared about Adri. If he had, there wouldn't have been any formal challenge, he would have just come directly to the estate and killed me.

The sound of a breaking branch brought me back to myself before I completely gave way to my other side. I'd snapped the tree branch I'd been holding onto in half. Adri's eyes were wide with fear, but it was obvious she didn't understand the strength required to do what I'd just done from a sitting position. All the leverage had been against me. If she'd really understood how close I'd just come to losing control, she'd be running away in terror.

It was only the spark of confusion in her expression that allowed me to continue. The confusion and the fact that in some ways she'd tamed me. I couldn't give myself over when there was still even the slightest chance she wasn't rejecting me.

"You're saying that because you're worried for me? Not because you really want to go back to him?"

She shook her head slowly and I shoved my beast back down to my center with relief.

"No, I want to stay, but how can I knowing it will mean you're going to be fighting to the death?"

I realized I was still holding the branch and tossed it away with a sigh.

"I've spent years learning control, but sometimes I still forget just how breakable everything around me is. If you go back to

Brandon, you support his claim that you belong to him, and I'd still be forced to challenge him. If I didn't, he would be justified in killing whichever two of my friends he wants."

"So there's no way you can avoid fighting him?"

"No, but it's not too late to save you. I can have you on a flight to Paris tonight. It's the only way to guarantee your safety."

She shook her head with such resolve that I realized for the first time I was going to have to overcome more than just my own reluctance to send her away. Looking at her, most people would never imagine the steel at her core, but it only made sense. Whatever she'd been through had nearly destroyed her. All loss wasn't equal and for whatever reason it'd represented nearly her entire world, but she hadn't given up, hadn't curled up and died.

And now she was showing that steel again.

"I'm not leaving. I believe you when you say my going back to Brandon won't solve anything, but I'm not going to run away and leave you all to deal with the mess I created. I wish you'd stop asking me to."

I nodded, wishing there were a way to convince her to flee to safety at the same time I was internally sighing in relief that she wanted to be here.

"You have as much right to see this through as anyone else does, but it's almost certainly going to get a lot uglier before it's over. Your freedom is going to be incredibly restricted, at least as bad as it was today. We'll escort you to school, stay just long enough to ensure we don't get in trouble, and then hurry back to our territory. At least if Brandon's pack does come after us there, we're within our rights to do something about it."

Chapter 26

Somehow we'd all made it through the last hour of school despite an increasing pattern of provocations from Brandon's people. In addition to failing Biology, Adri was also failing Spanish. I'd heard enough bad things about Mrs. Tiggs that I pulled Dom aside as soon as she and Adri met back up with the rest of the pack.

"Alec, that woman is terrible. She seems to have something against poor Adriana."

I nodded as I passed her the graded tests Donovan had procured for me. Fax machines were an incredible thing. One of them was Adri's, the other two belonged to people who were doing very well in the class.

"Can you look these over quickly and let me know if you see any discrepancies?"

I'd spent most of Pre-Calc going through the biology tests that'd been scanned into the school system, so I already knew the kind of stuff she was going to probably find.

"Alec, this is not fair. She's marked Adri off for many things that she didn't dock these two for. See, the tilde here and the accent mark there. Not only that, Adri's is a more technically correct answer on the essay question."

I nodded as I accepted the tests back from Dom. Adri needed a few minutes to talk to Mrs. Campbell, so I took the opportunity to pay Mrs. Sorenson a visit.

"More blank checks from the administration, Alec?"

At one point it'd bothered me that certain teachers took an instant, inexplicable dislike to me, but I'd long since chalked it up to something I couldn't control. If someone was determined to hate you there generally wasn't much you could really do about it.

"No, but I'd like to discuss Adriana Paige's grade in this class with you."

"That's none of your business, young man."

I felt a smile cross my features ever so briefly. Her pulse and breathing all but screamed that I was right. She was trying to hide the fact she'd been holding Adri to a different standard than the rest of the students.

"Be that as it may, I came across some information that causes me to worry about the quality of teaching in this school."

I held up the tests and sighed.

"I remember a fair amount about this section, Mrs. Sorenson, but more importantly I've noticed that John and Teresa's answers to several questions aren't substantially different than Adri's, but you marked hers wrong."

"How did you get those?"

"That's irrelevant. The question is what you're going to do about this? I'd hate to have to take these to the school board. Once I do that there'll be the inevitable witch hunt and who knows what they'll turn up, or what they'll do about it."

It always made me a little sick to threaten people's livelihoods, but the way her breathing spiked told me there were plenty of other discrepancies to turn up.

Her voice dropped to a pale shadow of its normal, arrogant tone.

"What do you want from me?"

"I just want you to do what you're paid to do. Go back and re-grade Adri's test the same way you graded the rest of them. Given how well she's doing in the rest of her classes I expect that you'll probably find her work deserves an A."

I left Mrs. Sorenson trembling at her desk and went straight to the Spanish classroom. Things were even easier there. Mrs. Tiggs had been skating on the brink of getting fired for years. I'd never had a class from her but even I knew she spent more time with the television on than she did actually teaching.

I met everyone out in the parking lot and smiled at how Adri's face lit up when she saw me. Despite all of the reasons to be worried or unhappy I spent the next hour or so in a pleasant haze as the pack crowded around the table in the informal dining room and consumed a respectable dinner.

Donovan caught my eye as I stood up from the table. I followed him back to his office and felt a surge of surprise as he flicked on the white noise generator that would shield our conversation from the ears of the rest of the pack.

"Master Alec, I hold you in the greatest of respect but feel I must caution you against what you're doing with the young lady."

I stomped on a flash of anger. It shouldn't be this hard to keep my temper, but for whatever reason it was harder to control myself when it came to Adri.

"I haven't even kissed her, Donovan. I haven't behaved in the slightest bit inappropriately."

Donovan made himself smaller, assuming a submissive pose in an attempt to help me leash the anger.

"I didn't mean to imply you had, Alec, but you need to understand what you're doing to her. You have strong feelings for her, it's only natural that you want to touch her, but it would be wrong to do so. You'll form the Ja'tell bond with her!"

His words slowed my wrath, providing something for reason to work on.

"You supported my father's decision to marry Mother. Out of the entire pack it was only you and Addison who did so. Why would you deny me Adri now?"

"You know how you feel about her, but do you really know how she feels about you? If you addict her to your touch before you truly know she loves you, you'll be no better than the drug dealers Jasmin ran out of town last year."

It was like I'd been struck a physical blow, one I reeled back from mentally as I tried to regain my footing.

"I never meant to harm her."

Donovan came forward and clasped me on the shoulder.

"I know, Alec, but the only way you'll be sure of her love is to keep her at arm's length. Otherwise you'll always wonder if she would have chosen differently but for the Ja'tell bond."

Chapter 27

I went through the rest of the evening in shock. Donovan had meant to slow the growth of my feelings but it had the opposite effect. I'd stopped denying my love for Adri inside the privacy of my own thoughts.

His efforts hadn't been entirely fruitless. I'd spent my entire life watching my mother pine over something she'd never have again. She'd loved my father, but she'd also been addicted to him. It was a potent combination that would never be replicated again, and so she lived out her remaining years a ghost in corporeal form.

I'd sworn never to do that to anyone. It'd supported me for years, kept me clear of any number of girls my age who'd been willing to throw themselves at me, but I'd forgotten my resolve in the rush of emotions Adri had awakened.

I went through my nightly ritual like a sleepwalker. I completed homework, grimly reviewed our far-flung enterprises with Donovan, and then dutifully endured my time on the machine.

Adri had spent most of that time with Dom studying her Spanish homework. I made myself scarce until the rest of the house retired to bed, and then finally returned to my room. I'd wanted desperately to spend the evening with her, but couldn't risk her normal ability to read me.

I watched her sleep for several minutes before finally showering and then lying down next to her. I salved my conscience by making sure there was a thin sheet between us, but couldn't silence the nagging suspicion that I was just too weak to cut myself off completely.

My retiring so late meant I woke up only a few minutes before Adri did. I was lying on my side gazing at her when her eyes first flickered open. I couldn't resist smiling at her, but her response was entirely unexpected. She smiled back and then moved in as though planning on a kiss.

I pulled back. I didn't want to, but I wasn't going to leave her a broken shell once I was gone. I avoided her advance and hoped her ESP was up and running enough to realize it wasn't that I didn't like her.

It was silly really. The quickest way to ensure I didn't destroy her with an uncontrollable addiction would be to ensure that she hated me, but I couldn't bring myself to do it.

The first half of the day proceeded in more or less the same fashion. Biology started off a little shaky, but I put Mrs. Sorenson to rights fairly quickly. Despite our conversation the night before she'd thought she could get away with grilling Adri again. I'd spent a few minutes before I finally went to bed reviewing the chapter we were going to be covering, so I promptly tripped her up and made her look foolish in front of the rest of the class.

After the second time it happened we lapsed into an uneasy silence. She left Adri alone and I stopped making her look like an idiot. We'd spent the rest of the class trading messages via Adri's notebook. I expected to be able to keep her distracted by asking her questions about herself, but partway through she'd gotten obstinate and refused to answer another unless I promised to begin answering hers in return.

I should have said no and just stopped asking her about herself but I needed to know where she'd come from, what had created the thoughtful, vulnerable person who more than ever had me wrapped around her finger.

The only thing I managed to hold over her was a promise to pack her onto a plane if she touched onto things that were better for her not to know. She seemed to take the threat seriously. She went back to answering my questions, and I tried to touch on everything I could think of short of the recent events that still haunted her.

I was surprised when the entire pack showed up during lunch to wait while Adri took her makeup test. Apparently she'd been behind from starting out the year late, and Mrs. Campbell expected her to make everything up.

It was hard to tell how much of the pack's support was because they genuinely liked Adri and how much of it was due to increased harassment from Brandon's pack. Dom, Rachel, and even Jasmin seemed to fall into the former category which was no less than Adri deserved.

I'd been considering the latter problem for a while but hadn't hit on any likely solutions. They still outnumbered us, but the actual balance of power had evened out when I'd killed Nathanial and Simon. If they poached our territory again we could probably kill more of them, but they'd been very careful to avoid provocations since I'd challenged Brandon.

We could always assume a more aggressive stance in our own patrols, but that'd decrease the pack's chance of survival when the Coun'hij finally decided to get involved.

I pushed the problem away long enough to watch as Adri handed her test in, had it graded on the spot and then all but jumped up and down as Mrs. Campbell put a large, red 'A' at the top of the paper.

The pack crowded around her, full of congratulations, and I somehow found myself holding her hand again. I regretfully let go as we finished up lunch, and then headed off to my English class.

Physics flew by with extra speed, almost as if to make up for the fact that each of the classes I didn't have with Adri now limped by with unbelievable slowness.

Mrs. Alexander was still absent, so we were able to spend the entire time conversing. I hit upon an unexpected nerve when I asked her about her best date. She instantly blushed and looked away as if afraid to meet my gaze. I waited a couple of seconds and then finally reached out and lifted her chin up so I could see her face.

"What's the matter, afraid I'll be jealous?"

She slowly shook her head, obviously wishing she could look back down.

"No, there isn't anything to be jealous of. I'd never been on a single date before Sanctuary, and you know all about what's happened since I arrived."

"That sounds like the easiest one I've asked you yet. Why the sudden bashfulness?"

She sat silently, her heart pounding erratically for several seconds and then finally looked away and whispered.

"Because I'm worried once you realize just how much of a loser I was back home, how much of a loser I still am, you'll decide you don't belong with me."

It boggled the mind that someone so attractive hadn't dated before coming to Sanctuary, but it hardly seemed like a cardinal sin.

"Why would you not dating very much have any impact on how I feel about you?"

"Because in addition to being the most thoughtful boy I've ever met, you also happen to be rich enough to buy a small country. You're so incredibly gorgeous girls swoon when you walk into a room. How can I possibly compete against the kinds of girls who'll continue throwing themselves at you for as long as you're breathing?"

She'd started out at a whisper, but quickly gotten louder. By the time she finished talking she was loud enough to cause heads to turn back and look at us. I probably should have been concentrating on calming her down, but whenever she got really animated she started talking with her hands, which triggered all kinds of pounce instincts.

I reached out and captured her hands before responding.

"Please don't do that. The fact you didn't date until recently doesn't mean you're some kind of nerd. Even if it did, that wouldn't matter to me. Also, other girls who may or may not find me attractive are irrelevant. I don't want them, I want you."

It was completely the wrong thing to say given that I was supposed to be giving her room to decide whether or not she really liked me, but the words just slipped out of their own accord. It was so startling I accidentally let go of one of her hands, which promptly began gesturing as she tried to come up with a response.

I stomped on the urge to snatch her hand out of the air, and instead gently recaptured it. It was obvious she didn't believe me, so I opted for the appearance of arrogance.

"It's okay that you don't believe me yet, I'm equal to the challenge of convincing you."

She chewed on my answer for a moment and then jumped backwards in the conversation.

"Don't do what?"

It was a second before I realized what she was talking about.

"Your hands, you tend to talk with them when you're excited or angry, and it's very distracting. I mean for us. All of the motion results in a hundred tiny signals flooding my brain as my instincts try to decide whether you're prey to be chased, or a bigger predator that I need to flee from."

Adri's eyes went so wide I worried maybe I'd actually scared her.

"Oh, I didn't realize it was a problem. I'll stop."

"It isn't actually that bad. More like an itch you can't quite reach. Although, if you ever want to drive Jessica absolutely crazy, spend a few minutes around her fidgeting. She's the most naturally high-strung out of anyone besides Jasmin. The fact she's also a submissive only makes things worse."

I could almost see the gears spinning inside her head. Even when she was thinking about being vindictive she still looked sweet. She looked up at me with an innocent smile.

"She won't eat me if I do that?"

"No. If you're really worried about it just make sure that one of the others are in the room at the same time with you."

"Now that has some real possibilities."

I found myself pulling her to her feet as the bell rang, and mentally castigated myself for indulging in physical contact. Dom had promised to meet us at Mrs. Tiggs class, so we stopped by our lockers and then I escorted Adri to Spanish. We were halfway there when Brandon and Vincent sauntered into view.

I casually shifted Adri around so I shielded her, but they split up as they drew nearer. It was a classic flanking maneuver, but that didn't make it any less effective. Brandon's arrogant smirk said that he knew exactly how limited my options were.

Vincent exuded anticipation, which only increased as Adri's pulse wound up. I held her up with one hand as we closed the rest of the distance between us and them. I could feel that she wanted to lag back, wanted to turn and run even, but the moment we showed that level of fear we'd be lost.

I angled towards Vincent as the hall all but emptied of other students. Predictably Vincent stationed himself exactly in our way. He stuck his hand out and placed it against my chest to stop our progress. He followed the contact up with a burst of energy.

"You're in our way, half-breed."

Reference to my mother was probably an implied threat to what they wanted to do to her once I was out of the way. It was all I could do to keep my hands from balling into crushing fists. The course I did pick wasn't the most prudent, but anger overwhelmed my normal decision-making ability.

I let my right hand manifest a half-hybrid shape that was achievable by only a few shape shifters. The long, semi-retractable claws sank into Vincent's chest just far enough to draw blood. It was still a calculated risk, but someone would have to come by in exactly the right spot to be able to see anything out of the ordinary around Vincent's sizable form.

I joined the physical threat with an unseen menace, letting a spike of power free itself from my being. It was nothing in comparison to what Brandon was capable of, but I didn't have to scare Brandon, and Vincent's expression indicated he was suddenly remembering just how mortal he was.

"You forget yourself, mutt. As the leader of another pack, I'm due more respect than that. Should you or your dominant wish to push things further, I guarantee that your heart will decorate the floor before he can come to your aid."

The calm words carried just far enough for Brandon to hear them, and he stopped moving as he began calculating the odds. He could kill me, but if I was really willing to take Vincent with me then the packs would once again be evenly matched.

Before Brandon could make his final decision Dominic came rushing around the corner. She wasn't Jasmin, but apparently she tilted the balance far enough in our direction.

I returned Brandon's lazy grin with a tight smile of my own as I returned my hand to normal and shoved Vincent back into his alpha.

"Now why would we do a thing like that when we all know you're a dead man?"

Brandon's smile had turned into something more threatening, but he wasn't about to act on the implied threat. Dominic stopped just outside of attack range of Brandon and gathered herself, but I waved her back.

"If I ever really decide the outcome is a foregone conclusion, you'd better start watching out for your people. You'd be surprised just how many of them could disappear if I no longer worried about the consequences of my actions."

Everyone greeted my announcement that the harassment was going to stop with relief, but they'd taken too much abuse during the course of the day to get very excited about it. As expected, Jess had taken some of the worst of it, which meant she was shooting both Adri and me nasty looks the entire way home.

By the time we finally pulled up to the house, it was all I could do to keep my shape in place. Donovan felt the tension arcing between the various members of the pack and offered to push dinner back, but I told him to proceed with plans as normal. I turned to leave and then paused and asked Adri if she'd accompany me out to the garden.

The invitation hadn't been something I'd been contemplating, but the craving for her company continued to grow the more time I spent with her. She followed me out to the northwest corner of the carefully-tended refuge and took a seat next to one of the reflecting pools.

I'd expected her to ask what was wrong. That was the usual girl response, but she just sat quietly for almost thirty minutes until I finally calmed down enough to put a true leash on my beast.

I looked over at her, absently toying with a stalk of grass, and felt something inside me push unplanned words out of my mouth.

"Will you do me the honor of allowing me to escort you to the Ashure Day festivities?"

Several minutes passed before she responded. I was half convinced that she was going to refuse me when she did finally turn back to me.

"Is this because of earlier? Because I told you I don't expect you to stay with me?"

I opened my mouth to respond to her and found a truth I hadn't realized before.

"I've actually wanted to ask you for quite a while. Hearing that Brandon was taking you was harder for me to accept than you might imagine. My asking you now has nothing to do with our conversation from earlier today."

"Why are you doing it now then? I half expected you to try and send me out of the country again. An invitation to the local equivalent to Prom was the last thing on my mind."

"My taking you to the dance is one of the more selfish things I could be doing. It represents so much of what I want, but is wrong for you on almost every level. I guess I've just decided I'm tired of trying to be good when I have so little time left."

"Why is that selfish? Most people would think you were being quite charitable taking the new girl to the big dance when you could have your pick of anyone in the school and half the females in the state."

She was so focused on everyone else she couldn't see how amazing she was, but it wouldn't do any good to try yet again to convince her. More important was ensuring that she understood what exactly was at stake. I reached over and took her hand, purposefully exposing her to the addictive sensation of my touch.

"Can you feel that? I mean, it feels good, doesn't it?"

She looked like she was going to giggle, but managed to keep a straight face as she stroked my hand.

"I think it's supposed to feel good, silly."

"Have you ever wondered about my mom? I mean, why she's the way she is?"

She was obviously confused; I waited as she looked for a way to respond.

"What do you mean? I've only met her the one time. She seemed normal enough. I guess a little distracted..."

I found myself laughing at her answer. It wasn't a happy sound, but I couldn't help myself.

"She's definitely distracted. You could even say utterly disconnected from the world. Completely free from the present, always living in the past."

"I don't understand how any of this ties together."

It seemed utterly cruel to come right out and say it, but she wasn't leaving me any other choice.

"It's all the same thing. Our touch, my touch, it's like a drug. It's addictive, subtly, so subtly most humans never even realize what is happening to them. I've seen what it's done to my mother. How can I say I love you if I turn around and do the same thing to you?"

Apparently I'd finally managed to break through the distraction of being so close to me.

She looked like she'd been struck. I waited once again for her to say something, but this time it seemed as though she wasn't going to find the words she was searching for. I could see the condemnation and mixed horror growing in her expression as she realized exactly what'd been done to my mother, what I'd been doing to her.

"We're where the legends of succubi originated. Irresistible demons who drain their victims dry, who leave their lovers a hollow shell of what they were before. Do you understand now? My getting closer to you is the ultimate form of self-gratification. It's the worst possible thing I could do to you. If you somehow survive everything that's about to happen, it would leave you forever hungering for another touch, but never able to fulfill that desire."

She shook herself as though awaking from a nap and placed a hand on my lips.

"None of that matters. All I want is to be with you, and if we're as likely to all die as you seem to think we are, then the state of my mind after you're gone is hardly something worth wasting worry on. I accept your invitation. As much as I hate the very thought of going to any formal dance, I can think of nothing better than going with you."

"That's the addiction, the Ja'tell bond talking."

She sighed in regret, or possibly frustration, as she released me and moved back several inches.

"There, I'm not touching you, and I still want to go to the dance with you. Want it more than anything else."

I knew I should tell her no, but I'd been willing, wanted even, to go when she hadn't known. Now that she understood and still wanted to go with me how could I do otherwise than take her? Only she didn't really understand, couldn't understand until it was too late.

"This is a mistake. The worst kind of mistake because we both know it's wrong and we don't care."

"I don't think it's a mistake. I don't even think it is wrong."

"But if you did, would you care?"

"Probably not, but that doesn't change the fact that this is what I want to do."

I should have said no, but we both knew I wouldn't, that I wasn't strong enough to do the right thing. I wouldn't have felt as guilty if I'd had a plan to get her away to safety. Instead all I could think about was just how little time we had left together.

Chapter 28

Rachel found me a short time after I asked Adri to the dance.

"Did you finally do it?"

"What are you talking about?"

She grinned up at me with a mischievous glimmer in her eyes.

"If you haven't done it already, you need to get a move on and ask Adri to the dance."

Rachel laughed at my shocked expression, waiting as I scrambled for an answer.

"How did you know I was going to do that?"

"That's easy, Alec. You needed to ask her. I could see it in a dozen different ways, but they all boiled down to the fact you couldn't be you and not go to the dance with her. We need to start making plans immediately. I bought a dress for her while we were down in Vegas, but we need a ton of other stuff. Oh my gosh, I forgot to get her shoes!"

I stopped Rachel before she could run away in a panic.

"I think I can take care of the shoes, sis. Just don't say anything to her."

She looked for a minute like she thought I was coming down with something, but instead of reaching up to take my temperature she shrugged and skipped away to find Adri.

Donovan was my next stop. He wasn't exactly ecstatic about the implications of the fairly large donation I'd asked him to make to the community committee tasked with organizing the Ashure Day festivities, but it hadn't been the amount that'd bothered him.

The family assets had long since grown past the point where a mere forty thousand dollars really meant anything. The sum wouldn't even dent the interest we'd receive this quarter off the main operating bank account.

The donation wasn't even entirely out of character. The family had been making donations to fund the Ashure Day festivities for as long as there'd been a Sanctuary, but the size was more than enough to tip him off as to what I'd done.

In the end though Donovan was loyal to the family, and he'd see that the arrangements were made. I left him muttering something about ensuring proper dancing, and then went to find Adri.

The next few days passed with a blur only matched by the joy of spending so much time with Adri. Left up to her, we'd have completely skipped school, but I hadn't entirely resigned myself to causing her death. If she somehow survived what was coming, I wanted to leave her with something more than failing grades and bitter memories.

In our downtime I drilled her mercilessly on Biology. Dominic was doing much the same, although taking a gentler approach, with Spanish. Any time we weren't studying, or otherwise spending time with each other, I was with the rest of the pack sparring, or by myself lifting weights.

I searched desperately for something that might give me an edge in the fight against Brandon, but in the short amount of time we had left there was nothing that promised to serve as a true equalizer.

I'd studied with a number of different martial arts instructors over the years, but most of them weren't capable of anything more than parroting the exact things they'd learned from their teachers. I needed someone who truly understood the underlying principles to fighting, but even that wouldn't help very much. The joints and reach of a hybrid were just too alien to the human body and the fighting systems developed for it. I'd already seen that creating new reflexes optimized for my human body wouldn't serve me well when in my other forms.

It was part of why Jasmin was able to mop the floor with anyone else in the pack in a fight involving our wolf form. She worked exclusively in that form and was able to react without thinking with exactly the right response to almost any situation. James, Isaac and I on the other hand invariably didn't commit strongly enough when on four legs.

We were too used to the movement, the sudden slashes and lightning strikes of hybrid combat. We'd see the appropriate opening, but not take it where Jasmin lunged in without even considering the fact that a miss would mean she was dead.

Without any other options, I'd spent hour after hour sparring with Isaac and James, but there was only so much you could learn from fighting the same two opponents when they were your same skill level.

It made me long for the days of Jaldul. In addition to breaking the southern shape shifters at roughly the current-day border with Mexico, he'd created a school for his sons and his most loyal hybrids.

It was one of the many things that'd fallen apart with his death. We'd become little more than barbarians. Each pack passed on the tricks and techniques they learned over the centuries, but when a pack was as decimated as ours had been, relatively little expertise survived.

Mallory hadn't been able to demonstrate any techniques, but at least she'd been able to describe them to me. It wasn't much, but it was part of the reason we'd survived against Brandon's larger pack as long as we had.

I'd expected the infighting among our pack to get worse as we got closer to Ashure Day, but instead it seemed as though everyone made their peace with what was coming. There was no telling how much James' mother had come through on her promise to calm him down, but he'd settled into a grudging acceptance that we were all likely to die. Even Jasmin had stopped haring off unpredictably.

If the pack had been one bit more unsettled I never would have agreed to let Adri come to one of our last remaining training sessions, but they weren't and I couldn't deny her. We'd been in my room reviewing her Biology when she'd looked up at me with those clear blue eyes and all but begged to be let a little further inside our terrifying world.

I never really had a chance, but once I'd agreed, I put in place as many safeguards as I was able, and made sure I'd have plenty of time to wear the rest of the pack out before she arrived. We went up to the north end of the estate where the two spurs that cradled the family land came back in and attached themselves to the mountain.

It was our usual spot, deep enough in that stray hikers wouldn't chance upon us, just like the unusually dense canopy also served as protection from discovery by flyovers. The trees had been planted almost simultaneous to the original pack's arrival in what came to be known as Sanctuary. It showed astonishing foresight for a time when the idea of human flight had been so fantastic as to be completely unbelievable.

TORN

Once we'd all arrived and discarded our normal forms I set James and Jessica in particular against each of the other pack members in turn in an effort to wear them down to tractability before Adri arrived.

The half hour passed incredibly quickly. It seemed only moments before Donovan was leading her into view. The breeze had been out of the north all day, so her arrival came as a complete surprise to everyone but me. The other five turned to watch her hesitant progress up the cultured gravel path, but I spared only the briefest of glances for her. My attention had to be on the pack, and I'd felt my beast roar up with surprising strength at the prospect of Adri being injured.

Donovan led her to within twenty feet of the sandy square Jasmin jokingly referred to as 'Donovan's Zen garden.' Jess had been tensing up with each step that Adri took towards us, but when she growled I struck out before my conscious, human mind realized what was happening.

I managed to turn my hand, catching her with the back of my fist rather than the deadly claws that otherwise would have disemboweled her, but even so I sent her flipping end over end with a yelp of pain that brought Isaac around with alarming speed.

I'd counted on Isaac's control withstanding whatever it took to keep Jessica in line, and for several seconds I thought things were going to devolve into a bloody mess, but Jess rolled back to her feet, apparently no worse for the wear, and Isaac calmed back down to something more near his usual demeanor.

The threat of sudden death having lapsed, I turned back to Adri and felt a pang of concern over how she would respond. This was the first time she'd seen this form since I'd killed Simon and Nathanial, and there was still a chance she'd run away screaming.

Dom slowly passed Jessica, who was pacing back and forth with her hackles raised. Adri gasped slightly as two hundred pounds of midnight-furred jaguar slowly stalked towards her, and I let a low growl make its way out of my throat.

Everyone was well aware of just what would happen if they harmed Adri, but Dom was the only one I'd have let get even that close to her. Dom dropped to the ground at the sound, rolling onto her back in a clear display of submissiveness as she looked back at me for permission to proceed.

I let her remain for several seconds before finally nodding. I could have spoken, but I found myself oddly unwilling to speak around Adri in this form. Maybe if I could keep this me and the other me safely compartmentalized she'd be able to continue to ignore the savage animal that didn't belong in her world.

Moving with caution so as not to spook either Adri or I, Dom stood up and walked over to Adri. She reared up onto her back legs, rested her paws on Adri's shoulders so that they could look each other in the eyes, and then walked around Adri, reminiscent of a common house cat in the way she rubbed up against Adri's legs.

Adri didn't really relax until Dom butted her head up against Adri's quivering hand. An obviously bewildered Adri watched as Dom then bounded away to change shapes.

Dom could no more speak in her cat form than Jess or Jasmin could as wolves. The hybrids being able to speak was one of the few advantages we'd had over the southerners. Body language could communicate an awful lot, but it still left room for the kind of misunderstandings that led to people killing each other.

With no 'generals' among their ranks to serve as voice for the pack, the cats had reverted to a solitary existence. All of South America was a complete snake pit and had been for years. The last feline uprising had been put down by unknowing Spanish conquistadors who'd done the weakened wolves an incredible favor. Most of us prayed every day that there wouldn't be another one in our lifetimes. There were plenty of other things that needed killing without us wasting ourselves killing cousins.

My thoughts served as a distraction until Dom reappeared, gingerly picking her barefoot way back to the sand. She had shoes on the other side of the court, but it was typical of Dom not to want to make anyone else wait on her.

Donovan gave both two-legged ladies a bow, nodded to the rest of us, and then retreated back towards the house and the mountain of duties awaiting him there.

Confident that Dom could handle Jess if she tried anything, I turned back to Isaac and James and motioned them to begin.

The rest of the sparring session went about like normal. We practiced every permutation of wolf against wolf, hybrid against hybrid and wolf against hybrid before moving to uneven groupings where one of us was up against more than one opponent.

The three hybrids were careful to use fists instead of claws, but even so things got heated nearly every fight. James could be counted on to lose his temper anytime things didn't go his way, and Jasmin and Jess weren't much better.

I took nearly as much damage separating combatants when things boiled over as I did when it was my turn to spar. I was careful to stay between the rest of the pack and Adri, but the worries proved to be for naught. It was a tired, bloody group that finally shifted back to human form, pulled shoes on and then walked back to the house carrying their clothes.

Adri had been exceptionally quiet on the way back through the tall hedge maze that Andrew and Donovan took such pains to maintain. It wasn't unusual for her to spend fairly significant chunks of time quietly thinking though, so I didn't worry until it extended through dinner. It only took a few minutes of thought to realize the likely cause of her mood.

The sight of the five of us fighting had finally been too much, and she'd realized we really were monsters. I'd been too busy to listen to her conversation with Dom, but maybe there'd been some indicator there.

I was sitting on the bed, waiting while she changed in the bathroom when the realization struck me. I was still looking for the right words when she came out clad in her usual shorts and tank top.

She paused momentarily before the massive, two-handed sword hanging from my wall, and then went silently to the bed and took her usual spot on the left side. I turned the lights off, and then went back and stretched out next to her.

"Alec, what's the sword for?"

Past experience had shown she didn't always remember our conversations when she got this tired. Still, it wasn't the kind of thing I should be telling her.

"It was forged in the days of Jaldul. He was the first king over the northern shape shifters, the wolves. Our people were strong and fast, but we were faced with enemies who were still stronger and faster. The king feared his people and the dayborn he'd been charged with guarding would be destroyed, so he ordered the creation of swords that could be wielded by the hybrids, and they swept their enemies away before them."

She was quiet for so long that I almost thought she'd fallen asleep. When she did speak her words were quiet, almost indistinct.

"Why don't you use it in your fight with Brandon?"

I suddenly felt every blow I'd taken over the last several days of sparing. I'd been tired before, but now it was as if even breathing was too much effort for my battered body.

"I'm not really trained in its use. My father was the last of the royal line who could have trained me. More than that though, it's been outlawed. It's a symbol of nobility in a world where depravity now rules. I can keep it as an artifact of ancient times, but to take it out and wield it in battle would be a death sentence for the entire pack."

Adri sighed in puzzlement but didn't comment so I continued.

"Even the beasts it was created to destroy have become untouchable. It really is nothing more than a relic of the ancient, dying past. Not even worth an equivalent weight of scrap metal."

Adri turned her face slowly towards me but didn't open her eyes.

"It's not worthless because it reminds you of what you need to do, of who you really are. I trust you. You always do the right thing, no matter the cost."

She'd slipped into true slumber which precluded further conversation, but I remained where I was nevertheless. She'd once again said exactly what I needed to hear.

We hid now for fear of humanity, its countless numbers and terrible technology. It hadn't always been that way. Once we'd protected them because might was responsibility, we'd had the ability and accepted the obligation.

The exhaustion was gone. I'd still need to sleep before the night was over, but I no longer felt the leaden listlessness that'd nearly overcome me just minutes earlier. I quietly rolled out of bed and padded across the carpet towards my studio.

I might not have time to finish this particular piece, but it was pulling at me, demanding to be brought into being. It would be the crowning achievement of my life so far, but at least I'd have my subject close at hand for the short time remaining me.

Chapter 29

It'd become almost painful to be separated from Adri. I'd driven myself away from her long enough each day to take care of the most important of my duties, but it was becoming harder and harder.

Ashure Day dawned clear and sunny. By the time the pack finally finished a light training session I was trembling like a heroin addict two days into forced abstinence. I raced ahead of everyone else and returned to find Adri studying in my room.

Her smile warmed the icy spot in my chest that woke each day convinced she was going to finally decide it was time to leave while she still could.

"How was training?"

The lilting sound of her voice pulled me back from the mental precipice.

"Fairly well, all things considered. We took it easy though..."

It was more and more work to keep her in the dark regarding things like the Coun'hij and the bloodsucker plague that was slowly taking over the eastern seaboard. She read me more easily even than Donovan or Rachel. She knew I was leaving stuff out, but didn't press me anymore.

"Only you would come back dripping in sweat and say you took it easy."

The mischievous curl to her lips pulled at me in ways that felt simultaneously good and bad. I nearly reached out to her, but instead shook my head in resignation.

"I don't know what I'd have done without you these last few weeks."

She didn't respond, so I changed the subject before things could get awkward.

"How's your homework coming?"

The question earned me a frown. "I think my mind's going to explode if I look at my Biology book even just one more time this weekend. Other than that things are great."

Only Adri could manage melodrama without becoming ludicrous. I chuckled almost despite myself. I'd convinced myself that taking Adri with me to see Mallory would be the wrong thing to do, but now that I was here with less than twelve hours until the challenge match, I couldn't bring myself to be parted from her again.

"I take it you'd be up for a brief field trip then?"

She perked up just like Rachel at the mention of shopping.

"A field trip sounds great. Except I have to be back at least three hours before the dance, or

Rachel and Jasmin will eat me. At least that's what they said, and I tend to believe them."

She was so casual about it all that I couldn't help myself. This time I did reach out and run a finger along the side of her face.

"Only you could manage to make a joke out of having fallen in with monsters."

She shrugged easily. "What else is a girl to do?"

I returned the shrug as I headed towards the bathroom.

"Be that as it may, I think you don't give yourself enough credit for just how amazing you are."

I hadn't realized Adri had never been on my motorcycle with me. She'd spent the entire time I was in the shower chomping at the bit ready to go, and then almost backed out when I took her out to the bike. She tried so hard to be brave that I didn't have the heart to tell her that it was obvious she was terrified of the low-slung sports bike.

I started to give her a way out, but she pulled the helmet out of my hand and crammed it onto her head with hands that had only the barest trace of a tremble. I took the first part of the drive well under the speed limit, and then as I felt her start to relax and lean into the turns with me, cranked it up to triple digits.

Once we were at something closer to my normal speed the rest of the trip passed quickly, and all too soon we'd arrived at the abandoned shed I used to hide the bike. I felt a brief surge of disappointment as her hands loosened around my waist and she leaned back. It had been a rare moment of guilt-free contact. There'd been plenty of clothes between our skin and consequently no risk of increasing the Ja'tell bond.

I killed the power to the bike and then listened for several seconds for any sound of pursuit.

"Are we here?"

"Disappointed?"

She blushed, but stuck her tongue out. I suppressed a grin and shook my head.

"No, we're not quite there yet, but before we continue on, I need your promise not to discuss this with anyone. Not even the rest of the pack."

As always, her scent told the story her face was so good at hiding. She was a little offended that I felt like I needed to remind her, and, unless I was very mistaken, starting to get the least bit dehydrated. I fished around the magnetically attached tank bag and pulled out a bottle of water for her.

"I'm sorry, Adriana. I know I can depend on you, this is just important enough that I needed to make sure you understood what's riding on your discretion."

She took a long pull from the bottle and nodded.

"I won't say anything. What exactly are we going to see?"

"Not a what, but a who."

I carefully picked her up and shifted her around so she was riding piggyback. It put her arms in contact with my neck, but the touch couldn't be avoided. It would take more than half an hour for us to make the journey at merely human speeds.

A couple of minutes later I pulled up in front of Mallory's cabin and felt the first pang of remorse at bringing Adri. I knew she wouldn't betray my trust, but the secret I was including her in wasn't just mine.

Donovan had left a sealed envelope on his desk with my name on it, but for all of his preternatural abilities of anticipation he couldn't have expected that I'd endanger Mallory like this.

I loosened my grip on Adri and helped her slide down to the ground. I steadied her, and then watched as she looked around, finally noticing the cabin, set well back into the mouth of the cave so as to blend into the hillside.

Her expression of pure delight at the discovery helped banish some of my fears and I walked over and knocked on Mallory's door. Mallory's characteristic shuffle sounded from inside and then she appeared wearing a simple blue dress Donovan had ordered for her last year.

She gave me a hug, and then stepped back so she could look up at me without craning her neck and pulling on the scar tissue that laced the front of her throat.

My worries that she'd be angry with me for bringing Adri evaporated as she flashed a dazzling smile and carefully moved back out of the way so we could enter.

"Mallory, I'd like to introduce you to Adriana Paige. Adriana, Mallory."

Adri smiled hesitantly as she offered Mallory her hand.

"I'm very happy to finally get to meet you, young lady. Alec is better company than most, but it's nice to have a new face around here."

I helped both ladies into two of the worn chairs in Mallory's living room, and then nodded at Mallory's command.

"You go ahead and do your chores. We girls will just get to know each other, and then once you're done, you can bring me up to speed on the latest developments."

Donovan had arranged a food drop a few days before, so I went around behind the cabin and picked up the heavy bar and two baskets that would allow me to carry more than would easily fit in my arms.

The food cache was replenished on a semi-regular basis by a driver from out of town. He had strict orders to come from the opposite direction. It was a brutal four-hour drive over some fairly rough terrain, but he was paid very well, and had a significant amount of money set aside in escrow. As long as no rumors were ever circulated about his activities he continued to draw a substantial bonus each year. If he ever said anything about his trips it would eventually make it back to Donovan and his golden goose would dry up overnight.

So far the arrangement had served to keep Mallory's existence a secret shared by a grand total of three people. Four, now that Adri knew.

I set out at a brisk pace, not a run, not with nearly one hundred pounds of metal balanced across my shoulders, but something that would allow me to cover ground fairly quickly. I found the food in short order. We'd set a heavy-duty steel box, almost a mini-shipping container, back inside one of the caves where it would be safe from observation.

The task was one I'd done hundreds of times, and I loaded up the baskets with practiced efficiency. I picked them up to check the balance and found that they weren't as heavy as I'd expected. I added another forty pounds to each basket and then lifted the burden and headed back toward Mallory's.

I heard Mallory's voice as I took the first load around to the back of her cabin and unloaded it in the steel vault we'd installed last year. It wasn't especially convenient for her, but it more than doubled her pantry space; and if the worst happened, I wanted her to be provided for as long as possible.

Donovan had set aside enough money to ensure that the deliveries continued well beyond Mallory's likely death, but there was no reason to force her to take the journey out to the cache any sooner than she had to. The wounds Agony had inflicted left her unable to lift heavy objects, so she'd be reduced to moving the food stores one or two cans at a time.

From my position at the back of the cabin I could make out her words.

"Nonsense. If I am kind, it's no doubt because of those very experiences that I would've been the most desperate to avoid. I think most of the best people are that way exactly because of the things they've endured. Individuals like Dominic, Rachel, and Jasmin don't just happen. They're the result of a native goodness being tempered and refined by terrible experiences."

The baskets once again empty, I headed back outside for a second trip. I'd made more of a dent in the stores than I'd realized. I was going to be able to carry the rest of the delivery in one load. It was heavy enough that the baskets creaked only slightly louder than my shoulders, but it all fit.

Adri looked so amazed when I carefully maneuvered the load through the door into Mallory's cabin that I decided almost twisting my ankle on the way back had been worth it. I gently set the baskets down and went to unload them as Mallory shook her head.

"That was almost as quick as normal."

I nodded absently as I opened the pantry door and started putting cans away.

"I've been lifting weights for a while, but present circumstances dictated a more aggressive program."

Mallory clucked at me and waved me over to the couch.

"You'll put them in the wrong spots. Just leave that, and I'll put it away later. Don't go all mulish on me, I may be old and feeble, but I'm still able to move a can of food. Come over here and let me look at you."

She was right, we didn't have much time. There was a limit to how long of an absence I could explain away the day of the fight. I suddenly felt as though I was weighed down with the entire food shipment at one time.

I slowly crossed the distance between us as I pulled Donovan's letter from my pocket. More than the food, or even the letter, this was the reason we'd come out here. There was little if any counsel she could give me at such a late date. All that remained was to lay the last bit of hope to rest; to verify that my latent power hadn't manifested.

Mallory gently accepted Donovan's letter and then waited as I knelt before her. She placed a hand on each side of my head and then called for her beast.

Mallory's power seemed to arc back and forth like an electrical discharge, and then she released me and sat back. I slowly looked up at her, but wasn't truly surprised when she shook her head at me.

I suppressed the disappointment that would just make her feel like she'd failed me. I must not have succeeded, or possibly she just knew me well enough to know exactly what must be going through my mind. She reached out as if to comfort me, but I gently returned her hands to her lap.

"Nothing's changed. We'll just proceed as before. Rest now, and should the worst come to pass I'll send Donovan to you."

It was unlikely, and we both knew it. Donovan would be loath to leave my mother, even for the woman he'd risked death for so many years before, but I'd give the order and leave it up to him to choose.

For the first time I felt a glimmer of understanding at what he must go through. It was a terrible thing to be forced to choose between your duty and the thing you wanted most in the world.

Chapter 30

Rachel hustled Adri off as soon as we returned. Based on the stern look she shot me one would have been justified in thinking that I'd shown up fifteen minutes before we were supposed to leave rather than with nearly three hours to spare.

I watched the pair of suddenly giggling girls disappear around the corner and then followed the hall to my bedroom. Rachel had already laid my tux out on the bed. I'd reviewed the expenditures sheet Donovan had brought by for approval at the end of the credit card cycle, so I knew it had cost more than some small cars, but Rachel had been adamant that nothing less would do.

At first look it seemed like a fairly straightforward standard black tux, but the material was something I'd never seen before. Almost shiny, but not really, it managed to create a sense of depth that reminded me of what I should be doing rather than standing around staring at my outfit.

I pulled a pair of old, paint-stained jeans on and headed into my studio with a frantic haste that only grew as the minutes passed. Everyone had opted for privacy after the dance, dealing with their fears or anxiety in various ways, but I'd decided it was the last chance I was going to get to do the right thing and convince Adri to leave town.

Every item needed to be perfect to guarantee she'd understand just what she'd be giving up if she didn't flee to safety. Donovan had already taken care of most of the details. The lights were already set up in the grotto, and I'd slipped out before the sun came up and made a few last-minute adjustments to the illumination. The flowers had already been moved out of the green house and arranged to perfection, which left only one last piece lacking.

I pulled out my paints, quickly mixed them to the shades I needed, and set about filling in more of the details. The grotto had been easy, I'd been there thousands of times under nearly every conceivable condition, and my memory allowed me to recreate it in near perfect exactness.

As always Adri was the hardest piece to translate into mere two dimensions. I could close my eyes and see her in glowing perfection, hands outstretched towards me in concern, but her beauty didn't translate exactly to such an imperfect medium.

The silvery light of the moon blended with the unearthly glow of her skin, turning her into a creature constructed of shadows and light, but that wasn't the difficult part.

The sound of the girls laughing while they did each other's hair and makeup had been a distraction, but one I'd been unwilling to give up. Someone turned on their white noise generator and the chance of hearing Adri talked disappeared, taking with it the last reason to allow myself distractions.

I flipped on my own privacy box, and let the white noise lull me into a trance-like state where I at least had a small chance of recapturing her expression. Acceptance, compassion and a near saint-like desire to mend wounds were all there along with a host of others that even after a month's time I couldn't interpret.

I threw myself into the work, and the minutes spun away into hours. Donovan had to knock on the studio door to finally break me from the mania of my work.

"Master Alec, you'll be late! Go now and shower. I'll clean up your brushes and ensure that the piece is set out in the grotto, safely protected from the elements."

I nodded, handing him my brush and palette as I left the room without looking back. I'd failed. Only a pale sliver of her perfection had been captured, but it was the best of which I was capable and there was no time to dwell on the failure.

Donovan was right concerning the lateness of the hour. I showered and dressed with as much speed as I was able. The tux went on, feeling only slightly too snug, and the next thing I knew I was folding the green pocket square that Rachel promised exactly matched Adri's dress. I was ready.

Before I left I reached deep into the back of my closet and pulled out three shoe boxes, two brand new, one battered with more than seventeen years of age. The new shoes were there as nothing more than insurance despite being incredibly expensive, custom pieces. If the fates smiled down on us, Adri would perfectly fit the originals that the newer pairs had been so carefully designed to reproduce.

Donovan was waiting impatiently outside of the South Receiving Room. As soon as I came around the corner, still hidden from view of those inside, he strode out into the room and cleared his throat with a slight half-bow.

"The gentlemen have at long last arrived."

Isaac followed on Donovan's heels, obviously concerned about Jessica. I caught only the barest flash of a black tux with understated silver threads worked throughout before he disappeared into the room.

James had been pacing back and forth. He'd probably much rather have been out tuning up his car, or possibly watching re-runs on the TV, but in an effort not to disappoint Dom he'd donned a tux as well. It was the kind of edgy thing Rachel never managed to get anyone else into, but James already felt like a laughingstock, so once he was finally convinced that dressing up was called for he usually let Rachel cram him into whatever she wanted.

The number of times that had happened were incredibly few and always corresponded to something particularly important to Dom. Whatever else might be said about James, he was very careful to keep Dom happy, which said more about his character than almost anything else.

I took a deep breath, set the newer boxes down on a nearby table, and followed James out into the receiving room. The girls were all even prettier than normal. A small corner of my attention checked to make sure Rachel had picked something suitably modest, which her mauve formal was, but mostly I just stared at Adri.

She was dressed in a strapless green dress that perfectly matched the accessories Rachel had selected for me. It was simple, while still managing to appear frothy and delicate, and I felt my pulse speed up as I took in the perfectly proportioned body it displayed to incredible advantage.

Jessica, in a silver sleeveless dress, and Dom in a form-fitting red gown both turned away from their dates for just a moment to watch as Adri smiled at my appearance, and then I'd crossed the distance between us.

Adri looked wonderfully dazed for just a moment as I took her hand and brushed my lips across the back of it. It took her several seconds to focus down on the opened box I'd brought with me.

"Rachel said you needed some shoes."

I went down to one knee and pulled the left shoe out, carefully slipping it onto Adri's foot while she was still contemplating the way the light played off of the nearly transparent surface. She absently shifted her weight over and let me slide the other shoe onto her right foot, and then looked down at me with bright eyes.

"They're perfect. Thank you."

Before I could respond Rachel hurried over and smiled at the sight of Adri in Mom's shoes. She leaned in and whispered despite the fact that everyone in the room would still be able to hear her.

"Mom wore those to the Ashure Day Dance, the one where she fell in love with Dad."

Adri pulled back as if to protest but I refused to relinquish my grasp on her hand.

"She wanted you to wear them. They were meant to be worn again tonight."

I offered Adri my arm as she nodded in acquiescence, and followed Jasmin out to the limo. As always she cut a beautiful figure, this time in a blue-streaked backless black dress with matching gloves. She and Rachel were the only ones without escorts, so I was relieved to see her smile at Adri before exiting the room.

The car was waiting for us. Donovan had spared no expense, importing an SUV-based stretch limo from Vegas. I helped Adri up into the car and then everyone else piled in behind us.

Rachel of course was excited about the wet-bar, but she knew better than to argue when I shook my head at her. Once she was old enough to legally drink she could make that decision, but until then it was off limits, especially in public.

She got her parting jab in though by leaning into Adri and stage whispering.

"Stupid shape shifters. None of them can get drunk, so they deprive the rest of us of the best parts of being young and stupid."

Jasmin rolled her eyes at Rachel as she fidgeted with the shoulder-length gloves. I had just a moment to wonder why she was wearing the gloves when she so obviously didn't like them, and then we were pulling up to the city park.

The dance committee had done a good job with the donation Donovan had arranged. The central, covered pavilion had been transformed into something that belonged in another world.

Hundreds of soft lights and dozens of candles, moving only slightly in the still night air, cast a multi-pointed glow over the area. Liberal bolts of silk had been hung from nearly every surface, turning the diffuse light into a sourceless glow that seemed to come from everywhere.

Well off to the west, only just audible over the hum of conversations, I could hear the burble of the town's one and only free-flowing stream.

TORN

Conversations died away as the rest of the town turned to watch our party disembark from the limo, but each member of the pack was more than used to being stared at. The humans never really understood why they felt slightly different around us, but nearly all of them responded to their instincts, and almost unconsciously excluded us on a day-to-day basis. This was just that exclusion written large for the evening.

Adri clutched at my arm in nervousness but I placed my left hand over hers and let the calming influence of the Ja'tell bond begin to work on her as we walked up to the greeters.

I handed the aged couple at the 'door' tickets for the entire party, and then we were inside and the illusion was complete. Adri gasped slightly, and then pulled at my arm until I'd bent close enough for her to whisper.

"That was you, wasn't it?"

"What if it was?"

"It's too much. I mean it's really nice, incredibly gorgeous in fact, but it must have cost you a fortune."

I felt a smile tug at my lips as I shrugged in supposed indifference. Despite knowing we had amazingly keen hearing, she continued to treat me like a normal person. It was illusion, but a welcome one. Being able to communicate with the rest of the pack while the humans around us remained unaware was too valuable of a tool to pass up, but for a moment I wondered if things would have been different if we'd kept up the illusion between ourselves instead of just for our neighbors.

Adri was still looking up at me, and half a dozen responses warred for prominence. The donation had been but a small part of the effort that went into the night, but that wasn't what I found myself saying.

"A paltry sum if it helps ensure a perfect night for you."

"You've done so much. I mean the dress, the shoes, and now this. Thank you, but you really shouldn't have."

How many girls would have remained grounded enough to say that? Dom certainly, Rachel, Jasmin, but not Jess, and no more than a couple of others I could think of in the entire school. Definitely not a Cassie or a Britney.

I smiled once again and bent down to whisper into her ear.

"I'm glad you like it. The fact that everyone else gets to participate is nice, but really it's all for you. Of course I did make a couple of stipulations."

The commencement of the music simplified the explanation of what those stipulations were, and I gently brought her into my arms and began the waltz-like dance that had been part of Ashure Day for more centuries than humanity had possessed written language.

It was enough different from a normal waltz that most girls couldn't have kept up, but Adri just relaxed in my arms and let me spin her around the room in a blur of green perfection. The rest of the pack fell in around us, James and Dom, Jess and Isaac, while Jasmin danced with Rachel.

Jas looked surprisingly disappointed. I knew it wasn't because of Adri, she'd demonstrated that earlier. I was missing something there. I filed the thought away as Adri became comfortable enough with the steps to talk.

"You're all such good dancers. How did that happen?"

I looked around at the rest of the pack and then spun her out and back in.

"Donovan has very inflexible standards when it comes to some things. Dancing happens to be one of them. In fact, I don't think I'll ever forget the expression on Jasmin's face when he told her she could go clubbing all she wanted *after* he judged her suitably proficient in real dancing. He said he wouldn't have her 'seduced by throbbing beats and soulless contact' before he'd at least exposed her to proper dance steps."

Adri cut off a giggle before it could truly escape and then shook her head in wonder.

"That's amazing. My dad thought knowing how to dance would make my first dance easier. It turned out to be a complete waste of time. Nobody asked me to dance and his lessons wouldn't have helped even if they had. Still, now I wish I'd done a better job of learning."

There it was. We'd tip-toed around the subject of her father for days, but the sickly, desperate scent she'd assumed each time he was mentioned had largely subsided. It was foolish to worry about helping her come to terms with her loss when we only had a few more hours together, but I found myself trying regardless.

"I don't suppose either of us talk about our dads much. I'm not pushing, but if you ever need to talk about him, about what happened, I'll listen. I'll even try to suppress the natural male instinct to present advice or solutions."

She instantly turned to wood in my arms. I had to pull her closer to prevent her from falling as we completed the last few seconds of the dance. She seemed to relax slightly into me as the music stopped, but it was obvious I'd made a mistake.

I cast about for something safe to say as the music changed to something Donovan wouldn't have approved of.

"Sorry, the stipulation was two decent songs, and then the DJ could play three of whatever he was in the mood for."

"It's okay, I actually need to sit down for a minute."

Completely at a loss for what else to do, I led her over to where Jasmin and Rachel had staked out a number of seats. Rachel looked up with a sigh of frustration as we approached.

"Big brother, will you please take Jasmin out on the dance floor so she can get some practice following? I tried to lead last time and she kept tripping me."

Jasmin was my oldest friend, but the last thing I wanted to do was leave Adri if she was on the point of a panic attack. I sampled her scent at the same time I listened for the telltale signs in her pulse and breathing.

Adri looked up to meet my gaze, and flashed a nearly-convincing smile as she waved me off, so I nodded and offered Jasmin my arm. As we walked out to the dance floor, I could hear Rachel and Adri conversing.

"I swear she's going to explode..."

Whatever else Rachel said was drowned out as Jasmin cocked her head at me.

"You don't have to do this you know. I'm fine."

Her voice was wrong, too loud, and rushed slightly, but she met my questioning gaze with a truculent set to her chin.

"I really will be fine. Rachel's great company and it isn't fair for me to steal you away from Adri."

I shook my head as we picked up the timing of the music and launched into the East Coast routine that we'd learned back when it'd been a minor form of rebellion against Donovan.

"I don't mean to neglect you, Jas. You, Rachel, me. We've been the odd ones out ever since Dom showed up and paired off with James. I shouldn't let what I feel about Adri get in the way of my friendship with you. It's not fair to leave you and Rachel alone all of the time."

I'd spoken nothing more than the obvious truth, but hadn't expected the strength of Jasmin's reaction. She missed the timing on her spin out, and suddenly looked as though she wanted to run back to the seats.

The music sped up slightly and I led her through the next few movements of our routine before she got herself back under control. Almost anyone else wouldn't have realized anything was wrong, but I'd known Jasmin her entire life. I'd been the one she'd run to when her dad had gotten high and turned into a monster.

I'd been the one to tell Donovan about the bruises and scrapes, and ultimately it'd been me who'd taken responsibility for her once she was orphaned and homeless. You couldn't spend that many years with someone, even just as friends without coming to know them on levels that nobody else did.

"Jas, what's wrong?"

"Nothing. I told you already. I'm fine."

I shook my head as we launched into the last quarter of the song in a blur of steps that only Isaac and Jess would have had any chance of matching, but Jasmin steadfastly refused to meet my gaze. When she finally spoke again, she was subvocalizing, much too quiet for those around to hear over the music.

"You're going to send her away tonight, aren't you?"

It was my turn to miss a cue, but it shouldn't have surprised me that she'd anticipate my intentions.

"I have to. We're going to die tonight and the only way to guarantee her safety is to get her out of town."

"But you're not planning on bringing her back if you win?"

Something inside me withered as I realized Jas was right. I hadn't ever thought that far because I'd never expected to survive the night, but I couldn't bring her back, couldn't expose her to the level of danger she'd be in once the Coun'hij found out about her.

Jasmin watched my thoughts stutter across my face and then shook her head.

"Don't send her away. She needs to be here as much as you need her to be here."

"Jas, you were the one who said I shouldn't have saved her in the first place."

The song was nearing the end, but Jasmin clung to me with incredible strength, momentarily refusing to be led.

"I was wrong, Alec. Sending her away would be a terrible thing for both of you. I don't want to see you pining away after something you want more than anything else, something you can never have."

There was a raw, bleeding pain to her voice that I'd never heard from Jasmin. She'd taken the worst abuse her father had been able to dish out and dried the tears away as soon as the pain had left. This was something else. Something new, or possibly just buried deeper than anything else she'd ever shown me.

The music ended and she released me, but her eyes pleaded with me to understand as she turned and headed back to Rachel and Adri.

Brandon's pack chose that moment to make their appearance. I'd overheard enough whispered gossip at school to know Britney had finally conquered her Everest. She was hanging off of Brandon like he was oxygen, and I spared a moment to wonder if she'd started realizing he wasn't what he pretended to be, or if he'd already addicted her to his touch.

Vincent and Cassie trailed along behind their alpha, and it was obvious the date was nothing more than a matter of convenience. Cassie had only ever had one target since Brandon had manifested his power. Vincent would do for an escort, and possibly even for more, but it was Brandon's arm she so desperately wanted to be on. It was part of what kept the rest of the pack in line.

Even if they hadn't been scared of Brandon they would have been scared of Cassie and the lengths she'd go to in order to secure his attention.

Jasmin muttered something about an over-dressed trollop and then pulled Rachel to her feet and gently shoved her towards me.

Adri was still looking brave, if somewhat distracted by the other pack, and I felt the briefest surge of jealousy as I led Rachel out onto the dance floor. Every reasoning part of my being knew the elevated pulse was nothing more than fear, but a niggling corner of my mind couldn't help but point out just how easy it would be to mistake fear and attraction.

The music was big band once again, and Rachel was an easy lead. For the briefest of moments I managed to forget about Brandon, about needing to send Adri away, about just how few hours of life I had left.

As the music ended once again I noticed that Jess and Isaac had drifted off into one corner where they could practice their air steps without taking someone's fingers off.

Adri was done being brave. Her head was slightly bowed and she'd given up any pretense of conversation with Jasmin, who looked concerned when she wasn't scanning the pavilion like she was expecting someone.

I escorted Rachel back to the seats and then reached out and carefully pulled Adri's chin up so I could meet her eyes.

"Dance with me?"

She smiled and nodded as she allowed me to lead her out into the center of the crowd. It was a slow song, and she leaned into me, wrapping her arms around my neck with surprising strength. It was the wrong thing to do, but I hugged her close to me, burying my face in her hair.

"I know you don't want to hear this, but it isn't too late for you to change your mind. Even now, it'd be a relatively simple thing to have you halfway across the country by the time the challenge actually occurs."

Adri cleared her throat as though trying to speak, and then just settled for shaking her head wordlessly. I wanted to press the point even as the rest of me wanted to follow Jasmin's advice. Now wasn't the time though, not surrounded by so many people, not with both packs present.

Instead of arguing with her I held her close, enjoying the feel of her pressed up against me as we swayed with the music.

There was no way they could have planned it, but the entire movement came together as though they'd been rehearsing it for days. I should have seen it coming, should have warned Jess and Isaac about going off by themselves. Not only did I not see it coming, I nearly didn't react quickly enough to intervene in time.

Vincent and Cassie appeared out of the crowded dance floor almost as if they'd been invisible, and suddenly they were squarely between Isaac, Jess and the rest of us.

James reacted exactly right. He shoved past Vincent, knocking him into Cassie and clearing the way for the rest of us. Jasmin was ahead of me, already cutting through the crowd with Rachel in tow, and then it was only Adri and I that hadn't joined the rest of the pack.

TORN

I picked Adri up, rushing along behind Jasmin as Brandon and his fellows materialized only a split second behind us.

We were moving with more than human speed, but there was nothing to be done about it. Isaac and Jess had chosen one of only two corners that actually had enough walls to be trapped in, and if we didn't stand together Brandon could cut us down individually.

Adri still hadn't had a chance to fully grasp what was happening as I tried to set her down without taking my eyes off of Brandon. I failed, and heard a slight gasp of pain as Jasmin handed Adri back to Dominic.

Jess was the most mentally fragile member of the pack, and being so nearly in Vincent's power had done something to her. I could hear her sobbing quietly as she rocked back and forth in the corner. I had a brief second to wish there was something I could do for her, and then Brandon and Vincent edged to within a hair of attack range.

Vincent was one of the vilest people I'd ever met. There was very little he hadn't done, and he was proud of every defilement or murder he'd achieved. I'd always sensed that Brandon was his mirror, but never had true proof.

Brandon was cautious, always presenting a good front, always careful to remain just to one side of the law. Only there'd never been any way that he couldn't have known what Vincent really was.

Somewhere along the way since I'd last seen Brandon he'd begun shedding the facade. There was a hunger for death, a yearning for destruction lurking behind his eyes like paired black holes. He was just hours from achieving his goal and stepping onto a path that was almost guaranteed to land him on the Coun'hij, but there was a real risk he wouldn't wait.

Vincent crowded in as close to Brandon as he could get with Britney between them, while Cassie rubbed up against Brandon's other flank, but my attention momentarily flickered out to the rest of Brandon's pack and I saw terror greater than even they should be forced to endure. They'd always feared their alpha, but it was the safe fear of something that could be avoided or somehow mitigated.

The safe fear was gone now. He'd become an unpredictable force of nature. Several of them were showing obvious bruises or otherwise moving gingerly, but they pressed forward eagerly in the hope that doing so would save them from further pain even for just a few minutes.

Isaac shifted ever so slightly, pulling my attention back to the more imminent threat and the unearthly level of power flowing back and forth between the two packs. James and Isaac were crackling pillars of energy to either side of me while Jas and Dom created a hum of background tingle just behind us.

Brandon exuded a white-hot torrent that left my skin tingling painfully as through I'd been bitten by thousands of insects. I reached inside for my beast but found a void instead of the answering rush of power we needed.

I could feel something stir weakly inside me. I let my hand elongate slightly towards its hybrid form, to verify that I hadn't somehow lost the ability to change forms, but the answering shift in my flesh did little to reassure me.

My beast had always been a half-feared specter that'd required a tight, eternally-vigilant leash. Only now that it'd been subdued did I realize just how strongly I'd leaned on it for the courage to stand up to Brandon.

For a second it was nearly more than I could do to remain where I was, but then I heard Adri whisper something too faint even for my ears to make out and there was no longer any choice.

I sank down slightly in preparation for springing at Brandon as his lips curled back in anticipation.

"Break it up! You kids back off!"

Mr. Paterson's voice cut through the gathered onlookers with surprising effectiveness. He hadn't been at the school long enough to understand the risk he was running. Eventually he'd be like the rest of the administration and faculty, like the police even. He'd eventually learn not to meddle in Brandon's affairs, learn to fear something he didn't really understand, but right now he was determined to make sure we didn't ruin the celebration for the rest of the town.

Vincent was edging ever closer. I didn't think that Brandon truly wanted the confrontation here and now, but they were like sharks with blood in the water. They'd scented weakness and had neither the will nor inclination to fight the instincts demanding they finish their foes while we were weak and vulnerable.

James and the others sensed it too. Losing control and shifting in full view of the gathered onlookers was as much of a death sentence as anything Brandon might have in mind for us, but James had already picked up the fine trembling of a shape shifter only heartbeats from changing.

I could see several of the others on both sides start shaking as Mr. Paterson shoved his way between the two packs. He didn't realize just how close he was to dying and whirled back and forth between Brandon and me.

"I said break it up!"

Things balanced on the edge of a precipice, and in the instant just before they slipped off the edge I felt my beast awaken with a roar of power. It sailed out from me with an almost physical force that pushed Brandon and the others' energy ahead of it. I heard a low, barely-perceptible growl that demanded obedience, and it wasn't until the wolves on both sides stilled that I realized it was issuing from my throat.

TORN

"This ends now. I don't care who started what, you guys are done dancing. Alec, you and your friends leave now. Brandon, you guys are out of here in the exact opposite direction and I mean now."

Mr. Paterson looked around expectantly, reacting as his training and fifteen years as an educator told him he should, but he didn't have the expertise to deal with this. Nobody moved. It was squarely in Brandon's court. We couldn't move until his pack had backed away to give us room.

"I'm not talking because I like the sound of my own voice, people. If you leave now, I'll forget this ever happened. If someone doesn't start moving in the next three seconds, I'll see the whole lot of you expelled and brought up on charges."

Vincent wanted to rip Mr. Paterson's head off of his throat. I could feel the blood lust radiating off of him, but Brandon waved him back and ever so slowly the rest of the pack followed.

We exited in a tight group, the hybrids on the outside in the most dangerous positions as Dom, Jasmin and Rachel tried to help the other two girls out.

I picked Adri up as soon as it was safe. Jasmin called the limo before we'd even hit the stairs, and it screeched to a stop as we made it to the road. Adri was trying to be brave but she obviously had a very nasty sprain. She hissed a little as I lifted her into the limo.

I pulled the soft pocket square from my front pocket and used it to blot away Adri's tears.

"I'm sorry. I didn't mean to set you down so hard."

Jasmin still looked mad. She was slipping her cell phone into a small purse.

"Any slower and you'd have been cut off from the rest of us by those mutts."

Adri still looked confused. She'd been looking the wrong way and events had evolved at more than merely human speed. Dom was helping Isaac, sandwiching Jess between them, crooning something soft and reassuring in an effort to calm her down. Dom looked up with unusual fire flickering behind her dark eyes.

"Vincent and Cassie cut Jess and Isaac off from the rest of us."

Rachel leaned in on Adri's other side, whispering so quietly there was even a slight chance that Jess didn't hear her.

"Jess is terrified of what Vincent and Brandon will do to her if they get a chance. She collapsed, and then everyone stormed the area."

We hit a particularly rough spot in the road and for a second I thought Adri was going to pass out. She even smelled hurt and I could only imagine the surges of agony traveling up her leg.

Jess sobbed quietly the entire way home, but Adri refused to cry. She whimpered a couple of times, but she somehow kept herself from breaking into outright tears.

As we pulled up to the house I lifted Adri out of the car, yelling for Donovan as I carried her into the closest sitting room.

I was nearly wild with concern by the time Donovan finally appeared with the industrial-sized first-aid kit. He nudged me out of the way and then stripped off Adri's shoe. I held my breath as he prodded the injury, releasing it only when I saw him relax slightly at what he'd found.

"Fortuitously, it's not broken, but I'm afraid it's one of the uglier sprains I've seen. I can take care of the pain though."

By the time we'd swabbed Adri's ankle down with alcohol, injected it in several spots and immobilized it, she'd calmed down fully.

Donovan surveyed our efforts with a nod of approval and then stood up and repacked the first aid kit.

"That should take care of the pain and immobilize it so it can begin healing, but it is vitally important that you don't put any weight on it, Mistress Paige. Please excuse me; I should go see to Mistress Jessica."

Even after everything she'd just suffered through, Adri was worried about others.

"We should go too. Poor Jess."

I gently stopped her from rising as I shook my head.

"They've already got her mostly settled down. James and Dom have already split off, and Jasmin and Rachel will leave next. She just needs some time. Time and Isaac."

She was silent for so long I almost couldn't bring myself to say anything else.

"I'm sorry to have ruined your night. I wanted it to be perfect. I should have known that wasn't possible. Not with everything hanging over our heads."

Adri's smile was so sincere that it loosened the tightness in my chest.

"Everything was almost perfect. If there was anything less than ideal, it wasn't your fault."

It was wrong for me to be so excited about what came next. It was a means to an end. Everything she'd just suffered through just made it more imperative I get her away to safety. I had to show her just how much there still was to live for.

"Still, I'd like to make it up to you. I suppose dancing is out, but I think I've got something that'll do just about as well."

I bent down to pick Adri up, only to find Jasmin staring at me from just outside the room as I stood up. Still clad in the dark dress she'd worn to the dance, Jasmin looked tired, but there was no waver in her gaze.

She was shielded from Adri's view, and she subvocalized, creating an odd sense of privacy as I shifted Adri around in my arms.

"Don't send her away, Alec. You need each other."

TORN

Jasmin disappeared as I turned and headed out to the garden, moving with a speed that I told myself had nothing to do with an effort to run from Jasmin's words.

It took only a brief time to arrive at the grotto, and find that Donovan had indeed outdone himself.

The lack of moon meant the only illumination was the floating lamps. There were almost forty of them, nearly motionless in the petal-filled pool. I'd torn the petals from dozens of roses in order to coat the surface of the water, and the purple edging around the white somehow lent the scene increased beauty beyond even what I'd expected.

The scent of the potted roses with which we'd filled the space between the stone walls had been divine all by itself, but once it mixed with Adri's natural scent it became something beyond description.

Adri's voice quavered slightly as she took in the results of our labor.

"Lagrimas."

I found my own voice less then normally clear as I responded.

"Nothing else would be appropriate. Not for you, not tonight."

I looked at the waiting easel, its black, velvet covering held safely away from the paint despite the cool breeze tugging at the fabric. I circled the grotto, listening to Adri's breathing and the quiet crash of the waterfall, and then found myself deviating from the script I'd spent hours agonizing over.

I shifted Adri around into one arm as I reached up to the velvet covering.

"There's something I'd like you to have. Something I hope will help you remember what you mean to me..."

They were the wrong words. Not the ones designed to remind her of her mortality, of other magical nights to come, but rather the truth. I carefully pulled the cloth away and then turned on the lights arranged around the border of the piece.

Adri's breath caught as she took in my efforts. I'd perfectly captured the grotto, the same one we stood in now. In the picture the moon's brilliance flooded down to meet with the soft glow of the greenery on the rock walls.

What I hadn't done justice to was Adri herself. She was the focal point, reaching out from the center of the painting with the compassion and acceptance I remembered, but the Adri I'd painted was a mere shadow of the beauty in my arms.

"She's beautiful. It's how I always imagined an angel would appear."

Something about her words told me she didn't understand, that she'd somehow failed to understand the identity of my subject.

"It's you, Adri. Of course it's beautiful."

It made absolutely no sense, but for the briefest moment it seemed as though she was going to argue with me. I watched her expression shift through a range of emotions I couldn't even begin to interpret, and then she turned back towards me with the barest hint of tears in her eyes.

"It's so beautiful. I don't know what to say. Are you sure you want to give it up?"

It was the last opportunity I was going to get. I tried to revert back to my script, tried to ignore Jasmin's words, still echoing inside my mind, but found myself unable to.

My need for Adri had somehow become something beyond conscious control. I could no more send her away than I could have stopped my lungs from drawing breath. In the short term I could override survival-level instincts, but in the long term they were always going to win out.

The emotions written plainly on my face despite my best efforts to conceal them caused amazement to flood Adri's face. She opened her mouth to say something, but I found myself lifting her chin as my lips hesitantly approached hers.

A sense of rightness washed over me as we kissed. My senses seemed to mix and intensify as she responded, clinging to me with all of her strength. I seemed to be tasting moonlight as her pulse sped up to dangerous levels.

I wanted to lengthen the gesture, to push her heart to even higher efforts as mine raced to do the same, but as it started skipping beats I came back to myself enough to pull away from her.

She'd tamed me utterly and effortlessly, and I wanted nothing so much as I wanted to kiss her again and again, but a tiny, vocal part of me knew I'd just committed a terrible deed.

Adri had only just barely regained her breath before she was pulling at me, seeking another kiss. Physically it was a small matter to hold her away, but it took nearly all of my willpower not to let her succeed.

I buried my face in her hair, wallowing in the scent of Adri and Lagrimas, and then finally found the ability to speak again.

"I'd like to, I truly would, but I don't think that would be fair to you. Even letting that happen was a mistake. I've never come so close to losing control."

The words came out without conscious thought, but they were truer than she could possibly know. I'd spent years learning how to control my beast, but somehow a simple touch from her almost cracked the corresponding control I'd created over the human pieces inside me.

Adri shook her head, looking somehow even more beautiful in her contentment than before.

"I don't think it was a mistake. I want to kiss you again, but I'll behave."

"You like the painting then?"

She nodded emphatically, but the motion was interrupted by a shiver and I suddenly realized how much the night air had cooled. She was probably in shock from the injury; the last thing I should be doing was letting her freeze to death.

"I'm sorry. I forget sometimes how much easier it is for you and Rachel to catch a chill. Let's get you inside where it's a bit more temperate."

She wanted to stay, tried to argue with me, but I deftly shifted her into one arm and then picked up the completed canvas with the other.

I carried Adri into the house, and then tried to convince her to fall asleep, but she refused. I let her pull me down onto the bed next to her, and then nearly sprang back up when she told me that she was going to come to the challenge with the rest of us.

The thought of exposing her to that level of danger brought my beast roaring back to the fore. Adri looked at my near-complete lack of expression and cocked her head at me.

"You weren't planning on bringing me, were you?"

"It's not safe, Adri. I don't want to leave you anymore than you want to be left, but it's the only option."

She fisted her hands as she shook her head.

"No, it isn't, just bring me along."

It was the wrong thing for her to be doing. Not only was she defying me, her body language was too aggressive. No dominant could let defiance become the general rule, it was against our fundamental wiring. I felt my fists ball up in response, but fought to keep my composure.

"You heard Mallory. The odds are very good that I'm not coming back. If the worst happens, the rest of the pack may very well have to try and fight their way out of there. They won't be able to get you out, they'll be lucky to survive even fleeing unencumbered. I can't ask them to run that gauntlet carrying you the whole way."

Adri unclenched one hand, slowly raising it up to my face where she could touch my cheek with just the lightest of sensations. It was like she was writing on me with fire.

"Then don't ask them. You'll either win, in which case it doesn't matter whether I'm there or not, or else I don't care what happens."

The thought of leaving her alone, completely at the mercy of the likes of Brandon and Vincent, bothered me on more levels than just the territoriality of my beast, but that was the side of me that currently was driving the fine tremble of a near-transformation.

"Don't be ridiculous, Adri. You should know at least a little by now what they're capable of. I can't let you expose yourself to the kinds of things Vincent or Brandon would…it's out of the question."

She looked up at me with eyes that showed absolutely no fear despite how close I was to losing control of the monster inside me.

"Alec, I need to be there with you tonight. If you leave me here, I'll head out on my own and look for you."

"I'll order Donovan to keep you here."

My voice had deepened as the barest beginnings of the change crept past my barriers.

"You can try. He may even do it, but I don't think so. He's far too much the gentleman to keep a lady captive against her will. Even if he does, do you really think he can watch over me every second?"

A sudden picture of Adri, broken and motionless while Brandon loomed over her, was too much and my hands shifted in a flash of heat and power. The semi-retractable claws that could mark steel tore into the foam and springs of the mattress as I threw all my will at stopping the change from going any further. She didn't even flinch at the sudden dismemberment of sections of the bed. Her eyes hadn't changed, they were still stubborn, still trusting and by far the most beautiful things I'd ever seen.

"You're not going to scare me off with cheap tricks. This is important."

She would have been a fierce shape shifter. I felt myself shake slightly as a powerful cocktail of emotions roared through me, but in the end I could no more force her than I could have forced Jasmin or Rachel.

She was volunteering for a death sentence, but it was her choice, and at least it would give us a few more minutes together than we'd have otherwise.

"All right. You can come. I don't like it. Don't like knowing you're guaranteed not to survive my passing, but it's your choice."

She smiled at my agreement, and then drew back as if she wasn't quite sure she could believe me.

"Not that I'm complaining, mind you, but why the sudden change?"

I found myself half-smiling. At least she couldn't read me enough yet to realize I was no longer capable of lying to her, no longer capable of denying her anything she really wanted.

"My death is nearly certain, but there's always a chance I'll somehow survive. As unlikely as that is, I don't want to survive and then find I've poisoned you against me. I won't stop you."

I'd been unconsciously listening to the sounds throughout the house as we'd been talking. The white noise generator in the suite shared by Andrew, Jess and Isaac was on. I'd heard James and Dom leave while we were still outside. It was surprising just how quiet things had become with two-thirds of the pack gone or behind privacy generators.

Adri reached over and took my hand. The movement was absentminded, as if she wasn't really thinking about what she was doing, but I should still have withdrawn my hand. I didn't, and when she spoke it was hard to tell whether she was talking about my having given her permission to accompany us, or whether it was because of the contact.

"Thank you."

"You must have driven your parents crazy with that refusal to back down."

She brightened up, something all the more incredible given that I'd just said *parents*.

"I suppose I might have frustrated them a time or two."

"And to think Rachel says *I'm* stubborn."

I almost returned her smile, but the sound of a familiar pair of feet exiting the house almost pulled me up out of bed. A second later Jasmin's Mercedes started up and squealed out of the garage.

Adri looked up, suddenly concerned.

"What's the matter? What do you hear?"

"Jasmin just left."

"What's wrong with that?"

"It's not safe for her to leave the estate. Brandon's pack could be waiting for her."

I went to roll to my feet, but Adri held onto me with all of her strength. She couldn't have physically restrained me, but I stopped regardless.

"Alec, she'll probably be okay. I know it isn't the best idea but please don't stop her. Not tonight."

It was suddenly clear, and I wondered that I hadn't realized what was happening sooner. James and Dom had each other, Isaac and Jess were together, and now, however briefly, I'd found Adri. I didn't have the first clue who Jas might have her heart set on. It seemed impossible that whoever it was hadn't swept her up already, but it must not have been reciprocated or the whole school would already be abuzz with the news.

I felt my heart ache at the thought of proud Jasmin standing in the darkness, utterly alone as the lights throughout the town slowly went out.

Adri watched me put the pieces together and held on even more tightly.

"Please don't let on that you know. I wasn't supposed to say anything. I just couldn't let you go after her."

I smiled down at Adri, and if my smile was a little bittersweet it held more joy than the situation really merited. So much hurt in so few people. Jasmin hauntingly alone, Adri with the scars of loss that I couldn't really understand. My own poor sister.

Adri seemed to read my mind. "What about Rachel, Alec? Where is she?"

"Rachel doesn't have anyone either, but she's still suffering from a deeper hurt. She's with my mother."

It wasn't my secret to tell, but Adri wouldn't use it to hurt Rach. Of that I was certain, and in a way this would allow someone to share just the tiniest sliver of what Rach was going through.

"No, Mother isn't going through a good episode. She's asleep. Rachel crept into her room and crawled into bed with her. It's a poor substitute for what she aches for, but it's all Mother can offer right now."

"Alec, there must be something we can do."

She released me and started gesturing wildly as her concern overcame everything else. I recaptured her hands and shook my head.

"Not right now. Rachel cherishes her few remaining illusions. One of the most important is the pretense that nobody knows just how hard it is sometimes for her to be the only human in a house full of shape shifters."

She was trembling now. All the pain she carried inside and it was Rachel's that nearly reduced her to tears. I brushed one hand across her lips.

"You've been a godsend for her, Adri. As badly as it hurts each time she sneaks away, it hasn't happened nearly as often since you got here. She's been improving ever since you moved into town, and the rate of change has increased over the last two weeks."

She'd calmed slightly, but I could feel the hurt rising up out of her battered heart.

"I suppose we make quite the pair, her and I. Two shattered little dolls trying our best to make sure the pieces don't blow away and leave us with nothing. An imposition to everyone around us."

I pulled her in tight, thinking only of comforting her.

"Not an imposition. Never that."

She nuzzled the hollow of my throat and then moving with human slowness that was still somehow too fast for me to stop, reached up and kissed me. It was the first kiss magnified a dozen times over, and it wakened my beast with a tingle of power.

For the first time I could remember, my beast and I wanted exactly the same thing. I desperately wished there was some way I could stay with her forever.

It seemed like we stood glued together for hours, maybe even days. When we finally parted it wasn't because I was satiated, but because it was the right thing to do, the only thing that promised even the slightest chance of me maintaining my control.

She was trembling as I held her at arm's length and finally managed to convince her to lie down and try to go to sleep. I told her ancient legends until she'd finally drifted off, and then curled up beside her and drank in her scent.

Chapter 31

I left Adri's side as I heard Jasmin return to the house. She shot me a defiant look as I intercepted her on the way to her room. I held up a hand to forestall the tongue lashing she was a heartbeat away from delivering.

"Jas, I'm glad you made it back okay."

She was so shocked I was able to pull her in for a hug, something I hadn't done in far too long.

"Thank you for helping take care of Adri for me. I know it's not fair, but if possible please try to get her out tonight."

Jasmin nodded as she wiped away the moisture at the corner of her eyes before it could become actual tears.

"We'll get her out. Dom and I both love her too, and Isaac will do it just because it's the right thing to do."

I nodded in gratitude and then pulled out my phone.

"It's nearly time."

"I know. I'll go get Dom and we'll get Adri out of her dress and into something that'll keep her from freezing."

I sent a quick text to Isaac, and then went in search of Donovan. I found him in his office, a black and white movie playing on the TV.

"Yes, Master Alec?"

I waved him back into his seat and pulled the extra chair around so I could face him.

"Donovan, I want you to go to her tonight."

He shook his head, the perfect picture of a loyal retainer intent on going down with the ship.

"I'm serious. There's still a chance that I can hurt Brandon badly enough that the rest of the pack can escape. If that happens they'll pick up Mom and Rachel and try to disappear. There won't be anything stopping you from doing what you've wanted to do all these years."

Again a slight shake of the head, and then Donovan cleared his throat.

"I'm too much of a prize these days to be allowed to disappear and you know it, Alec. Under your guidance the family fortunes have grown by an order of magnitude. Brandon, the Coun'hij, none of them can afford to let that kind of wealth get away from them."

Donovan reached into his desk drawer and handed me a thin slip of paper with an address and a fifteen-digit code on it.

"If anyone survives they should go here. I've been steadily siphoning off untraceable funds for most of the last decade. It's a paltry sum, but it should be more than enough for all seven of them to disappear for the rest of their lives."

The thought of Donovan waiting patiently as Brandon arrived to capture him, of the torture that he'd be subject to so that Brandon could learn our financial secrets, was almost enough to bring me to my knees. Donovan misinterpreted the horror on my face and reached out to grip my arm.

"I can hold out long enough for them to acquire the funds and disappear. I know that much already. He'll eventually get the rest of the family holdings, but not that piece. Your family will be taken care of no matter what happens."

I shook my head. "That's not what I was contemplating. I'm sorry I let things come to a head. I should have done something different, should have bought us a few more months in the hope I'd manifest a power."

Donovan tightened his grasp on my arm as he shook his head.

"You have done nothing to be ashamed of. We all have our part to play and you've played yours better than most could have hoped. I'm proud of the man you've become, and I'll do my part now to protect those we love."

He turned back to the movie and I stumbled out of the room at his polite dismissal. Isaac, Jess and James were waiting for me in the East Drawing Room. James looked up as I entered the room.

"We're going to stay and fight no matter what happens. We won't let anything happen to Adri."

I shook my head. "No, James. I appreciate the thought, but the packs will be too closely matched. Unless I manage to hurt Brandon much more than I expect I will, the odds will be against you all. Just get out of there. Take Adri if you can, but run back here, get Mom and Rach and then get out of town."

Isaac looked for a moment like he would argue with me, but I pressed Donovan's paper into his hand.

"Everyone needs to memorize that and then destroy it. Donovan's arranged for enough wealth to be secreted there to sustain you all for your entire lives if you make it out."

I heard footsteps and turned to meet Jasmin, Dom and Adri with a smile. Adri was dressed in jeans and a white hoodie that emphasized the porcelain perfection of her skin. She managed a vague smile in my direction, but it was obvious she was still half asleep. I carefully picked her up and carried her out to the Hummer.

Donovan had displayed incredible foresight in having copies made of the keys for both vehicles we were taking and distributing them to the entire pack. Jasmin slipped into the front seat of the Hummer as I set Adri inside and the other four joined Jess and Isaac in her Jeep.

Despite a valiant effort to stay awake, Adri fell back asleep within moments of the engine turning over. She'd obviously been worried I'd be offended, but it was a silly fear. Spending time with her, awake or asleep, was divine. The pavement rolled away beneath us as I watched the rise and fall of her chest, the complete vulnerability of her face.

All too soon it was time to exit the vehicles. The last leg of our journey would be on foot. I grabbed the backpack Donovan had left on the floorboards and double-checked that everyone had secured their copies of the keys inside the tiny pocket sewn into their ha'bits. I cinched the backpack up tight against my shoulders, and then slipped my keys into Adri's pocket.

Jasmin frowned at the action, but we all knew I wasn't going to survive the night. I'd give the fight my utter best, and I'd lose. No single, normal hybrid could hope to stand against Brandon.

I waited while everyone shed their street clothes and shifted forms in a harmonious wash of power, and then I picked Adri up and followed them all off into the night.

The pack ranged about Adri and me, careful to keep close enough to be able to support each other, while still watching for ambushes. Being in my human form slowed our progress somewhat, but I was loath to give up the feel of her against my human skin.

Adri reawoke after we'd been walking for fifteen minutes. As she opened her eyes with the barest hint of a shiver, I realized she was cold and shifted her around slightly, wrapping my arms more fully around her in an effort to keep her warm.

"We've still got nearly half an hour, you should get some more sleep if you can."

She shook her head, but her eyes closed of their own accord despite her best efforts. A short while later we all caught the scent of the other pack. I nearly managed to get the flares out of the backpack without waking Adri. She stirred slightly as I handed Isaac and James each a pair, and then came fully awake as the first set of flares were ignited, bathing the clearing in green light.

I felt Adri's quick intake of breath at the same time she clutched at me, but gently disengaged from her as Jasmin and Dom came up and flanked her.

I stripped my clothes off in quick, economical motions, and then surveyed the pack. Isaac and James had calmly taken up station on the outside of the group, with me in the center, the girls slightly behind me. I chanced a quick glance at Adri and saw her attention completely focused on Vincent, a dark-furred figure who'd materialized in the center of the clearing almost as though he expected to be the one to face me.

Just beyond Vincent was the ever-shifting clump of four-legged figures that was the rest of the pack. There was a nervousness to their movements that made me wonder what they expected to happen.

Whatever threats Brandon had used over the last few days to motivate them were equal to the task and his entire pack turned towards us with a flood of power that surpassed anything they'd displayed previously.

One by one we responded with answering surges of power, and in less than a second the air between the two packs seemed to hum with potential violence. They still outnumbered us slightly, but the arcing tendrils of energy told a story in which the advantage was slightly on our side.

As always Brandon was the final piece that reduced the fight to one which we couldn't win. Brandon stepped into the circle formed by the two packs, and I felt the first surge of rage from my beast at his appearance.

He didn't intend on being reasoned with. He'd only remained in human form because skin was a better canvas for the bloody symbol he'd drawn on his own chest. I was one of few living shape shifters who could have hoped to recognize the symbols of the four main royal lines, but I didn't need the hours I'd spent pouring over my father's journals to know he hadn't copied any of the recognized sigils.

As bad as that would have been, this was utterly worse. He wasn't claiming a royal lineage, he was declaring himself the creator of a new lineage, and the jagged, bold lines he'd chosen boded for a bloody, terror-filled reign if he wasn't slapped down by the Coun'hij.

It was an insult to everything my family had ever stood for, and the chains with which I'd leashed my beast nearly weren't equal to the task of maintaining my composure. He looked at me with eyes that had finally began to show the depravity lurking in what remained of his soul and shook his head at me.

"While I appreciate the sentiment, it really is far too late to secure absolution by bringing me the girl."

I'd only thought his earlier gestures had tested my willpower. The thought of turning Adri over to him sparked a fire inside me that consumed the bindings I'd spent years erecting. Where before my beast had strained at my will, nearly tearing free, now there was simply nothing left between my two selves.

Had it been necessary to override the instincts that were so often anachronistic and dangerous in the modern world, I would have utterly failed, but there was no such necessity. Animal and man were utterly unified in protecting the one thing we both valued at or above anything else.

A ripple of movement passed through both packs as Brandon's beast called forth a cyclone of power and there was no answering surge from me despite the obvious rage coursing through my system. It was a cause for worry.

Brandon had long been more powerful than me, but a failure to respond, especially coming after a similar lack earlier, only tilted the balance further in his favor. Both packs were wondering how I could have even a chance of succeeding if I didn't have the native savagery of my beast supporting me.

"Adri is here solely in the capacity of witness."

He was grinning now at my perceived lack of power. I mirrored his actions of just a second before, stepping closer as his pack growled at me.

"Ah, and here I'd thought you'd once again settled on a course of appeasement."

"No. We've come for one purpose and one only. No more murdered hikers, no more convenient accidents. This ends tonight."

Brandon's clap played to the observers from both packs, but it was a hollow gesture. He wasn't going to sway anyone tonight. Both sides were far too entrenched in their positions to change now.

"Always observing the old forms, aren't you, Alec. Well now it's time for a whole new batch."

His hybrid form exploded out from the center of his being even as he finished speaking. He was moving towards me in a further rush of power while most everyone else was still trying to process the fact he'd shifted.

It was an impressive display but ultimately nothing more than posturing. He'd started too far away from me to have any hope of true surprise. I let my own form shift into something that had a prayer of standing against him and charged towards him.

I heard a slight gasp from Adri and then my full attention was on Brandon. He was fast. It was almost more than I could do to block his attacks. Each blow landed with the force of a freight train, and my limbs smarted despite the unnatural vitality coursing through my system.

I was the strongest I'd ever been. The strength training regime had yielded unexpectedly large gains, but simple flesh and bone could never hope to match Brandon's gift.

I reeled away from the first exchange with blood showing on a number of places. Brandon was the ultimate bruiser, using his superior size and strength to hammer away at me like a tireless golem.

A quick feint lured his leading hand out of position and I raked my claws up his arm but took a slash to my shoulder in return. He moved out of the way before I could capitalize and turn the opening into a clinch that would allow me to inflict true damage.

A low, guttural growl answered my success and suddenly Brandon was driving me before him. I reeled away from blow after blow, only just avoiding giving him the opening he'd need to finish the fight instantly.

Heat lightning lit up the area, and I used the momentary spots it left in his eyes to savage his side as I dodged past him back towards the center of the cleared area.

The fight had already lasted longer than I'd expected. Most deadly violence wasn't the endless sparring enacted in movies. He was satisfied to bleed me out for now, but eventually

I'd make a mistake and then it'd be up to the pack to get Adri out.

The flares were dying down. The change was almost imperceptible but seemed to march in time to the increase in tempo Brandon was driving.

I saw my opportunity as Brandon let one of his blindingly quick slashes travel too far. I charged him with all of the momentum of several hundred pounds of bone and muscle. In a flash I was inside his right arm, and I managed to grab his left and immobilize it as I slammed into him.

Both feet were already clawing at his legs, tearing into them as I tried to immobilize his free hand so it couldn't cut at me. I'd executed the technique perfectly. It should have borne him to the ground, I'd used it on both Isaac and James in the past, but Brandon absorbed the impact and freed his left hand after less than a second of struggle.

I found myself flying through the air, propelled by one hand that sliced all the way down to my ribs as I sailed away. By all rights he could have gone for a clinch and ended it there, but I'd had superior positioning with my feet and the win would have left him immobilized while my pack fled.

Those thoughts flickered across my mind in the fraction of a second my flight lasted, but they were an insubstantial wraith in the face of what happened next. The ground reached up and slammed into me with bone-crushing force that sent bloody droplets flying as Adri screamed.

Something inside me tore, and then suddenly the entire world seemed to be trying to force itself inside the void that'd opened up in my being. The amount of pain was incredible, and I opened my mouth to scream, but the metaphysical wind crashing into me drowned out any sound.

My beast screamed his own defiance at what was happening, but all our rage couldn't stop anything. The wild, bestial power of each of the shape shifters in the clearing had somehow become focused on me and the hole inside me gobbled the energy up, channeling it and sending it elsewhere a split second before it would have consumed me.

Even over the pain I could feel the different signatures of each of the moonborn, and for the first time I realized how unique each of them felt. I felt the barest taste of Adri, the power willingly offering itself before James' energy moved to the fore of the torrent. There was a wariness there, but it was nothing compared to the hatred that flowed in from Vincent.

Channeling the power from my pack mates was relatively easy, it was the others who caused me to burn up my own strength in ensuring their hatred didn't consume me. Each pain-etched second seemed to stretch out into infinity as I waged a war on the unseen plane.

I should have been worried that Brandon would kill me while I was incapacitated, but I could feel him. Somehow I knew he'd collapsed to the ground only just after I'd stopped rolling.

TORN

They were all arrayed motionless around me, and a detached portion of my mind spent an eternity contemplating the scene. I was drinking down a painful collage of each of them. Each was familiar and yet new at the same time. I was surprised to find the depth of Jasmin's feelings, the range of James' suffering over his torn loyalties, and the utter profundity of Isaac's calm control.

The need inside me was far too powerful to ever be satisfied, but with an abruptness that was all the more amazing in contrast to the frozen eternity of my pain, suddenly there was nothing left to feed it.

Left with nothing else to draw inside me, the splintered pieces of my soul snapped back into place.

I didn't want to move, feared in fact that I wasn't capable of motion. It seemed impossible that what I'd just been through could have left anything but a charred wreck in place of my body, but I felt compelled to do something. In the sudden silence I could hear the heartbeats of all those gathered around me, and there was something subtly wrong with one of them, a pulse that was oddly more important to me than even the pain I would doubtless endure on its behalf.

I opened my eyes, took in the last of the harsh light of the flares, and was surprised to find that I could still see.

I was too weak to stand, but I began crawling. Movement hurt nearly as bad as I'd feared, but I couldn't remain still. The acrid tang of the flares permeated everything, but under that cacophony was a sickly melody of blood. Mostly mine, although Brandon's was nearly as pervasive, but neither of those was what compelled me to move.

I could have happily stayed in one spot and bled to death, but the smell of Adri's blood was as unmistakable as it was alarming, and my whole world narrowed down to the pale, only barely breathing, mound.

Chapter 32

More than once I'd thought we were going to lose Adri, but as impossible as it seemed, we all survived.

I'd planned on bypassing Brandon, utterly focused on getting Adri's bleeding stopped, but as I'd neared him he'd began moving again, and my beast had suddenly roared back to life. We still shared a common purpose, but once again we had different priorities when it came to carrying that purpose out.

The thought of Adri bleeding out while I was busy ensuring Brandon never threatened her again should have compelled me to leave him until after I'd tended to her, but in this my beast refused to be tamed. I struggled to bring my limbs back under my control, but the efforts bounced off a will that at least for that moment was stronger than even my need to save Adri.

Only after Brandon was finally still was I able to tear my clumsy limbs away from what was left of him and totter the rest of the way to Adri.

My discarded shirt served as a barely adequate pressure bandage, and I'd packed it into her wound as I prayed that we'd be able to get her to safety.

Brandon's wolves had streamed away in ones and twos as soon as they were able to move, and I'd ordered Isaac and James not to give pursuit when they'd finally been capable of standing and fighting.

We had them outnumbered, but saving Adri was the first priority and there was nothing to stop Vincent from reassembling them and swinging back to kill us in detail if we split up. Even days later I remained convinced he would've pressed the attack when he regained consciousness if not for the fact that most of his fellows had already disappeared into the darkness.

Adri's makeshift bandage had been completely soaked through by the time we made it back to the cars. Jasmin had piled into the back seat where she could keep pressure on the wound. Isaac threw me his spare key as I tore around the side of the Hummer and then we were off in a spray of gravel.

I flogged the powerful engine the entire way back and pushed the tires to the very limit of their capabilities as I threw the massive vehicle around turns at speeds that would have made Adri shriek if she'd been aware of her surroundings.

Donovan was waiting for us at the house, already scrubbed and ready with a blood transfusion prepped.

Dom scrubbed and then pushed me out of the way so she could help our resident doctor stitch Adri up. I paced anxiously around the operating room until Donovan finally ordered Isaac and James to move me somewhere else.

It was a dangerous move considering just how frayed my control was, but apparently both parts of me realized that distracting Donovan would just result in Adri bleeding to death. A half hour after I was ushered outside to the garden, Dom came out and reassured me that Adri would be okay.

"The branch she fell on just barely nicked one of the veins near her kidney. She wasn't bleeding that fast, but in the time it took us to get back she lost a lot of blood. "

I thanked Dom for the update, and then feigned enough composure to convince her to leave, but I didn't truly calm down until Adri was safely resting on my bed.

Isaac, James and Jasmin started asking for permission to go out hunting the remnants of Brandon's pack almost as soon as it was confirmed that Adri was going to survive. I finally agreed provided that they took Jess and Dom with them.

Under normal circumstances it would've been foolish to leave the house so uncovered. It would be all too easy for Vincent to circle around with a couple of wolves and kill our dependents while everyone but me was away, but faced with my newly-awakened power, nobody seemed to doubt but that I could lay out an entire pack all by myself.

The others weren't any more sure of what it was I could do than I was, but it'd sufficed to bring Brandon and the others down, and the dominants were anxious to do something to ensure that we wouldn't continue to have to worry about attacks.

It was a relief when they all finally left and let me turn my attention back to Adri. I was careful not to touch her, but I stayed by her bedside for nearly the entire twenty-four hours it took her to regain consciousness.

I'd erred drastically by allowing the Ja'tell bond to deepen as much as it had. I'd given up fighting my selfish desires because I'd been so convinced I was going to die, but maybe it wasn't too late to reverse the damage. Maybe long months from now she'd make up her mind to be with me of her own free will. Maybe she wouldn't. It wouldn't be the first time that someone thought themselves in love while exposed to extreme danger, and it wasn't likely to be the last.

The thought of her turning away from me, of her choosing another was nearly more than I could stand, but my course was fixed. Whatever she decided where I was concerned, I knew I loved her. No matter how bad things might get, the thought of sending her away would never cross my mind again.

Author's Note

I do hope you enjoyed reading Torn as much as I enjoyed writing it. I have to admit that this is a book that almost never got written. A few years back I sat down with the intent of writing about a girl that was slightly damaged, and a boy that for all he was a bit more than just human, faced odds too insurmountable even for him to conquer.

Seven or eight months later, I finished up what I would later come to call Broken, and breathed a sigh of relief that Adri had finally been able to tell her story. Despite being 'done,' I couldn't shake the idea that there was a huge swath of the story that hadn't been told.

It wasn't until I read the excerpt of Midnight Sun that Stephenie Meyer put on her website that things finally clicked. The best way to tell all of the cool parts of Adri and Alec's story that hadn't made it into Broken was to tell everything again, but do it from Alec's point of view.

I knew on the outset that it was going to be a tricky project. I wanted something where it didn't matter which novel you picked up, you still came away with questions that you had to then pick up the other novel to get answers to. I couldn't just write *Torn* as much as I needed to go back to *Broken* and carve away some of the bits that would be better told from Alec's point of view.

I'm incredibly pleased with how *Broken* and *Torn* each turned out individually, but they were always meant to be enjoyed in close proximity to each other.

If you haven't read *Broken* yet, that is the installment of Alec and Adri's story that you're going to want to read next. If you have read *Broken* already then you'll want to pick up *Splintered* to continue the series.

Finally, please consider going out to my blog, www.DeanWrites.com, and signing up for my mailing list so that I can keep you in the loop as I continue to release more books set in the *Reflections* universe.

Acknowledgements

As always, thanks need to go out to everyone that continues to provide support in dozens of different ways. When an author chooses to go the indie route, it means they absolutely rely on their fans to get the word out, and I'm very appreciative of all of you that blog, review, or otherwise help put Torn on the map.

There are a few individuals who deserve special mention. The Corbridge brothers and C-M2E all of who have gone way above and beyond the call of duty.

Additional thanks and acknowledgement need made to Obsidian Dawn, www.obsidiandawn.com, for brushes used in the creation of the cover for Torn.

Finally, the biggest thanks of all goes to my wife Katie, who serves as my cover artist, editor, and first reader, all the while keeping Hurricane Sage from destroying the surrounding countryside.

About the Author

Dean Murray is a prolific author with more than thirty titles across multiple pen names and more than half a million copies of his work currently in circulation.

Dean started reading seriously in the second grade due to a competition and has spent most of the subsequent three decades lost in other people's worlds.

Things worsened, or improved depending on your point of view, when he first started experimenting with writing while finishing up his accounting degree.

These days Dean has a wonderful wife and two lovely daughters to keep him rather more grounded, but the idea of bringing others along with him as he meets interesting new people in universes nobody else has ever seen tends to drag him back to his computer on a fairly regular basis.

Keep up to speed on Dean's latest projects at www.DeanWrites.com.

Frozen Prospects

The invitation to join the secretive Guadel should have been the fulfillment of dreams Va'del didn't even realize he had. When his sponsors are killed in an ambush a short time later, he instead finds his probationary status revoked, and becomes a pawn between various factions inside the Guadel ruling body.

Jain's never known any life but that of a Guadel in training. She'd thought herself reconciled to the idea of a loveless marriage for the good of her people, but meeting Va'del changes everything. Their growing attraction flies against hundreds of years of precedent, but as widespread attacks threaten their world, the Guadel have no choice but to use even Jain and Va'del in their fight for survival.

The Greater Darkenss

Dean writing as Eldon Murphy

Something powerful is stirring in the darkness. Something so ancient that even creatures who've been alive for hundreds of years have long since discounted this new threat as nothing more than myth.

Normal humans will be caught in the crossfire, but then that's always the way of things. Geoffrey has no memory of his past life or any idea how to survive in the violent, dangerous world in which he's trapped. Despite his best efforts, he's about to find himself in the middle of a conflict that threatens to sweep away everything, and everyone he's been fighting so hard to protect.